Charlotte Collins

Charlotte Collins

A Continuation of Jane Austen's *Pride and Prejudice*

Jennifer Becton

WHITELEY PRESS

A WHITELEY PRESS BOOK

Copyright © 2010 by Jennifer Whiteley Becton
www.jenniferbecton.com
10   3 4 5 6 7

ISBN-13: 9781453740477
ISBN-10: 1453740473

Printed in the United States of America.

Cover: *Lady Morgan*, portrait by René Théodore Berthon, held in the National Gallery of Ireland. (Image in public domain.)

The characters and events in this book are fictitious or used fictitiously. Any similarity to real people, living or dead, is coincidental and not intended by the author.

For

Octavia Clark Becton

I consider everybody as having a right
to marry once in their lives for love, if they can.

❦ Jane Austen ❧

ଏ Prologue ଛ

1818

The sun shone on the day of the Reverend Mr. Collins's funeral, and Charlotte knew that her husband would have questioned the wisdom of the Almighty for allowing such fine weather on the burial day of one of the church's devoted servants.

As the exceedingly devout rector of Hunsford, near Westerham, Kent, Mr. Collins had always preferred to conduct a funeral in dour weather, which he felt appropriately matched the solemnity of the occasion. A light drizzle was an additional benefit, for it forced mourners to wear heavy attire despite the season. In his estimation, a funeral was a weighty thing, and no lightness or warmth of any kind was to be tolerated. So he would have been properly horrified by the impious gaiety of his own funeral day.

Fortunately, in his extinguished state, he would not have to tolerate the day's infernal light, for he had already departed the earthly realm for the kingdom of heaven. Should he take exception to the fine weather, he could discuss it with the Almighty face to face.

And he probably would.

Charlotte, however, had seen to every earthly detail; her husband was attired in his most expensive suit, mourners had remained constantly beside his body, and she was seeing to his legal affairs. But the weather was out of her control.

Now, Charlotte stood in the doorway of Hunsford parsonage and watched the funeral procession begin its morbid journey as the unseasonably warm wind caused leaves of vibrant red, orange, and yellow to rustle on their perches and blew her somber-hued skirts, revealing more ankle than was strictly proper. Sun glinted off the hearse that bore her husband's coffin, highlighting the buckles on the horse's harness as he trotted briskly away from the house despite the driver's attempts to slow him to a more sedate gait. The mourners maintained a more dignified pace. Among those men who followed the coffin were her father, who genuinely mourned the loss of his son-in-law; Mr. Darcy, who did not mourn him at all; and a host of parishioners, whose grief fell somewhere between the two.

She watched as the procession disappeared down the drive, loath to return inside where the drawn drapes blocked out nearly all light. Even so, she fancied that her wretched light-swallowing bombazine mourning attire darkened the room still further.

She nodded to her companions, family and friends who were also clad in black gowns, gloves, and scarves. Like the men who escorted Mr. Collins's body to his final resting place, they too had gathered to grieve for a gentleman whom few had liked well enough to hold five minute's conversation.

As his widow, Charlotte felt a measure of sorrow at Mr. Collins's death; he had been her nearly constant companion these seven years. But she had not been in love with him. She could hardly even claim to have liked him.

Of course, Mr. Collins had not been in love with her either. Their marriage had not been his choice. The commandment for him to wed had come from on high: from his patroness, the Lady Catherine de Bourgh herself. And so, he had taken himself to visit his cousins, the Bennets, with the intention of securing a wife *en famille*. Upon discovering Mr. Collins's mission and the absolute revulsion of his intended fiancée—her dear friend Elizabeth Bennet—Charlotte had pursued him, quite literally.

Under the guise of easing Elizabeth's burden, she had put herself into Mr. Collins's path at social events and absorbed his conversation in private.

In truth, Charlotte had wooed him.

And when she spied him coming down the lane to Lucas Lodge, her family home, ostensibly to propose, she had rushed to meet him quite by chance so that he would not lose his nerve. Nearly seven-and-twenty, Charlotte was nigh on becoming a spinster and an encumbrance to her family, and marriage was the only option available to an educated woman of small fortune. And as a practical woman, Charlotte had seized the opportunity available to her, meager though it was.

Yet, somehow she and Mr. Collins had served each other well. Charlotte had removed herself as a burden to her parents and gained a comfortable home of her own, and Mr. Collins had pleased his patroness, lifting him in her esteem. And as long as they avoided each other most of the time, their marriage was quite pleasing.

In the early days, Mr. Collins had actually served as a somewhat tolerable companion, but after the death of their only child, Margaret, a beautiful dark-eyed replica of Charlotte who had not survived even the first year of her life, the couple had become even more disconnected, merely existing in the same household. Mr. Collins had sequestered himself with his sermons, fawned over the number of windows in Lady Catherine's home, and consumed all the biscuits in the parsonage before Charlotte had ever had the opportunity to eat one.

Skirting the company of assembled ladies, Charlotte disappeared into the kitchen where she discovered her childhood friend Elizabeth Darcy, the very woman who had spurned Mr. Collins. She had traveled with her husband from Pemberley, their grand estate in Derbyshire, to attend.

Elizabeth appeared unsure of words appropriate for the situation, but she offered her a sympathetic smile.

Charlotte broke the silence for her. "I am pleased that you have come." She gestured to a chair that was tucked beneath her small kitchen table. "Have a seat in here away from the others and talk with me."

Elizabeth sat while Charlotte produced a tin of biscuits and set them on the table between them. They both selected a treat and ate in silence until Elizabeth found her voice.

"My dear Charlotte, I am sorry for your current circumstances."

Charlotte smiled. "My current circumstances must not be so negative, for they have brought you to my kitchen, and I have missed you, Eliza."

She and Elizabeth had always been good friends, but Elizabeth had disapproved of her decision to marry Mr. Collins. And Mr. Darcy found him absolutely intolerable. Consequently, they had seen little of each other over the intervening years, and the separation had caused a certain level of detachment in their friendship.

"Tell me, Charlotte, for I have heard nothing of the particulars of what has transpired: What has happened to take Mr. Collins away so unexpectedly?"

"A carriage accident. He was walking to Rosings Park to pay his daily compliments to Lady Catherine and was struck by a runaway mule wagon."

"A mule wagon?"

"Certainly, if it had been his choice of the means by which to meet his demise, he would have chosen a vehicle of quality pulled by a perfectly matched team of horses."

"Indeed!" Elizabeth said.

"But we may not always choose our circumstances."

Elizabeth sobered and met Charlotte's eyes. "No, we may not. Sometimes society—and transportation—makes demands of us that we must do our best to meet. You, Charlotte, have always exceeded the demands of society, even if I have not approved of your choices. And now you have a new set of circumstances with which to deal, and I hope that happier choices will be available to you."

Tears welled in Charlotte's eyes. She had hoped for happier choices too. But with the death of her husband, her protection and place in society had also vanished. She was alone, without daughter and husband, without home. Those circumstances merited her mourning, if the loss of her husband's company did not.

"Perhaps one day *I* shall meet with another Mr. Collins."

"Do not even joke about the possibility, my dear friend, for I believe you have done your time in purgatory. It is time for you to experience the heaven that a marriage of true minds can be. I consider everybody as having a right to marry once in their lives for love, if they can."

Charlotte envied her friend's felicity in marriage, and though her example had taught her that romantic love existed, she had no plans to pursue it herself. Her sole aim was to secure what money she could from Mr. Collins's estate and create a small, but comfortable, home for herself.

"I thank you for your kindness. If I cannot manage happiness in my choices, then I will have to make the best of those indifferent choices that are before me."

"As you have always done."

Elizabeth fell silent, and at length, Charlotte nodded in the direction of the sitting room and said, "But now, I fear, I must do my duty to the assembled company." She had balked at calling them guests, for that denoted people who had been invited for pleasure. Those in the sitting room appeared anything but pleased. In fact, they appeared quite ready to depart, and Charlotte could not blame them.

Upon entering the room, her younger sister Maria Lucas came to her side and touched her arm briefly. It was the most meaningful gesture her flighty sister could manage. And her mother, now swaying under the effects of ill health, lurched to her feet and wobbled alongside. They managed to encircle her, and Charlotte wished they would have kept their seats.

Her mother pressed her hand in hers. "Oh my dear daughter, whatever shall you do now? For we cannot possibly afford you."

Charlotte understood well her worries. A woman alone was at a disadvantage in society. And Charlotte was now truly alone.

But she produced what she hoped was a comforting smile for her mother. "All will be well, Mama. Pray, take your seat and do not be concerned about my future. Worry does no good."

Charlotte restrained a wry smile. Indeed, it would do no good for her mother to waste feeble energies on concern for her. She was concerned enough for herself, but only decisive action would remedy her situation, and at the moment, she was rendered ineffective by duty.

Even now, she wished she could be about the business of securing her independence, of talking to her husband's solicitor.

Alas, she must fulfill her final obligation to Mr. Collins, though in her heart, she wished that the mourners would depart.

Why had any of them come? The scene was utterly nonsensical. No one lamented the death of the gentleman to whom she had been married, except perhaps Lady Catherine, and she could not even be put upon to visit the parsonage.

Perhaps they had come simply to verify that Mr. Collins had well and truly departed for the mansions of heaven, which undoubtedly had as many fine windows as Rosings Park, and to ensure that he would never again bore them with his tedious conversation.

✎ One ✎

1820

"Do not tell me that you intend to spend the rest of your days in this dreadful sitting room, Charlotte," Maria said, settling herself on the faded upholstered chair beside the fireplace with a flounce.

Charlotte set aside the letter she had been writing to her cousin Mary Emerson in London, abandoned the writing desk, and walked to the settee, knowing all too well that she would be unable to complete her correspondence now that her sister had joined her. In lieu of paper and quill, she picked up a cup and saucer from the mismatched tea set on the tray beside the settee. The cup was empty. She felt the pot; it had gone cold. Such a bother.

She rang the bell for beverage reinforcements, lowered herself to the settee, and regarded the room. She had to admit that it was rather dreadful, the furniture worn, and the rented cottage small, but at least she had such comforts, and two servants as well.

"I do intend to sit here in this room, for, despite its faults, I find it rather pleasant."

Indeed, it was the loveliest room in her cottage. Two comfortable chairs with curving wooden arms flanked a cream-colored settee, which had probably been white at one time. The seating area was situated in front of a modest but cheery hearth, and an old writing desk was tucked between two windows, facing south and opening toward an herb garden. As the sun made its course through the sky each day, it brightened the room and nurtured the plants outside and the occupants inside.

"How dull." Maria, who obviously did not feel nurtured by the small room, practical furnishings, or the sunlight, clucked her tongue as she glanced around her.

"I much prefer the quiet life, and now that Mr. Collins has gone to his reward, I feel that I deserve mine. I shall enjoy my little home and meager income, and I shall live out my days as a very eccentric old widow."

"Old? Bah! You are but five-and-thirty years old, and that is not so very aged." Maria leaned forward. "You must get out into society again."

Charlotte reclined against the settee. "Must I?"

"Indeed, sister, for you have worn your widow's weeds far longer than required, and you of all people deserve a happy existence after living with such an odious man as Mr. Collins."

Charlotte smiled at her sister, wishing for her sake that the world worked in such a manner, that people actually received that which they deserved, and knowing it never would. Maria had reached her early twenties and remained unmarried, but still she retained the hopefulness and innocence of youth.

Foolish girl, Charlotte thought as she studied her sister. Maria's blond hair had slipped its pins and now the loose strands glinted in the firelight. Without so much as checking her own coiffure, Charlotte knew that her dark hair remained neat and precise. She was never anything but neat and precise.

Maria blew a wisp of hair out of her face. "And it would fit in with my plans."

Charlotte narrowed her eyes. This certainly did not bode well, and she meant to interrogate her sister immediately, but before she could demand an explanation, the door opened, and Edward entered balancing a tray of fresh tea things.

Edward Effingham. His name was grander than his intelligence. And even if his family had managed to retain its fortune, he would not have married well. Edward was her housekeeper's son, a young man of fourteen years with thin strawberry blond hair and a body as sturdy as a fence post. A good servant, he tended to many household duties, but his mind seemed to be caught somewhere in early childhood.

He walked into the room with slow, metered steps and placed the tray on the table as though he carried royal porcelain and not chipped pieces from Charlotte's old set.

He made a deep bow and rather than exiting the room unobtrusively, he said, "Mama told me to make certain that your tea is properly set for you, Mrs. Collins. She told me not to open my mouth and speak a word to you, but I cannot know if the tray pleases you without asking, can I?"

Charlotte cast a cursory glance at the teapot and fresh cups. "Everything is as it should be. Thank you, Edward."

He grinned in relief and exited the room without remembering to take the old tea tray with him. The door closed with a click behind him as he returned to Mrs. Eff in the kitchen. Charlotte turned her attention back to her sister. She had been watching Edward's departure as well.

"He's forgotten the old tea tray," Maria said. "He is not the brightest lad, is he?"

"No, but he is kind, and that often makes up for mental facility." Moreover, Charlotte was grateful for her servants. Her family had been unable to afford much household help, and so she, Maria, and her other siblings had often been required to prepare meals or beat rugs. She certainly did not desire a return to household chores. She added, "Besides, he and Mrs. Eff have released me from most of the kitchen drudgery."

"It *is* nice to live in a home in which I am not required to cook." Maria's face had turned wistful, reminding Charlotte that something was amiss. "I wish to have servants of my own one day."

"Yes, now, tell me of these plans to which you have so subtly alluded."

"I know that my visit was intended to endure only a few months, but…" Here Maria paused dramatically and mustered a pouty expression. Trouble was certainly afoot. "I had hoped that I might come to reside with you here in Westerham. Mama and Papa are ever so feeble, and they have made arrangements for our brothers and sisters. I am the only child who was to remain at home. However, they will never again make proper chaperones, and I shall have no hope of meeting a gentleman suitable for marriage unless I can move about in society. I am virtually an old maid, you know."

Charlotte poured two fresh cups of tea and considered her sister's situation. Their parents' health had continued to decline, leaving Maria without the benefit of society during the prime of her young life. She had not had the opportunity to experience the exuberance of youthful courtship. Or its disappointments.

Indeed, Charlotte had never experienced love as such and had doubted its very existence until she had too late seen the evidence of it. Now, she believed that it was a rare commodity. "Better to be an old maid than unhappily married."

Maria's expression soured briefly. "Even you are not convinced of the truthfulness of that statement. Confess. You have always believed that it was better to be unhappily married than to be a poor old maid."

"Yes." Charlotte could not dispute that she had believed so in the past. Mr. Collins had certainly made her reconsider her previous philosophy, and now, she was less certain of her opinion on the matter.

Maria ignored her tea and picked up the bonnet that she had discarded earlier that morning. She began to arrange a bow of pale green ribbon. Concentrating on her task, she appeared to give little thought to her words. "I shall find security and love, I am certain of it, for I still have my beauty, but I require a chaperone to set a toe into society. Mama and Papa cannot do it, but you could. Though you continue to wear your ugly colored gowns, you are no longer in mourning and can attend balls and parties. You are an independent woman."

"My independence was hard won." Charlotte said, recalling the tediousness of her daily interactions with her husband that had resulted in her current situation. How many ponderous sermons had she been subjected to? How many simpering compliments had she endured? And worse, how many fireplace mantels had she heard him describe in painful detail? "Note the carvings, my dear, the fluting, the ribbons. All are of the finest quality. A masterful hand created this artful mantel." And on and on he would go until Charlotte wished humanity had never discovered fire, for there would be no fireplaces on which to lavish his praise. Yes, her independence had been hard won indeed.

"But without your help, I have no hope of winning my own or of finding love." Maria looked up from her bonnet. "You must be my chaperone."

Charlotte looked at Maria's shining face and wondered if she had ever felt so hopeful. Perhaps as a very young girl she had imagined meeting the perfect gentleman and falling in love with him. Perhaps, buried deep within her the hope existed still, but she was now too practical to live for something that might never happen. Her security had not come easily, and she simply did not have the will to go into society and become swept up, and then disappointed, by the quest for love, even if it were her sister's quest and not her own.

But then there was Maria with her head full of wishes, and Charlotte knew that for some people dreams of love did come true. Her friends Jane and Elizabeth Bennet had both had the good fortune to be able to marry for love. And by pure coincidence, their beloved gentlemen had both possessed great fortunes. Charlotte had not had the luxury of marrying for love, but perhaps her sister might.

"If Mama and Papa approve, and continue to send your allowance, you may keep the small bedchamber upstairs as long as you like, and I will serve as your chaperone."

Maria squealed like a young girl, leapt off her chair, and flung herself onto the settee and into Charlotte's arms. "And may we go to the winter ball in Westerham in two weeks' time?"

Charlotte groaned aloud. She had not expected the onslaught to begin so suddenly.

"Pray, say yes, sister. A gentleman will be there whose acquaintance I do so wish to make. An *American*." Maria said the word as though it were exotic and strange. "He is said to be just about my age and is traveling with his uncle on a tour of Europe. They are relatives of Colonel Armitage and are staying at his house for the duration of their visit."

Charlotte eyed her sister. An American? What could she possibly be thinking?

The Armitages, at least, were a well-respected family of decent fortune. Colonel Armitage had been in service to England, and he had elevated his whole family's status. Mrs. Armitage was a quiet, unassuming woman, who seemed to disappear when her jovial husband was near. Their children had made very good marriages. This American gentleman came from good English stock, and if he was on a European tour, he obviously had a good income as well, but Charlotte would withhold her good opinion until she had seen proof that he was not a barbarian, which was unlikely.

"He is said to be very handsome…"

There was the real inducement, Charlotte thought.

"…and Americans are reputed to be less particular about rank and age and other things about which we English are so concerned."

Supposing it could do no harm, Charlotte smiled in encouragement. "Indeed? Well, then I suppose you must meet him."

"Then we may go to the ball?"

"Yes, I suppose we may. Quite a picture I shall make in my somber attire among all the angelic white muslin and pale-colored gowns." She plucked at the drab gray fabric of her skirts.

"It has been two years, and it is perfectly acceptable for you to begin wearing other colors." Catching Charlotte's reproving look, Maria continued, "But somber shades quite flatter your coloring. You will not make such a dour picture as you suppose. You may be the belle of the ball yet."

Maria was being kind. Absurd, but kind. Charlotte was an old widow, no matter in how loving a light her younger sister viewed her.

However, against Charlotte's will, a tiny thrill of forbidden delight coursed through her at the prospect of attending a ball, of meeting new people and conversing with old friends without the weight of Mr. Collins always about her shoulders, and of dancing again. But who would dance with her now? Her days as a debutante were over years ago, Charlotte reminded herself, quickly squashing her excitement under the weight of reality. She was just coming out of mourning for her husband and must perform her duty as chaperone to her sister.

"No one will spare a second glance at me. And certainly no gentleman."

"I would be happy if a man would only look once at me."

Charlotte sighed. "You desire a marriage so much even after seeing my own less than ideal one?"

"I do. Honestly, I do. For I have seen what is possible when one marries for love."

Charlotte understood Maria's reference perfectly, and she did not blame her one bit for desiring the same love that Jane and Elizabeth had found. "Then we shall ensure that you meet your young American, but we will do so with the utmost decorum and propriety. Otherwise, straight back to Mama and Papa you go."

Maria straightened and blinked. "What a thing to say! I shall behave myself very well."

༄ Two ༄

An odd mixture of scents is present in the air of any ballroom: wood smoke, perfumed flesh, cold meats, watered wine, and humanity. Charlotte had forgotten the precise combination of pleasant and unpleasant aromas. Now she inhaled deeply, attempting to ignore the stench of body odor that existed beneath the other, more pleasant, smells. The scents seemed to hold memories, and Charlotte endeavored to ignore them. Memories would do her no good. She must attend to Maria, not to her own past. Instead, she focused on more tangible elements of the chamber.

Two large fireplaces loomed at one end of the ballroom, and the sheer number of wax tapers, probably donated by Lady Catherine, who never attended a public ball but who liked to make her charity known, leant a feeling of opulence to the assembly.

Arm in arm, the two sisters wove their way through the crowd toward an empty spot near the fireplaces where they could observe the dancers. Maria sparkled in her white gown with its puffed sleeves and pale green trim around the neckline, and though she would never admit it, Charlotte felt somewhat attractive in the modestly cut lavender gown with black trim, which seemed to flatter both her face and her slim figure.

Maria jabbed Charlotte in the ribs. "That must be him." Her voice was sharp, but at least she had bothered to whisper.

Charlotte scanned the ballroom for the gentleman who had captured her sister's attention so forcefully. Maria gestured with a turn of her pretty blond head and giggled. Charlotte looked but could see no one spectacular. "Who?"

"The gentleman. The *American*." Again the word was spoken as though it denoted something unusual and not just an ordinary man. "The one standing next to Colonel Armitage."

Charlotte found Colonel Armitage easily enough, for he had a memorable physique, large and jolly, and always stood out, even in a crowded room. Beside him was a young man, who appeared to be rather tall and had dark blond hair, which had been styled to convey unconcerned wildness. She was certain that such perfectly tousled wildness actually took his valet hours to achieve. He spoke to Colonel and Mrs. Armitage, gesturing broadly, and smiled just as broadly. He appeared to have engaging manner, for the Armitages attended to his every word, as did many guests, but Charlotte thought she sensed a cocky air about him.

No, she must not believe the worst of him. Not yet. Perhaps her own poor experience with gentlemen was coloring her opinion of the young man. "He looks quite…" She searched for the word. "…nice."

"He certainly does. I expected him to appear different somehow, being that he is an American. Perhaps more uncouth. But he is dressed in proper English attire."

She was quite correct. His striped waistcoat, tan trousers, and dark coat caused him to blend with the other gentlemen in attendance. "He seems to fit well indeed, but we shall see how well he gets along in society."

Maria tore her eyes from the American and turned to her sister. "You must arrange a meeting for me before another young lady steals his attentions for the evening."

How quickly Maria had forgotten her promise of good behavior. Charlotte would have to guard her carefully indeed. "I shall do my duty as your chaperone and arrange an introduction, but everything will be done in a proper manner. I certainly will not rush straight to the colonel and demand a meeting."

There were rules of behavior that must be followed without question. Appearances meant everything for a woman who hoped to gain the protection of a husband. Was she naturally witty and a good conversationalist? No? Then she must learn to be so. Was she a natural musician? No? Then she must practice until she seemed to be naturally gifted. Was she happy? No? She must pretend to be so.

A woman must be an artist, a seamstress, and a great reader, and this she must do with an air of gentleness and decorum. She must behave *comme il faut* even if she wished a thousand times a day to do otherwise. It simply had to be done in the name of keeping oneself from falling low in society and being forced to accept charity from those formerly called equals.

Maria's gaze rested again on the American. Her voice was wistful. "No, indeed. That would not do at all. I do not want to appear to be overeager."

"The best way not to appear overeager is not to be overeager in the first place."

Maria groaned. "Please do not take the pleasure out of this for me."

Charlotte took Maria by the hand, gently turning her away from the American. "I do not intend to rob you of pleasure, but neither do I intend to sit by and allow you to be injured or to injure yourself socially."

"You fret too much."

"You do not fret enough." She glanced at the gentleman out of the corner of her eye. He did not appear to be a ruffian.

Maria said, "Then together we will fret just enough."

Charlotte hoped it would be so. "We must act decorously."

The frustration Charlotte had felt from her sister seemed to vanish. Perhaps her warnings had taken hold.

"I suppose you are right, but I am so tired of being alone. I do not think a little indecorous behavior would destroy my reputation."

Perhaps her warnings had not even been heard.

Charlotte was about to offer a stern rebuke when old Mrs. Farmington and her young granddaughter sidled up to them. Mrs. Farmington maintained a powdery, aged appearance even in the generous softness of so many candles. The pattern and color of her dress, a fleshy background with a subtle chevron pattern, were also reminiscent of powder, causing Charlotte to wonder if she ordered her entire wardrobe after the substance. She groaned at her approach, for Mrs. Farmington's mind was as dusty as her appearance, and she was forever speaking out of turn.

Polite curtseys were offered and the older woman began the conversation. "Such a lovely ball, is it not, Mrs. Collins?"

Thankfully, a safe subject. "It is indeed, Mrs. Farmington."

"It has been quite some time since we have seen you out in society."

"Yes." Mrs. Farmington had put together two sentences of good sense, and Charlotte wondered if a third could possibly follow.

She gestured to Charlotte's half-mourning attire. "You do Mr. Collins credit by your devotion to him. And it was such good fortune that he was able to leave you a little something on which to live."

Apparently, two reasonable sentences were her limit.

The old lady was rude but correct. Mr. Collins had left her some money. Before their marriage, Charlotte had the foresight to maneuver him into arranging a jointure, a fitting sum of money left to her in the event of his death. Charlotte's father had encouraged her not to make any such request, believing it wisest not to be troublesome before the marriage was official. But she had ignored his advice, and at first blush, Mr. Collins, being very much against the idea, had proven her father right.

Mr. Collins had railed against the idea. A woman inheriting money was unbiblical, he said.

Then, she had reminded him of Mr. Bennet, who had made similar arrangements for his wife and children and whose house Mr. Collins himself would inherit. Of course, Mr. Collins could not allow his relation to appear to be his better. And so employing the straightforward and uncomplicated tactic of exploiting her husband's desire to keep up with his relations, Charlotte had contrived a jointure.

Straightaway after Mr. Collins's funeral, she had visited his solicitor and invested her small inheritance in the Funds, and with good luck and a high rate of interest, Charlotte had been satisfied that she would be able to exist in her widowed state.

She then sought suitable accommodations, for she was forced to vacate Hunsford parsonage so that Lady Catherine could prepare it for its next occupant. However, hoping to spare herself the embarrassing task of making inquiries of those whom she had formerly considered her social equals, Charlotte asked after another structure on Lady Catherine's estate: an unused hunting cottage inconveniently located on the fringes of Rosings Park.

Lady Catherine had agreed to rent it to her at a greatly reduced rate, a circumstance that Charlotte suspected had arisen not from charity or kindness but from a feeling of responsibility. But she did not care why Lady Catherine had given her such charity, and she certainly did not intend to jeopardize it in any way. And now that she was a lowly tenant of Lady Catherine, she was no longer invited to attend the tedious social functions at the great house.

Truly, the situation could not be more agreeable.

But it was none of Mrs. Farmington's affair. Charlotte certainly had no desire to discuss her situation with this old crone or anyone else, so she chose to deflect her line of inquiry. "Mr. Collins's death was quite a shock, but I am coping with it as best I can."

Mrs. Farmington's smile oozed pity. "Yes, yes, my dear, it is good to see you out amongst society again though I doubt there are any suitably unattached gentlemen in attendance tonight to give you a turn around the dance floor."

Charlotte did not know what reaction was proper in the face of such indiscreet comments. She could not laugh or manage to muster anger. She simply stared at old Mrs. Farmington and wondered if it were possible for her to attain the coveted blunder trio and discuss not only income and matchmaking but to comment on her out-of-fashion attire as well.

She meant well, Charlotte was certain, but rather than allowing her to direct the conversation any longer, she gestured to Maria, who stood quietly beside her. "I am acting as my sister's chaperone. And is this your granddaughter?" She nodded at the woman who stood at the old woman's side. "She looks far too grown up to be little Miss Farmington."

Mrs. Farmington beamed. "This is indeed our Constance. She is quite a good deal bigger, is she not?"

A quick glance at Miss Farmington revealed that she did not appreciate being called a good deal bigger, but she said nothing as her grandmother continued. "This is her first season out. Is she not lovely?"

Constance Farmington was a lovely young lady with chestnut hair and a sprinkling of dainty freckles across the bridge of her nose, but she rather reminded Charlotte of the red roan pony her family had owned when she was a girl. She hoped that Miss Farmington was like the pony only in appearance and not in manners, for the beast had ignored her protestations and dragged her all over the countryside in search of the most delectable grasses. That pony had taught Charlotte a great deal about the complexities of social interaction: most people—and horses—behave in ways that benefit themselves and care little for the wishes and feelings of others.

Charlotte glanced again at red roan Miss Farmington, who was clearly thrilled to be among members of the opposite sex. She leaned forward conspiratorially and spoke to Maria loudly enough for the group—and perhaps the entire assembly—to hear. "Have you had the pleasure of meeting Colonel Armitage's relatives yet?"

"No, indeed, we have not." Maria shot Charlotte a haughty look under her curving blond lashes.

"Oh, you must, for they are the most fascinating—and handsome—men as I have ever seen." Miss Farmington gestured across the room to where Colonel Armitage, the young American, and an unfamiliar gentleman were surrounded by a large group of people. "Mr. James Westfield stands there beside the colonel." She indicated the young man Charlotte and Maria had observed earlier. "He is a bit older than I, but still very handsome, do not you think?"

Maria agreed perhaps too wholeheartedly. "Yes, quite handsome. And so tall."

"His uncle stands beside him. He is quite old indeed, and his attire is certainly not up to the standard of his nephew. His name, I believe, is Mr. Benjamin Basford."

Charlotte looked at the very old Mr. Basford who was probably not more than a few years older than herself, and although his dress portrayed a certain rawness not usually seen in an English ballroom, she found him to be handsome in a rather untraditional way. His hair was stylishly tousled, although she was certain that the wind—and not a valet—had arranged it. He seemed to find the ball to be very amusing and appeared to enjoy the attention he and his nephew had generated. His expression had a rather comical bent, and he did not appear to be a serious person. Charlotte disliked his smirk immediately.

But Mr. Basford was insignificant. Mr. Westfield was the prize.

"How charming they look!" exclaimed Maria.

"Oh, they are!" Miss Farmington said. "Mr. Westfield is said to have a fortune awaiting him in America, and his uncle is apparently of no little means as well, although he certainly does not dress the part."

"Oh, how lovely. They are rich as well as handsome."

Charlotte too was pleased to hear that Mr. Westfield was of substantial means. If her sister were successful in making a match with him, she would have security, and if the dewy expression in her eyes were any indication, she might have love as well. Indeed, the situation was quite possibly ideal.

The girls continued to speak about Mr. Westfield and Mr. Basford until Mrs. Farmington became bored and, claiming a parching thirst, bustled her granddaughter away into the crowd toward the refreshment room, where lemonade, negus, and white soup awaited.

Ever the dutiful chaperone, Charlotte was soon left to stand alone to watch her sister dance with Mr. Jonas Card, an acquaintance she had made on her early visits to Hunsford. He stumbled good-naturedly through the quadrille while Maria laughed.

Though he was a well-looking gentleman, always polished and elegantly dressed, Mr. Card's fortune and property caused many of the young ladies of his acquaintance to view him as more handsome than his features warranted. Maria, however, had never looked at him twice, fortune or not, and Charlotte had always been rather sorry for that, for he was a genial sort of man who would tolerate her sister's frequent flights of fancy and was capable of financing her shopping trips.

Charlotte was contemplating Mr. Card as a potential suitor for her sister when she felt someone bump into her. Slightly off balance, she reached to steady herself against the side of the mantel and turned, annoyed, to find the offender to be a large gentleman with a shock of red hair and piercing eyes. The gentleman's gaze was intense, and he offered a slight bow. "Pray excuse me."

"It is nothing, sir." She turned politely away. They had not been properly introduced, and she did not want to invite his acquaintance by meeting his eyes again. But the man continued at her side. She could sense his gaze upon her, and she began to feel slightly uneasy.

"I do not believe we have been introduced, but I do not see how it is so wrong for an introduction to take place now that I have nearly caused you to fall. I am Lewis Edgington." He offered a proper bow. "I am an often forgotten relation of the de Bourgh family. A distant cousin actually."

Charlotte was reluctant to break with convention, but he was a relation of Lady Catherine, so she curtseyed with extreme decorum and what she hoped was a foreboding expression.

He continued undeterred by her countenance. "Lady Catherine promised to introduce us. I understand that you rent the old hunting cottage on her property. She said that you are the widow of her former rector."

Stubborn man, Charlotte thought as she stared at him. He knew very well that she had no desire to continue the acquaintance, no matter to whom he was related. Her manner exhibited that truth as clearly as if she had spoken the words aloud. She had no chance to generate a reply before he spoke again. "I am sorry to hear of the Reverend Mr. Collins's death."

"Thank you." It had been two years since he was buried. Why were so many people commenting about him tonight?

"It is good for you to venture out into society again and to mingle with others now that you are coming out of the mourning period."

Well, she was certainly glad he thought so. She often concerned herself with the inappropriate opinions of strange men. She narrowed her eyes. "I still mourn Mr. Collins, sir."

"Yes?" He considered her for a moment, and an odd expression came into in his eyes. "Well, I am very sorry to hear that."

What precisely did that mean? She did not know quite how to respond to his reply, which had been uttered with an undertone of…of…she knew not what, and could only manage to say a brief "thank you."

Relieved when he bowed and left her, she leaned against the wall. She was unused to male attention, and something about Mr. Edgington caused her discomfort. Suddenly, she wanted nothing more than to return to the safety of her home.

Thankfully, the quadrille soon ended and Mr. Card delivered Maria back to her side, bowing to her so deeply Charlotte worried that the seam of his coat would split. "Thank you for the dance, Miss Lucas. May I procure lemonade for you and Mrs. Collins?"

"How kind—" Charlotte began, but Maria spoke over her.

"—but we do not require a beverage at the moment. Thank you, Mr. Card."

At her dismissal, Mr. Card's face fell into a downtrodden expression, which he quickly covered with a bright smile. He was an obliging gentleman, and her sister really ought to have a care when dealing with him. She planned to say as much to her when he departed, but the very moment Mr. Card's coat disappeared into the crowd, Maria demanded, "Will you not go speak to Colonel Armitage now?"

Charlotte glanced through her eyelashes across the ballroom at the three gentlemen. They finally had managed to divest themselves of the crowd that had been around them all evening. "In a moment." She searched for an excuse to depart for the evening instead of seeking an introduction.

Maria was openly staring at the American. Anyone in the room might read her obvious interest. When would her sister learn the art of subtlety? Charlotte reached out to take her hand and divert her attention to a more appropriate object, but Maria spoke. "It is my good fortune, then, that Americans are a brash sort of people, for here they come now."

Colonel Armitage led his relations straight toward them, and Charlotte allowed herself only the briefest of glances, but Maria shot them an open, welcoming smile.

"Mrs. Collins, Miss Lucas, will you allow me to present my long-lost relations from America?" He indicated the older gentleman with entirely too much dark hair for his age and a witty look in his eyes. "This is my nephew Mr. Benjamin Basford, the son of my elder sister who, you will remember, disappeared to the American colonies some years ago to get married. And this is his sister's son, Mr. James Westfield."

The gentlemen bowed.

"It is a pleasure to make your acquaintance," Charlotte said with a sedate curtsey and a jaundiced eye.

She looked to Maria, who had also greeted them with a curtsey, but her eyes were wide and locked with those of Mr. Westfield. They seemed to take no notice of the others around them or to mark the pleasantries they uttered.

This was trouble indeed.

The young man spoke first. "May I have the pleasure of the next dance, Miss Lucas?"

Maria beamed. "You may."

And with that, Mr. Westfield offered his arm and led Maria, who practically floated at his side, to her place in the set.

"What a charming pair," Colonel Armitage said. "And he is just as taken with Miss Lucas as I predicted."

Mr. Basford looked at his uncle. "I heard you make no such prediction."

The colonel appeared incredulous, one hairy eyebrow raised. "I said as much just this morning at breakfast. Did you not mark me?"

"I heard you speak only of your eggs and toast, also a charming pair but hardly my nephew and Miss Lucas."

Colonel Armitage gave a frustrated snort, and Charlotte wondered that his eyebrows did not flutter in the breeze. "I mentioned Miss Lucas as a possible acquaintance for him, I am sure. Perhaps I only thought it. Ah! The joys of aging. One day you shall understand."

Charlotte murmured something polite having to do with maturation bringing wisdom, but she did not quite believe her words applied to the colonel, for tonight he seemed more confused than wise.

But Mr. Basford only laughed and said, "I hope that I never age so much that I'd begin to confuse people with breakfast items."

Colonel Armitage snorted again and turned to Charlotte. He took her hand and patted it. "All this talk of food is making me hungry, and I can take no more of my nephew's wit on an empty stomach. I must excuse myself for the buffet."

Charlotte hoped Mr. Basford might excuse himself as well, but he remained at her side, studying the room with a silent smirk while his uncle squeezed his way through the crowd. She followed Mr. Basford's gaze, which alighted on a young couple obviously being introduced by an elderly chaperone. He looked back at Charlotte, his dark eyes mischievous. "Don't you find these English introductory rules to be a little confining?"

Already shaken by her impromptu conversation with Mr. Edgington and recalling her ruminations on that very subject earlier that evening, Charlotte was taken aback at his selection of topic. She recovered herself quickly and congratulated herself for saying, "Indeed I do not, for they keep one from being thrown into the company of inappropriate, dangerous people."

He grinned at her attempt at a cutting remark. "Well, it's a good thing, then, that we met in the proper way. Since we were introduced by my uncle the colonel, you can be assured that I'm neither inappropriate nor dangerous."

Charlotte was fairly certain that he did not present any danger, but she was as yet uncertain about deeming him appropriate. She examined him for a moment. "We shall see."

"Then, while you are deciding, shall we have a dance?"

She stared at him now, mouth agape. "Can you not see that I am in mourning attire, sir?" She gestured to the black trim on her gown.

"Are you?" He looked her over once. And then once more. "My apologies. I assumed that you wore that shade because it suits you."

"I am just coming out of my mourning period, if you must know," she ground out.

"Ah, then it's fortunate that the prescribed attire suits you so well. It brings out the lovely color in your cheeks."

Was it possible that he paying her a sincere compliment? She hardly thought so, for she knew very well that she only had color in her cheeks due to embarrassment or as a result of remaining too long out of doors in the summer. He returned her gaze with an open expression, and she wondered if he was awaiting an appropriate feminine response. A swoon perhaps. Well, she certainly did not intend to concede to his expectations.

"Are all Americans as brash as you?"

"No, some are as stuffy as you. Are all English bound by pointless manners and meaningless social conventions?"

"Our manners and customs do not bind us but protect us."

"They prevent you from living freely."

Charlotte's teeth clenched momentarily. She was beginning to believe that he was, at the very least, inappropriate if not dangerous as well. She unclamped her jaw. "If living freely means bringing disrespect to Mr. Collins and being ostracized by my friends and family, then I will remain bound by convention, as you say. And while you are in England, it would be better if you followed our customs as well."

"Would it?" He spoke as if their conversation was pleasant and not laced with discomfort. "Then I fear I will not make a good impression on Westerham society while I am here."

Charlotte decided to turn to a polite subject. "And how long will you be in our town?"

"Quite some time. My sister wants James to be introduced to your English society. I am to be his chaperone."

"Then you will be forced to attend many of our tedious social functions." She certainly did not relish the prospect of meeting Mr. Basford with any frequency.

"Yes, I am afraid so, but I do find certain aspects of them rather amusing. I assume you'll be attending with Miss Lucas."

Her reply was a reluctant "yes."

He gestured to the dance floor where Maria and Mr. Westfield stood up together. Their two blond heads were easy to view among the other dancers. "My uncle was correct. They do look well together, don't they?"

Charlotte was forced to admit that they did make a handsome couple. As she watched their sunny heads bob with the movements of the dance, an imp seized her, and before she could censor herself, she said, "Like eggs and toast." Mr. Basford leaned back his head and fairly shouted with laughter, causing Charlotte to regret her allusion. She glanced around, thinking to find the entire ballroom focused on them, but no one seemed to notice his outburst or her complexion, which was certainly a ten shades of crimson.

His laughter abated and he studied her. "I find that I like you, Mrs. Collins. Perhaps at the next assembly, we can see how well we do on the dance floor."

Charlotte gawked at him before schooling her features into a mask of impassivity. Mr. Basford did not appear to comprehend the forward nature of his remark, and when she attempted to lance him with a look of disdain, he only smiled, causing her to wonder if a man such as him could possibly be cowed by anyone.

Mr. Basford bid Charlotte a polite goodbye, bowing, his eyes never leaving her face, and against her will, she noticed that he was a tolerably handsome man.

৩৩ Three ৩৯

The sisters visited their parents' home in Hertfordshire for the Yuletide. The journey of fifty miles was cold, and the public coach was cramped and unpleasant. The wet weather turned the roads to mud during the day, and the cold transformed them into a partially frozen slurry at night. The horses labored before the coach, and Charlotte fancied that she could hear their groans of protest at being forced to work in conditions that were not suitable for man or beast.

If Charlotte had not had a true fondness for her family, she would have never attempted the trip, especially accompanied by a sister who was struck dumb by love. Charlotte wished Maria had been struck mute by love instead, for she spent the duration of the voyage speaking of Mr. Westfield, Mr. Westfield, Mr. Westfield. His hair, his eyes, his wit.

They had not been enclosed within the carriage for more than half an hour before Charlotte began to fear that one of their fellow travelers might toss her sister out the window at the next mention of Mr. Westfield's name.

Briefly, very briefly, Charlotte had considered doing so herself.

When they had finally arrived at Lucas Lodge, Charlotte pulled Maria aside and said, "Do not overtax Mama and Papa with tales of romance."

But Maria had only looked at her and asked, "Why ever not? They will be pleased that I have attracted the attention of a gentleman such as Mr. Westfield."

And upon their first moments in the sitting room, which was kept uncomfortably warm to assuage their parents' fear of drafts, Maria had relayed all the details that she had been able to discern about the gentleman. Beginning with his appearance and finishing a summary of their most intimate discussions, which had apparently focused primarily on fashion.

And for the next few weeks she had elaborated.

Between Maria's discourses on Mr. Westfield, the Lucases managed to celebrate Christmas, relax together *en famille*, and eat as lavishly as their budget would allow. And Charlotte would have found her time in Hertfordshire to be restful had it not been for Maria's chatter and the obvious concern it elicited in her parents.

Aware that she would eventually be asked to account for Maria's involvement with Mr. Westfield, Charlotte had attempted to avoid the subject altogether when alone with her parents. She hardly knew how to convince them that Mr. Westfield was an upstanding gentleman when she was yet unsure.

One evening shortly before their departure, the subject could not be avoided. A fire roared in the hearth while her parents huddled under heavy blankets to keep out the non-existent drafts and Charlotte perspired.

"Now my dear," said her mother. "Do tell me about this gentleman Mr. Westham."

"West-*field*, Mama." How could she possibly get his name wrong? Maria had only spoken it with shocking regularity for the past five weeks.

"Yes, yes. Your papa and I are very concerned. He is American, is he not?"

"Indeed he is."

Lady Lucas groaned.

Sir William raised his eyebrows. "I know we have had our trouble with them in the past, but certainly they cannot be completely disreputable. If he is quite taken with our Maria, he cannot be thoroughly bad, can he?"

Lady Lucas's face was drawn into skeptical lines, her mouth pulled downward into a small frown. "But is this gentleman—this *American*—good enough for our daughter? Surely not."

Charlotte had asked herself the same question, but she did not want to worry her parents over much. So she told them the same platitudes she used to reassure herself. "Although we have not long been acquainted with Mr. Westfield, he comes from a well-respected English family and he is traveling Europe with a proper—" she was unsure if proper were the correct word to describe Mr. Basford—"chaperone. I will ensure that nothing untoward occurs."

"Yes, yes, but has he any money?"

"I understand that his family wants for very little. They are travelling our country quite at their leisure."

Lady Lucas appeared relieved and snuggled deeper under her blanket, but Sir William leaned forward. "That is reassurance indeed, but I only wish he had a title. An appointment to the knighthood. Maria is quite pretty enough to marry a person of rank."

Charlotte regarded her father. He knew very well that America did not operate under a system of rank. Perhaps his mind had dimmed more than she had realized. "I fear that titled gentlemen are rather difficult to come by in America."

"Oh, of course." Sir William looked momentarily confused and then he took Charlotte's hand. "You are a good daughter, my dear. You made a good marriage yourself, and I am certain you will ensure that Maria will also be so fortuitously settled."

Charlotte only smiled.

❧❧ ❧❧

In the new year, Charlotte and Maria returned to the warm—but not stiflingly so—walls of the cottage in Westerham. Foul weather caused social invitations to arrive infrequently, and Maria heartily lamented her empty calendar and spent her hours planning future perambulations in sunny gardens and picnics by the river with various and sundry gentlemen. She was determined to fall in love. With Mr. Westfield if possible.

Love was also on Charlotte's mind. In her youth, she had not believed that love existed, but she had seen the proof of it. Now, she wondered at its nature. How did it feel? Maria seemed wild and willing to be wooed. But did love overwhelm or coax? Did it break in like a thief and steal one's heart? Or was it patient and kind?

Charlotte did not care for poetry, and she did not often turn her thoughts to it if it could possibly be helped. But Shakespeare's question came to her mind, "Tell me where is fancy bred, or in the heart or in the head?" Love in poetry was one matter, but what of the real world? What was love?

She was contemplating poetry! She was in desperate need of some diversion or she would certainly begin composing some lines of her own.

So when Mr. Jonas Card and his mother paid a call on them one overcast afternoon, Maria and Charlotte were both quite pleased, for Maria had gained society and Charlotte had been able to forgo her poetical musings.

Mr. Card and his mother had only just entered the sitting room, when Maria decided to enact her plotted escape, although only out to slog along the damp country roads in Mr. Card's barouche.

"Why do we not pick up Miss Farmington and drive into Westerham for a while this afternoon?" Maria asked Mr. Card in a pleading tone. "I am desperately in need of some amusement outside this house, and the weather is not so cold as to make the trip unpleasant."

"Our driver is along to chaperone, so if it is agreeable to your sister, let us be off," Mr. Card looked to Charlotte for permission. With a proper chaperone, there was no reason to thwart her sister's escape plot. Even though she did not wish to be alone with Mrs. Card for a protracted period of time, it was better than the alternative.

So she nodded her consent, and soon the young people had departed, leaving Charlotte with Mrs. Card and a pot of tea. Jonas's mother was a diminutive woman of little meaningful conversation but many words. Moreover, she was of single-minded purpose, much like a terrier. She was determined to fetch a daughter-in-law who would bend easily to her will with regard to the running of the Card household.

They had already discussed the weather and the upcoming change of seasons, and the conversation lulled, causing Charlotte to await Maria and Mr. Card's return with some eagerness. Why had she not reminded them not to tarry too long in town?

"We have not seen you and Maria about this winter. We had worried that you had disappeared into Hertfordshire for good."

"No, we still reside happily here. We merely chose to enjoy a quiet holiday with our relations. As you know, our parents must keep to the house due to their ill health. We felt it unkind to leave them during Christmas."

"A noble thing to do, but we missed you at our assemblies."

"Thank you. It is very kind of you to say. I know that Maria longed to attend those functions. She missed her companions greatly."

"I believe it is also safe to say that Miss Lucas was missed as well, especially by Jonas."

Charlotte sipped the tea, desperately hoping for a turn in the conversation, but Mrs. Card spoke again.

"It has always been my fondest wish that Miss Lucas would one day marry my Jonas."

Charlotte set her cup daintily in the saucer and then placed it on the table, giving herself time to consider a proper reply. Was there a proper reply? She was hardly in a position to negotiate a marriage contract for her sister, especially to a gentleman whom she had no wish to marry. "It is flattering to know that you consider Maria suitable match for your son. He is an upstanding gentleman."

"Indeed, they are a fine match, and I have said as much to Jonas."

This conversation was not at all to Charlotte's liking. She knew very well that her sister's affections lay with the American Mr. Westfield and not with Mr. Card, whom she viewed as little more than a toy to be discarded at her whim.

"Mrs. Card—"

"I suppose Miss Lucas is in love with that dreadful young American, like every other young lady of our acquaintance."

Charlotte sat up rigidly. Were her thoughts so obvious? Her words teetered too close to the truth. "To the best of my knowledge, Maria is not in love with anyone at the present time, and I do not believe that this is a suitable topic of conversation."

Mrs. Card's eyes hardened to something between granite and steel and then softened slightly. "Forgive me. I just worry so about my Jonas. I do want him to be happy."

Finally, some relief. "I do understand. I want Maria to be happy as well."

"I must confess that I have heard nothing negative at all about Mr. Westfield. In fact, I have heard just the opposite. It was indecorous of me to say such things, but it does feel good, now and again, to say bilious things about other gentlemen. It makes my Jonas stand out as the deserving gentleman that he is."

"Your acknowledgment does you credit." Charlotte hoped the conversation would soon land on even footing. "Mr. Card is indeed a fine gentleman and a good catch for any young lady."

"How kind of you to say. And I must say that by all accounts, Mr. Westfield is a testimony to his English lineage. He behaves in a civilized manner and is always pleasant at a party." Here Mrs. Card leaned forward in the manner of a conspirator. "It is his uncle whose behavior is questionable."

After her conversation with Mr. Basford at the winter ball, Charlotte could well believe that.

"Oh?"

"I had it from Mrs. Holloway who had it from a relative of the colonel's that Mr. Basford behaved as quite the libertine in America."

"Oh dear." Libertine was not the description she had expected. Clown or jester, perhaps, but not libertine.

"They say he was thrown out of America for indecent behavior. And to be thrown out of a country as indecent as that is really saying something."

Charlotte could believe him rude and flirtatious, but she could not believe him to be such a man as that. "Can one be thrown out of a country without some sort of trial? That seems rather unlikely, do not you think?"

"Not after the things he has done here. He is often impertinent and overtly plainspoken. He seems to laugh at us all. I would put nothing past a man such as him. Have you not marked his behavior?"

Charlotte nodded her assent and refilled her cup of tea.

"It is utterly incomprehensible to me that he would be chosen to chaperone young Mr. Westfield. He does not set a decent example at all. What could Mr. Westfield's parents have been thinking to send him across the world in such a man's care? Some people, it seems, simply do not understand the way of the world."

Charlotte leaned back, and curiosity forced her to ask, "Are you at all acquainted with a Mr. Lewis Edgington? I encountered him some months ago at the winter ball."

Her face brightened at the prospect of relating more gossip. "Now there is a man who is reputed to be thoroughly good."

"It is nice to hear a man is said to be so."

"He is a widower. He lost his wife about the same time as Mr. Collins's accident, I believe. I have heard that he keeps a very nice sort of house with a respectable number of servants, and it is said that he rarely gambles."

Charlotte was preparing to make a suitably disinterested reply when the sitting room door burst open and Maria entered followed by Mr. Westfield and Mr. Basford.

Charlotte and Mrs. Card stood abruptly, surprised at their calamitous entrance.

Maria flung herself on the settee where Charlotte had been sitting. "Lord, you will not believe what has happened to us!"

"Good heavens, Maria! This is very untoward," Charlotte said and then turned to welcome her new guests. "Please do sit down."

Mrs. Card sat down on her chair rather heavily for a person of her small size. "Where is Jonas?"

Mr. Westfield took possession of the other upholstered chair beside the fireplace, and Mr. Basford sat in the small wooden chair beside the writing desk, immediately tilting it back on its rear legs.

Charlotte stared at the airborne chair legs and imagined that she could hear the wood creak in protest, causing her to question not only the integrity of the chair's structure but also of Mr. Basford's character, for only a questionable gentleman would show such disrespect for the furniture of a lady.

No one had responded to Mrs. Card's inquiry, so she repeated herself. "I demand to know what has happened to my son."

Mr. Basford concealed a smirk, Charlotte was certain of it.

"You will never believe it, Charlotte," Maria said, "but poor Mr. Card's carriage broke down on the way out of town. Fortunately, we were soon discovered by Mr. Westfield and Mr. Basford, who summoned help and then offered us a ride home in their carriage, for it is threatening rain."

Concern crossed Mrs. Card's features. "Oh dear. Rain! Where is Jonas? He shall be quite soaked through if he does not hurry!"

Mr. Westfield replied, "The repair has been made to the carriage, and he should be not fifteen minutes behind us. He was fortunate to be so near town when the break occurred."

"I do hope he beats the rain, for I cannot bear a wet ride home." Mrs. Card arose and walked to the window, her hands clasped in front of her. The gentlemen arose as well, Mr. Basford slower than his nephew.

"Do not worry, Mrs. Card, he will be along soon," said Mr. Westfield.

"What has become of Miss Farmington?" Charlotte asked Mr. Westfield.

Mr. Basford answered. "We deposited her at her home on the way here."

Charlotte nodded and was just about to suggest another cup of tea to her new guests, and hoping her supply would stretch to accommodate so many, when Edward entered the sitting room to announce Mr. Card, who stood beside him looking somewhat embarrassed.

The gentlemen bowed, and Mrs. Card appeared to be restraining herself from going to him. "Jonas, are you well?"

"Yes, Mama, I am quite well, only a little ashamed at putting out Miss Lucas and her friend especially in such threatening weather."

"Does it threaten still?" Mrs. Card turned again to the window. "It is quite dark. Jonas, we must return home immediately."

Mr. Card smiled apologetically at Maria. "As you wish, Mama. Pray excuse us, and Miss Lucas, please accept my sincerest regrets over our ruined ride."

Maria barely tore her eyes from Mr. Westfield when she said, "The incident is already forgotten."

And Charlotte could well believe it. When Mr. Westfield was near, it appeared, her sister forgot nearly everything, good manners included.

After the Cards departed, the gentlemen were once again able to take their seats, and the party became quiet.

"Shall we have tea? Maria, ring the bell and inform Mrs. Eff that we require another pot."

Maria went obediently.

"Why do the English have such an obsession with tea?" asked Mr. Basford, still leaning precariously on the back legs of the chair. "It is nothing but a few dried leaves after all."

Charlotte studied him. "Indeed, your censure is unwarranted, for I have heard that Americans are quite mad for the stuff as well. Particularly in Boston, I believe."

Charlotte was pleased with her retort, and so was Mr. Basford, who leaned his head back, causing the chair to tilt even further, and laughed heartily.

"She has you there, Uncle."

"Yes, indeed, she does."

"Mr. Basford seems to believe that the customs of our country are quite stilted and unnecessary," Charlotte said to Mr. Westfield.

"I confess that I do," Mr. Basford replied, letting the front legs of the chair return to the ground. "Take for instance the custom of calling people by their family names. I've seen close friends referring to each other as Mr. or Mrs. Whatnot. It's ridiculous."

"In your opinion, perhaps, Mr. Basford. I have never called social acquaintances by their first names unless I have known them since childhood. It is too familiar and uncomfortable."

"That is only because you have not practiced. Call me Ben, and you'll soon see how nice familiarity is."

Charlotte looked at him with horror. "Indeed, I will not! That sort of familiarity is only permitted in private moments between married couples, and perhaps not even then!"

He spoke as if she had not. "And I'll call you Charlotte."

"Indeed you shall not!" she objected, leaning forward as though to apprehend his words.

Mr. Westfield came to her rescue. "Uncle, do stop tormenting Mrs. Collins." He turned to Charlotte. "He is still reacting to your tea comment. He does not like to be bested in a battle of wits."

Regaining her composure somewhat, Charlotte asked Mr. Westfield, "Are all people in America this informal?"

"No. In truth, the rules of propriety are somewhat relaxed in our country, but many of us are almost as formal as you. However, Uncle believes strongly in informality and fancies himself ahead of his time."

"Someone ought to tell him that it will do him no good to be ahead of his time if he is rejected by society in the present. He will have no acquaintances to speak of and even fewer friends."

"You are probably correct," Mr. Basford said conversationally. "I care nothing for mere acquaintances, but a true friend will accept my eccentricities, Mrs. Collins."

He emphasized her name, causing Charlotte to flush. "With such appalling manners, it is unlikely that you will ever develop true friends, Mr. Basford." She emphasized his last name in the same manner.

Edward entered just then with the tray, and he deposited it on a side table. He looked very pleased at having accomplished his task successfully. Charlotte smiled, while Maria began to serve the tea, beginning with Mr. Westfield. She did not concentrate on pouring, but smiled at the American, and Charlotte hoped she would not overfill his cup and spill on the rug. It was such a bother to clean rugs. The room would be in upheaval for days.

She was about to admonish her to take care, when Maria righted the teapot and spoke. "Have you heard, Charlotte? We are all invited to Colonel Armitage's house for an evening of cards."

No longer concerned that her rug would be destroyed, Charlotte considered the invitation. Maria knew that she did not enjoy cards and would not blame her for turning down the invitation. She was on the verge of doing just that when she saw the look Maria gave Mr. Westfield and the look he returned.

"We will go, of course, will we not, Charlotte?" Maria asked, still looking at Mr. Westfield.

"I do not see how I could refuse."

ஒஇ Four ஓஇ

"I should have refused," Charlotte said as the team of large-bodied gray horses pulled Mr. Card's lovely barouche—though not half so fine as any of Lady Catherine's elegant conveyances—along the well-rutted roads. "This rain has all but destroyed the lanes, and it is a dreadful evening for being out."

Maria scowled. "Do not be so sour, Charlotte."

Mr. Card looked quite discomfited and shifted in his seat. "We will soon be in a pleasant room with pleasanter company."

"That is a subject worthy of debate," Charlotte murmured to Maria. It was unlikely that the weather, or Charlotte's temper, would turn for the better before the night was out. She had passed a very taxing week. She had been obliged to call upon Mrs. Card, and after a dull quarter hour in her company, she had spent the rest of the week going over her finances, which always dampened her mood.

Maria leaned forward and asked in a hushed tone, "Why are you in such poor spirits this evening?"

In truth, Charlotte did not relish being in the company of Mr. Basford, but she did not want to confide in her sister, who could keep nothing secret. "I do not intend to be. I am certain the weather has depressed my spirits. I will be less gloomy, I am sure, when we are in company."

"Then it is quite fortunate that we arrive at Colonel Armitage's home soon, for Mr. Card and I will not have to bear your mood very much longer."

Charlotte stared out into the gathering darkness and remained silent. The sun was hanging low, and its light filtered through the cloudy, rainy sky, casting the world in a gloomy haze.

Beside her, Maria fidgeted with her dress, adjusting the dove-colored fabric across her lap so that there were no wrinkles. Charlotte observed her preening gestures, and then she looked at her own dress. She had worn mourning attire for so long that she felt odd wearing this gown of pale colored cotton with a subtle dusky blue floral motif. The decision to relinquish her mourning garb entirely had been difficult, but Maria, for once, had made good sense.

"Charlotte," she had said, "You have served your time and done your duty to Mr. Collins. No matter how much you wish to deny it, you are still alive, and as such, you need to retake your position in society."

"You speak as if I am some great lady. I am just Charlotte Collins."

"And while Charlotte Collins may not be of a noble family, she is the daughter of a gentleman who was appointed to the knighthood and is a great lady of a different, more meaningful, sort."

Tears had come to Charlotte's eyes. "How kind."

"It is not kind; it is the truth. Tear the black lace off your gowns and rejoin the world."

Charlotte toyed with the thought. "Perhaps I should."

"Indeed you should, and perchance you will find a new beau of your own."

Charlotte had laughed at the ridiculousness of that comment, for she could not hope in that direction, but she did remove the black lace and pack away her black dresses. She was going to live, and she would begin tonight, this dreary, damp, and dingy night.

At least, that had been her intention, but she could not shake off the darkness of her spirit as easily as she had dispatched with her dark clothing.

Mr. Card, who had been absorbed in watching Maria arrange her skirts, ventured a compliment. "I hope you do not mind my saying so, but you ladies look lovely tonight. You quite outshine the sun."

"I should hope we outshine the sun at such a gloomy time of day."

Mr. Card looked abashed and quickly attempted to correct himself, but Maria laughed off his words. "I comprehend your meaning, Mr. Card, and I appreciate the kind sentiment. I am afraid my sister has let the weather affect her spirits too much today."

"It is true. You should not mark a word I say this evening, Mr. Card. I hope that the fresh air will soon improve my mood."

"Good society, also, must be of some help. Pleasant conversation can certainly do no harm," added Maria.

Charlotte wondered if she would find pleasant conversation at a card party, for the most she had ever heard over a game of whist was "Aha!" or a disappointed, "How cruel you were to take that trick, Mr. Whatnot!" If her preconception held true, she was in for a dull evening indeed.

"We will pass a merry evening with our friends. I have heard such wonderful tales over a hand of cards," Mr. Card returned, and Charlotte had to smile at their very different opinions on the matter.

"Yes, Miss Farmington has promised to attend, and of course, Colonel Armitage's relations will be there."

Mr. Card leaned forward, gesturing broadly as the two continued to speak about the evening's society while the carriage finished its journey. Orange light shone out the windows of the Armitages' house, promising warmth and comfort, and Charlotte found herself eager to be inside and out of the gathering gloom.

Mr. Card alighted from the carriage, his boots making a splatting sound as they hit the damp ground.

He assisted them from the carriage. "Take care, ladies. It is moist, but we will be inside soon enough."

Charlotte picked her way to the front door, and she turned in time to witness his careful aid of her sister. She remembered the words of Mrs. Card. He did love Maria.

And this fact was certainly lost on her sister, for in her excitement to be among the others, she barely touched his arm as he escorted her to the door.

Their party had arrived slightly late owing to the poor condition of the roads, and when they were shown to the drawing room, they discovered that many games were already in progress. Maria went directly to the table where Miss Farmington and Mr. Westfield played at whist with Colonel Armitage and Mrs. Holloway, a woman with whom Charlotte did not share a particular acquaintance. She and Mr. Card overlooked their game and chatted with the players.

Charlotte received a cup of tea and took it to the window seat, where she could observe the whole room. It seemed a pleasant party even if it were an evening of cards. Wreathed in flickering yellow candlelight, the group took on an ethereal glow. Yes, the room looked quite pretty, but still, Charlotte would have rather remained at home. Leaning back into the cool darkness of the window alcove, Charlotte sipped her tea and reminded herself that she was here for Maria. She must focus on her sister's happiness. Soon enough, Charlotte could be back at her little cottage enjoying her solitude.

She heard Maria laugh loudly and glanced up at her. Her sister absolutely shone under the attention of Mr. Card and Mr. Westfield. Her blond hair was like a halo around her delicate face, and Charlotte wondered how long she would remain unmarried now that she was out in society on a regular basis. Mr. Westfield looked quite enchanted, and Mr. Card was just as enamored as ever. Would her sister ever recognize the love of a man whom she counted as merely a friend? Most likely not. Maria was a careless young woman, and Mr. Westfield distracted her completely. Poor Mr. Card was in for a hearty disappointment now that Mr. Westfield was in Westerham.

The side door to the salon opened, admitting Mr. Basford. He made quite a striking figure in his simple attire. His neck cloth was done in a simple knot compared to the more complex creations of the other men in the room, and he appeared to be dressed for a comfortable evening at home instead of entertaining a party of guests.

Not wanting to invite his attention, Charlotte looked away before he noticed her appraisal and turned again to the card game, in which Miss Farmington apparently made a decisive play and clenched the win, causing a roar of mixed happiness and disappointment to erupt from the table.

Mrs. Holloway and Colonel Armitage excused themselves, graciously allowing Mr. Card and Maria to take their places. Colonel Armitage noticed Charlotte's position at the window, paused briefly by the biscuit tray, and then, encouraged by her welcoming smile, joined her. "Mrs. Collins, how do you do this evening?"

"Very well, thank you, Colonel."

"I hope you find it a very pleasant party. I only regret that my guests were required to venture out in such wet weather."

"My sister and I are thankful for your invitation, and I can assure you that the journey was quite worth it, sir."

"Well, I am glad to hear it."

"Please have a seat." Charlotte made room for him beside her on the ample window seat.

"Thank you." He lowered himself beside her.

"It was very kind of you to give your places to Maria and Mr. Card."

"It is good for young people to gather together, do you not agree?"

Charlotte nodded.

"And we older people, having virtually no vitality left in us, must be content to bask in their youthful vigor."

On such a night when Charlotte felt the gloom so personally, she was forced to agree with the Colonel. "At a certain point in life, we all must endeavor to entertain ourselves."

Colonel Armitage sighed. "Is that not the truth? I find it a surprisingly difficult task, this business of entertaining of oneself. I fear that if left completely to my own devices I might bore myself into oblivion. That is why I host evenings such as this. By surrounding myself with youth, I fancy that I become more interesting by default."

Charlotte laughed.

"What nonsense is my uncle telling you?" Charlotte and the colonel looked up to find Mr. Basford leaning against the wall.

Appalling manners! "On the contrary, he speaks common sense."

"We were discussing the behavior of people of a certain age in society," the colonel explained.

"Just as I suspected. Utter nonsense."

Charlotte was surprised at the derogatory tone he used with his uncle, but Colonel Armitage, apparently used to such loving disrespect, laughed. "How very much like your mother you are."

"Many have said as much, Uncle."

"What is your opinion on the subject?" Colonel Armitage asked him.

"As you may well believe, it is quite different from yours. And Mrs. Collins's as well, I imagine." He looked at her for assent.

"I have no doubt that our opinions diverge, for they have not been on the same continent since we have been introduced."

"Quite so," he said. "I believe that we who have attained some maturity of years have an advantage in society. We shouldn't cut ourselves off from it. Rather, we should use the benefit of our experience to enjoy it, for we are no longer desperately seeking our mates or worried about impressing our companions. We've already done these youthful things, and now we may simply enjoy ourselves without these distractions."

Charlotte contemplated the matter for a moment. "Perhaps this is a wise way to view life, but I am afraid this will prove to be an unpopular opinion."

The colonel snorted. "My nephew cares nothing for popularity."

Mr. Basford waved his hand dismissively. "It's not a matter of popularity. I simply do not allow the opinions of others to guide my behavior."

"Perhaps circumstances are different across the Atlantic, but here in England, we have great respect for others and show it through appropriate, acceptable behavior."

"We behave very charmingly in America. We simply do not allow etiquette to rule us."

Colonel Armitage was then summoned by Mr. Westfield, and he stood to make his excuses and take his leave. "I see I must go play host for a moment. Ben, take my place at the window and you may continue your debate."

Charlotte suddenly wanted to issue some excuses of her own and escape before Mr. Basford could accept or reject the colonel's offer. She searched her mind franticly for a plausible excuse. Did she hear Maria calling? She glanced at her sister, who sat on the far side of the room and was clearly much engrossed in her conversation with Mr. Westfield to be sufficient pretext for departure. Mr. Basford would never believe it. Did she leave the kettle on the stove at home? That would not suffice either. He would probably simply tease her about England's love of tea. Perhaps she could use an old excuse—the need for refreshment. Yes, refreshment. Not even Mr. Basford would prevent her from a beverage and a biscuit.

Too late! Mr. Basford was sitting beside her.

Even though Mr. Basford's girth was half that of his uncle, the widow seat seemed to shrink and the walls closed in, and Charlotte scooted as far to the side as possible. He only leaned toward her—the cretin—and grinned. "Hello, Charlotte."

"I have asked you not to call me that, and there is no need for another greeting, for we have been conversing for several minutes."

"The proper response would be 'Hello, Ben. How nice to see you tonight.'"

Charlotte scowled. He infuriated her by smiling back.

His voice softened. "I do not mean to make you uncomfortable, Mrs. Collins. Let's speak of a friendly subject."

"I did not think there was a subject we could discuss in a friendly manner."

"Then I'll choose the topic and prove to you that I can behave properly."

"Amaze me."

"Well, now that was very rude."

Embarrassed, she apologized, and they remained in silence a moment. At length, Mr. Basford cleared his throat. "My nephew seems to be enjoying the company of your sister."

"Yes, Maria speaks about Mr. Westfield with only the kindest terms."

"I am pleased to hear that."

"I am certain that he will miss her company when we travel abroad," Mr. Basford said.

"You go abroad?" Charlotte asked, both pleased and disappointed at the prospect.

"Yes, we depart in a fortnight. James's mother believes that a visit to the continent is essential for every young gentleman's education."

"How nice for one so young to see so much of the world."

"We tour Paris and then return to England to finish with a stay in London," Mr. Basford said.

"London is very agreeable, with many occupations for a young man such as Mr. Westfield. It is also a place of rich history." Charlotte had been into town on occasion and had always taken pleasure in the exhibits of the British Museum.

"I am afraid James may be more interested in theater and fine dining than he is interested in history." Charlotte imagined she heard a touch of regret in his voice.

"Those are also admirable pursuits."

"I am glad that you approve."

She paused. "I find that difficult to believe."

He turned his head to look at her more directly. "I thought you wanted people to concern themselves with the opinions of others. That is all I am doing now."

"I do not desire falsity, Mr. Basford. I simply desire that you present yourself honestly."

"Then, at your request, I'll do so, and in turn, you must not complain about my casual attitude."

"And you must not chide me for my polite behavior."

"Then are we friends?"

He seemed quite sincere and Charlotte smiled. He would soon be gone—first abroad, then to London, and eventually back to America. She could see nothing wrong with developing a friendship, especially since her sister seemed to enjoy Mr. Westfield's company so much. "Yes, I suppose."

His smile widened and almost drew a blush to Charlotte's face, but before she could consider the repercussions of the ruddiness of her cheeks, she found Maria before her. "Charlotte, may I speak to you a moment?"

"I pray you will excuse us, Mr. Basford."

He nodded and then moved away to give them privacy.

"I see you are enjoying Mr. Basford's company," Maria settled herself down in the spot he had vacated and arranging her skirts.

Charlotte's first instinct was to deny her enjoyment of their discussion, but then she softened and said truthfully, "Surprisingly, I do enjoy conversations with him. He is…different."

Oblivious to the profundity of her sister's revelation, Maria was focused solely on herself. "I too enjoy Mr. Westfield. May we invite them to dine with us?"

"I am afraid not—"

"But we make such a charming party." Maria's eyes pleaded with her sister. Her tone was whiny, and Charlotte was sorely tempted to roll her eyes.

"That may be true, Maria, but Mr. Basford has just told me that they are bound for France in a fortnight."

"Oh, what a disappointment! Why has not Mr. Westfield mentioned that to me?" Maria slumped over, and Charlotte was tempted to correct her posture, but she kept quiet while her sister considered her situation.

After several minutes, Maria straightened. "I had hoped…"

"I know what you had hoped, but there is no sense in wasting this evening in mourning for a future evening. Leave me and enjoy your friends."

Maria seemed to deliberate, her brows knitted together. She looked very serious. "For once your unstoppable practicality actually makes sense."

Charlotte laughed.

For the remainder of the evening, Maria did enjoy her friends, and Charlotte joined a game of whist and indulged in more than a few confections. She did not speak with Mr. Basford until the end of the evening when he accompanied their party to the door.

He escorted Maria on his left arm, Charlotte—somewhat unwillingly—rested her hand on his right arm. Mr. Card walked ahead with Miss Farmington and her grandmother, whom he handed into their carriage while the others spoke in the entryway.

"Thank your uncle for his generous invitation," Charlotte said to Mr. Basford.

"I will, and in turn we thank you for coming."

"It was a grand time, Mr. Basford," Maria paused a moment to push a curl from her face. "Perhaps when you and Mr. Westfield return from your tour of France, we shall all meet again at a ball."

Maria's addendum elicited a firm look from Charlotte.

Behind them, Mr. Westfield said, "I do hope so. Do you not agree, Uncle?"

Mr. Westfield stepped forward, took Maria's arm from his uncle, and led her to the Farmington's chaise to bid them farewell, leaving Charlotte alone with Mr. Basford, who turned to her. "I do agree. Will you be so kind as to save me a dance at the next ball, Mrs. Collins?"

Imagine having a gentleman reserve a dance at her advanced age. In fact, it had been years since anyone other than Mr. Collins had asked her to dance, and even then, dancing had not been a pleasure. Her husband had been awkward of foot, and eventually, Charlotte had begun to decline to stand up with him, pointing him instead to other suitable partners.

Charlotte was quite certain that Mr. Basford would prove to be a pleasanter partner. He at least had managed to escort her to the door without crushing her slippers.

"We shall see, Mr. Basford."

The Cards' barouche arrived before them, and Mr. Basford aided her inside. Charlotte could feel the warmth of his hand through their gloves.

"Good evening," he said with a slight bow, glancing at her earnestly.

"Good evening," Charlotte replied. His gaze really was too earnest. It caused her stomach to flutter. Odd.

Mr. Card joined them in the carriage, and it rumbled away, leaving Charlotte to watch as Mr. Westfield and Mr. Basford returned to the house. Just before the carriage rounded the first bend, Charlotte saw Mr. Basford turn and look toward the horizon. Was he looking at the carriage? She sucked back into the seat as if he had caught her spying and then chastised herself for her foolishness. He could not possibly have seen her. It was far too dark.

Mr. Card was seated across from Maria, and the two talked quietly about the evening. As the carriage wound its way closer to Charlotte's cottage, a pleasant quietness fell. The conveyance rocked gently while the rhythm of the horses' hoof beats sounded on the road.

When they arrived at the cottage, it felt warm and inviting, and Charlotte knew Mrs. Eff had awaited their return. She appeared in the entrance hall forthwith looking quite done in. Mrs. Eff had once been a soft, genteel lady, but now the palms of her hands were as rough as the course material of the apron she wore, and the hair that had once been fashioned in ringlets was now pulled into a bun at the nape of her neck. But her voice was always cheery no matter the time or circumstance. "Had you a pleasant party?"

"It was a lovely evening."

"For the most part," Maria added.

Mrs. Eff raised an inquisitive eyebrow as she helped to remove their cloaks. Although Mrs. Eff was her servant, she was a gentleman's daughter, a well-educated woman who had the misfortune to lose her husband without the benefit of jointure or relations to sustain her, and as such she had no means of support.

She was what Charlotte could have been, and she remained keenly aware of that fact.

Mrs. Eff had provided a measure of companionship and news from society while Charlotte was secluded in the early part of her mourning and she remained her friend despite the disparity in their current social positions.

"Miss Lucas's evening was full of amusements. However, I fear that she is disappointed by the forthcoming departure of an acquaintance."

"I had hoped we would be more than mere acquaintances."

Mrs. Eff patted her hand. "Ah, I understand, Miss Lucas, what it is to be thwarted in love."

"She is hardly thwarted in love."

Maria giggled. "You ought to speak to my sister about love, for she was much in the company of a particular gentleman this evening."

"Was she?" Mrs. Eff turned to Charlotte. "And may I ask who was the gentleman?"

Charlotte busied herself with removing her gloves. "Nonsense. No such gentleman exists."

"That was rather a tender farewell from Mr. Basford this evening, Charlotte. I think he is enamored of you."

"What a thing to say!" She dropped her gloves in Mrs. Eff's waiting hand. "Tender indeed. Mr. Basford was merely being polite, or as polite as a person such as him can be."

Thankfully, Mrs. Eff noticed her discomfort and changed the subject. "Do you require anything else tonight? Assistance with your gowns?"

Both Charlotte and Maria declined her offer, and Mrs. Eff retired to her chamber behind the kitchen while the sisters mounted the stairs. They stopped at their separate bed chamber doors.

"Mr. Westfield was quite attentive to you this evening."

"Yes." Maria had a strange, sweet smile on her lips.

"Mr. Card too showed great kindness to you."

"Mr. Card?"

"He sent his carriage for us."

Maria mistook her meaning. "It is ever so vexing to be always at the mercy of others for transportation. Surely we can afford a chaise at least."

Charlotte ignored Maria's desire for transportation of their own. She must make her message plain, for Maria was intent on misunderstanding her. "He is fond of you."

Maria yawned. "We have always been fond of each other, but there is certainly no attachment between us."

"Perhaps you have not noticed his attentions to you."

Maria opened her bedchamber door. "Perhaps you are the one who refuses to notice the attentions of a gentleman."

✍ Five ✍

Maria sat with Charlotte in their little sitting room with the sun pouring through the open windows. They had just finished a luncheon of cold meats, rolls, and butter and had been sharing what Charlotte had believed to be a companionable silence.

"What a crushing bore this town has become now that Mr. Westfield and Mr. Basford have gone."

Charlotte, who had been lamenting the amount of mending that had accumulated in her basket and contemplating another roll and butter, looked up from her stitching.

"Life went along quite well before they arrived. I am certain that we will survive now that they are gone."

"That is a subject that I am willing to debate."

"Well, I am certainly not willing to debate it. You will simply have to find something else to occupy yourself."

"Humph," Maria said in an unladylike manner. She had not seen Mr. Westfield since the evening of the card party, for he had been away from home when they had called on the Armitages soon after. Their visit had been brief and Maria had returned home quite put out and had been rather off ever since.

They sat a little longer listening to the tentative birdsong of early spring. Maria shifted on her chair and sighed.

"Shall we not pay a call on the Cards? It is dreadfully dull here."

Charlotte put down her mending and studied Maria. She appeared ready to fly from the cottage with the least provocation. Perhaps an afternoon out would improve her spirits.

"I can see you will give me no peace unless I agree."

Maria grinned. "You are quite right."

"Then we shall go, and since the weather is so fine, we will walk through the fields instead of the road."

"Charlotte, you know how to ruin anything that is remotely amusing."

"I find walking an amusement in itself."

"I do not know why."

"It is good exercise, it improves the spirits, and it is enjoyable to see the countryside."

"I can see the countryside just as well from the seat of a carriage or from walking the road on foot."

"Indulge me, Maria. I have not had a good walk through the countryside in quite some time. It is much pleasanter to walk with someone than to walk alone."

Maria agreed reluctantly to her sister's proposition. It was a short distance to the Cards' home, and Charlotte took great pleasure in the journey, enjoying the breezy spring weather. Maria complained incessantly. "My hair will be in such a state after walking in this wind."

"It is but a gentle breeze."

"My dress will be covered in mud."

"We have crossed no puddles."

"What if it rains?"

"It is not going to rain. The sky is blue and not a cloud in sight. Now do be quiet and leave me in peace."

The Cards' home was called Crumbleigh and was one of the finest estates in Westerham. Mr. Card had inherited Crumbleigh and a substantial fortune, making him one of the richest of their acquaintance. Maria always said it was a shame that all that money was wasted on such a man as Mr. Card, who was kind and obliging almost to a fault. She was at a point in her life when she believed that masculinity was defined by egotism, hardheadedness, and difficulty. While Charlotte appreciated both kindness and masculinity, she had rarely found them combined in the proper ratio in one man.

Mrs. Card received them cordially in a large, sunny sitting room.

"How glad I am to have visitors. And what a fine day for a long walk."

Privately, Charlotte thought that it must have been quite some time since Mrs. Card had indulged in a long walk, fine weather or no.

"That is precisely what I told my sister."

Mrs. Card smiled and then summoned the maid. "Go and tell my son that we have visitors." Then she turned to Maria. "Jonas will be very glad to see you. He has been quite dull these past few days."

"I am sorry to hear that. Has he been ill?" Charlotte asked.

"No, indeed. I believe he is in need of society. Young men these days seem to thrive more on society than sport. I believe that the two of you will do the trick."

Mr. Card arrived and was attired in a deep brown coat, tan breeches, and a creamy white cravat tied in a barrel knot. He appeared stylish yet sober and refined. He smiled as he greeted the assembled ladies and announced, "What a fine day! Shall we all not stroll through the gardens?"

"What a jolly idea," Maria said sourly.

Mr. Card's eyes widened to an almost impossible degree. "You do not wish to see the gardens? They are quite nice."

"Perhaps we could find a quiet bench and have a nice chat while Mrs. Card and Charlotte stroll. I am quite sick of strolling, and we must still walk home."

Mr. Card beamed. "There is a very pleasant bench in the rose garden, and I would enjoy sitting with you."

The four walked through the house, the women's dresses whispering as they walked, while Mr. Card's boots punctuated the quiet with gentle taps on the polished stone floors.

Charlotte had always loved Crumbleigh, although she could have wished for a less disintegrated-sounding name. She could remember visiting Mr. and Mrs. Card with Mr. Collins when they had first married. She had stood in the massive entryway and tried not to gawk even as she secretly marveled at the size of the hall and at her reflection in the sheen of the floor.

After she had been married to Mr. Collins for some time, she had lost some of her admiration for fine things. She could not recall all the times that she had listened to her husband discourse on such items as window dressings, vases, or furniture. Although they could only afford modest accoutrements themselves, Mr. Collins could not be prevented from praising the belongings of others. It had gotten to the point that Charlotte wanted nothing fine in her house for fear that he would boast about it to all he met.

Now, looking around the Cards' house, she felt not a twinge of jealousy. Maria, however, ran her hand along the cool marble trim and gazed longingly around her. Poor girl. It really was unfortunate that she had no feelings for Mr. Card, for he admired her, and she admired his home.

The group arrived in the rose garden, where Mr. Card and Maria tucked themselves on a little bench among the roses.

"Let us walk this way, Mrs. Collins." Mrs. Card directed her toward a small path. "We will leave them to speak alone for a time."

They chatted about the weather and then the subject turned to Mrs. Card's favorite topic of conversation—gossip. Mrs. Card's tongue was wicked and the breadth of her knowledge of the happenings in Westerham took Charlotte aback. Mr. Holloway had acquired a new sow, which he described to everyone as just as fat as Mrs. Holloway but better company. Apparently, Mrs. Holloway shared her husband's opinion of the quality of their time together, for she had become quite close, it was rumored, with an unnamed gentleman of their acquaintance. Mrs. Holloway had hinted at the affair but would not identify the man.

"Can you imagine? An affair amongst those of our acquaintance."

Charlotte was not very much familiar with Mrs. Holloway, but she found the idea of an affair implausible as well. "'Tis probably nothing but foul wind. Mrs. Holloway is certainly attempting to wound her husband for comparing her unfavorably to a pig."

"I must admit I quite agree with his comparison," Mrs. Card said. "She prattles on endlessly and indulges in too many confections, if you ask me. At the winter ball, I went to refill my wine glass again, and I observed her eating almost an entire tray of biscuits. Such gluttony."

Charlotte concealed a smile at Mrs. Card, who was often deep in her cups when in company. However, she could not quarrel with her assessment of Mrs. Holloway's conversation. She had to admit that she often found the company of certain barnyard animals more appealing than the prospect of an evening in the company of Mrs. Holloway—or Mr. Holloway for that matter—but incompetence in social settings did not mean that Mrs. Holloway was engaged in illicit behavior. That sort of thing happened in London, not Westerham.

Charlotte turned the conversation to safer topics, and she listened as Mrs. Card described her improvements to the gardens and Mr. Card's charity to the tenants on their land. Then Mrs. Card paused, glanced about as if expecting spies to appear from behind the shrubbery. Charlotte began to fear an uncomfortable change of subject, and that fear was not unfounded, for Mrs. Card grabbed her arm, nearly pulling her off balance. "Tell me this, and tell me truly, has Miss Lucas begun to feel tenderly toward my son?"

Charlotte was quite taken aback that she would broach this subject again and stopped midstride, causing Mrs. Card, who had not relinquished her grip, to be jerked backward. A reprimand leapt to Charlotte's lips, but she refrained and responded as politely as she could. Would this woman never cease meddling in her son's life? Not to mention Maria's. And Charlotte's for that matter. "Maria has not confided as much to me, and that is as it should be. Life is difficult to navigate without one's sister sticking her oar in. I feel that it is best to let young people work things out for themselves, do you not agree, Mrs. Card?"

Mrs. Card dragged her onward down the path. "I certainly do. It is ever so frustrating to watch people manipulating their relations, especially for monetary gain. I am only concerned with my son's happiness, but obviously he has the potential to make a desirable match among his own class."

"Maria is the daughter of a gentleman and certainly of Mr. Card's class!"

"Yes, but has she any money? Any dowry?"

Anger blossomed within her, but she responded with politeness. "Then why do you support the match?"

Charlotte knew very well why Mrs. Card was pushing Maria and Mr. Card together. She wanted a daughter-in-law who could be easily managed. And Maria, bless her, had more hair than wit.

"I have my reasons, and I may as well tell you that upon only the slightest provocation, Jonas will make an offer to your sister."

Charlotte's mouth dropped open and then snapped quickly shut.

"I can see that you are surprised, but I do not see why. Anyone may see Jonas's admiration."

"Mrs. Card—"

"Pray do not make yourself uneasy. As you said just moments ago, it is best to let young people work these things out for themselves. We shall just sit back and watch." Mrs. Card patted her hand reassuringly and then released her hold. "But I must say that I am quite disappointed in you, Mrs. Collins."

Charlotte continued walking calmly, but she imagined issuing any number of set-downs to the rag-mannered harridan.

"After our conversation on the day of that dreadful storm, I assumed you would have nudged Maria in my Jonas's direction."

There was very little to be said in response that was both truthful and polite. "I will encourage my sister to marry as she wishes, and she wishes to marry for love. She has spoken of no such feelings for any gentleman."

Mrs. Card's ears and nose turned an unflattering shade of red, and she crossed her arms in front of her. "You must see what an advantageous match this would be for her, and indeed yourself as well. I never took you for a fool."

The old cow was certainly in fine form. Charlotte took a deep, steadying breath. "I was once of your opinion, Mrs. Card. In fact, I was even more determined, for I believed in marriage primarily for the purpose of improving one's circumstances."

"And well you should have thought as much. It is a wise opinion for a woman to hold."

"I once agreed, but I have come to see the value of allowing love to color one's matrimonial decisions. If happiness in marriage is indeed a possibility, I am certain that it can only result from love."

"There is no such thing as a happy marriage."

Charlotte glanced over Mrs. Card's shoulder, willing some sort of interruption to occur. The appearance of Mr. Card and Maria. A carriage pulling into the drive. A regiment of soldiers marching through Crumbleigh on their way to battle. Any excuse to defer this conversation would suit Charlotte very well.

When none of those eventualities occurred, she unclenched her jaw. "I must disagree, for I have seen the evidence of them. I will encourage my sister to follow her heart. If her heart leads her to Mr. Card, then so be it."

Mrs. Card huffed, seeming suddenly to expand to twice her size and then deflating just as quickly. "Jonas is not the sort of man with whom women fall in love easily. He is the sort whom one comes to love over time."

Charlotte had nothing to say in response, and the two ladies walked in uneasy silence for some distance. The silence had the advantage of relieving Charlotte of both Mrs. Card's dreadful conversation and her tour of garden improvements, but it could not persist much longer. Charlotte selected a safer topic. "Have you heard that the Americans have gone to France?"

Not seeming to notice the lack of a segue, Mrs. Card's face lit. "Indeed I have."

"I understand that Mr. Westfield's mother encouraged it as part of her son's education."

Mrs. Card leaned in. "That is not at all what I heard."

"Oh?"

"I have heard that the true reason is that Mr. Basford wanted to visit," she paused and her voice dropped, "his Parisian mistress."

"Mistress?"

"Indeed."

The woman must be fabricating these stories. Two tales of such an illicit nature seemed improbable. "How could you possibly come to know that?"

"How does not matter. What matters is that I know it. We must beware of these Americans."

"If he were indeed joining his—" Charlotte could not speak the word and began again, "If indeed this were the case, why would he take Mr. Westfield with him?"

"Yes, poor Mr. Westfield. I believe it is safe to say that he will certainly return to Westerham a changed man. We may not trust him with our daughters. In fact, I would not be surprised at all to discover that Mr. Basford was Mrs. Holloway's mystery lover."

Charlotte stared at her companion. It was all so completely unbelievable. She acknowledged that evil existed in the world. She had seen it. But she did not believe Mr. Basford to be evil. She knew that stupidity existed in the world. She had seen even more of that. But she did not have the impression that Mr. Basford was particularly stupid. And Mrs. Card's accusations would mean that he was both evil and stupid.

Charlotte had no reason to mistrust Mrs. Card, however. Perhaps it was best to exercise extra caution where the American gentlemen were concerned. She had witnessed the effects of trusting untrustworthy men, and she would not allow Maria to become a victim. Society was often more harsh on the victim than on the perpetrator of the crime.

On the walk home, Charlotte was quiet, but Maria chattered on. "I am so pleased that I thought of the idea of an outing today, for it was just what my constitution required."

Charlotte trudged onward and did not bother to point out that she, not Maria, had suggested that they call on the Cards. There was not much point in correcting her, for she had already skittered on to the next topic.

"Mr. Card told me so many delicious stories, but I cannot seem to recall any of them. Have you ever had that happen? Your head is so full that nothing will come out? I suppose not, for you are far too sensible for that. Then we spoke of fashion. He said he very much hoped that the current enthusiasm over such tight fitting coats would soon pass, but I said I quite fancied a gentleman in a well-fitted coat. He seemed to value my opinion on the matter and vowed to see his tailor straightaway." Maria should have paused here, but instead she launched into yet another topic. "Mrs. Card seemed to be in spirits today. I believe I detected some color in her cheeks after her walk with you. Did you have a pleasant chat?"

"Humph," said Charlotte. It was the best response she could muster.

"Well, it was so jolly to be out, even if it was only with Mr. Card."

Charlotte regarded her sister as they walked. She wanted to clutch her arms and give her a good shake. "You speak of him too lightly, Maria. You should be careful of his feelings."

"Oh, pooh."

✦ Six ✦

Charlotte passed a restless night and arose early. She elected to enjoy a cup of chocolate, in the stead of her customary tea, as a consolation for her lack of sleep. The dark, bitter delicacy seemed to match her mood and yet also somehow brighten it. The house was quiet and cool at that hour, and the warm drink brought a measure of comfort to her restless spirits.

Knowing that Mr. Card desired to propose to Maria and that she was completely oblivious to that fact made Charlotte extremely uneasy. Maria was sweet, but she was an artless girl and ignorant of the feelings of others no matter how much her sister instructed her. She certainly would not have the presence of mind to spare the feelings of her long-time friend.

Charlotte contemplated simply telling her sister of Mr. Card's feelings. It had been a difficult temptation to resist, but resist it she did. She found it unethical for her to divulge Mr. Card's feelings even if his mother had been thoughtless enough to do so. This argument alone, however, was not strong enough to convince Charlotte to conceal the facts. It was her knowledge of her sister's nature that solidified her decision. Maria would only make a mess of the situation if she knew of Mr. Card's intentions. She could imagine Maria's obvious attempts to avoid him or to slough him off on other young women. It was a charade that Charlotte had no desire to watch.

In addition, it was quite clear that Maria did indeed harbor an interest in Mr. Westfield, and she was not going to be satisfied until she had made a fool of herself over him.

What a fix! A good man loved Maria, but she did not love him. She persisted in fancying another man, who may or may not be in the process of being corrupted by his questionable uncle. And Charlotte was caught in the middle. How had she come to be in this situation? After Mr. Collins's death, she had enjoyed a quiet life, and somehow her solitude had been replaced by vexation and confusion. Peace was nowhere to be found, and Charlotte was forced to search for solace in the cocoa plant.

After finishing her second cup of chocolate, she attempted to read, but still she felt restless. She considered a conversation with Mrs. Eff, but she was too jittery. Deciding that perhaps a walk into town and a browse around the shops would calm her, she notified Mrs. Eff of her departure and left a note for Maria, who was still asleep.

Charlotte walked briskly along the side of the road, and soon the hem of her dress was dampened with dew. Her spirits, however, were much brightened by the time she arrived in Westerham. She visited several shops but purchased nothing, and as noon approached, she walked to the Circulating Library.

She was considering a new novel when she sensed a presence beside her and glanced over to find Mr. Edgington, the red-haired gentleman who had bumped into her at the ball, perusing a volume several feet away.

"Good morning, Mr. Edgington."

"Good morning, Mrs. Collins," he said politely. "A pleasant morning for a browse around the shops, is it not?"

"Yes, quite."

"What do you read?"

"I am sorry to say that I enjoy novels."

"Why are you sorry to say that?"

"Are not novels considered to be a lower form of entertainment? Especially those whose content is comedic?"

"People who believe that must not comprehend the need for levity and release in our lives."

"You are quite right. Our lives are serious enough, and I find it odious indeed always to read books of great import."

Mr. Collins had been a dutiful student of sermons, and he had been displeased when Charlotte became bored of them.

Mr. Edgington smiled. "I concur. In fact, I am here for a book of travel narratives."

"Also an interesting subject. Far more interesting than a collection of sermons."

"Were you required to study sermons as a child as I was?" he said with a grimace. "I can vividly recall sitting in my room and reading Fordyce's tome while my friends were allowed to run free in the out of doors."

"I am also well acquainted with Dr. Fordyce's advice, but not from my childhood. Mr. Collins was a great believer in his tenets."

He looked at her earnestly. "I find many of his beliefs rather archaic. Even as a young child, I could not comprehend his idea of such severe subjugation of women. Those of your sex should be free to enjoy life just as a man might."

Charlotte was not certain that Mr. Edgington was speaking of entirely innocent subjects when he talked of release and pleasure. His tone was placid, but something in his eye seemed to suggest conspiracy. Or was she imagining it? Charlotte hoped to temper their discussion. "I find some of his advice for modest speech and action to be useful even today, but I have no scruples in admitting that I find his ideas regarding subjugation to the male of the species, no matter how worthy, to be very questionable indeed."

"Would you deem it questionable for me to invite you to dine with me this afternoon?"

Surprised, Charlotte analyzed him. Was it questionable? Was he flirting with her in an inappropriate manner, or was she imagining it? She had heard only positive reports regarding Mr. Edgington. Perhaps her feelings of unease stemmed from her suspicious mind. As long as they dined in a public establishment, what harm could there be in it? She was well beyond the blush of her youth, and it was acceptable for a widow to be in the company of a gentleman in public view. She placed the book back on the shelf. "I do not think it would be questionable, and I must confess I am famished."

He offered his arm. "Then let us dine, and if you wish to make any other confessions, about your reading habits or otherwise, you may feel free to do so."

Her face heated at his flirtation, and she hoped it was not obvious to those who observed her. Actually, Mr. Edgington was the second man who had brought a youthful blush to her cheeks in recent days.

If pressed, she would be forced to admit that she quite liked the fact that she was on a gentleman's arm. It must be a metaphor of some kind. Being escorted meant that she did not walk alone through the streets of life. Or something of that sort.

Charlotte and Mr. Edgington entered and were promptly seated in a public room where they were served some lovely bread, cheese, and tea. At first, Charlotte felt awkward, but as the conversation flowed, she found her ease and soon they were speaking like old acquaintances. When the church chimes sounded, Charlotte was surprised, for the hour was much later than she had anticipated. Charlotte stood. Mr. Edgington rose with her.

"Oh dear! I fear my sister will be worried at my long absence. I must return home. Will you forgive my hasty departure?"

"Of course, of course. Your sister will wonder where you have gotten yourself," he said solicitously. "May I escort you?"

"It is not necessary, sir, but I thank you for the meal." Charlotte picked up her reticule and exited the public room, and Mr. Edgington followed.

"It would be no trouble."

Charlotte turned, surprised to discover him so close by. She stopped. "Thank you, but it is not far, and I am not certain my sister will be up to receiving guests this afternoon."

He took her fingertips in his hand. "Then I shall allow you to go alone, but only if you allow me the privilege of calling on you in the future."

Charlotte did not know how to respond, but she had enough presence of mind to pull her hand from his grasp. They were in a public street! "Mr. Edgington, I am a widow…"

He did not appear abashed at her rebuke. "And I am a widower. Certainly we may be friends."

Charlotte began walking toward home, but he kept pace. After several more steps, she stopped again and turned. "Friends then if it will convince you that I do not need an escort." She spoke the words for his benefit, but she remained uncertain. Something seemed amiss with Mr. Edgington. She wondered why she had found being on his arm so pleasant only an hour earlier.

"May I call on you next week? We can discuss sermons."

"You may call on me provided that we do not discuss sermons."

She managed to divest herself of him only after she agreed to allow him to call, and when Charlotte finally arrived at her cottage, she was thankful that Mr. Edgington had not escorted her, for Maria was in high temper. Mrs. Eff, who had been sitting with her in the kitchen, looked relieved to see Charlotte. Even Edward, who was tending to the fire, seemed grateful for her appearance.

"Where have you been? I thought you were just doing some shopping," Maria demanded.

"I dined in town with Mr. Edgington."

"You dined with Mr. Edgington!" Maria's voice was barely under a shriek. "And just at the moment when I needed you most."

Maria stood abruptly, nearly knocking over the kitchen chair, and stormed out of the room. Charlotte glanced at Mrs. Eff, who only shook her head. She began to follow her, but Mrs. Eff stopped her. "Give her a moment to compose herself."

Seeing the value in her suggestion, Charlotte returned to her chair. "I am sorry, Mrs. Eff. You and Edward must have had a difficult day."

Mrs. Eff smiled at her across the table. "It was nothing, my dear."

"Nothing," Edward repeated, wiping his hands on his trousers and leaving behind dirty prints.

"I should have been here."

"You had to have your dinner."

"It was rather impromptu. I should have come straight home."

"You have to lead your own life." She paused. "Were you with Mr. Edgington lately of London? The relation of Lady Catherine?"

Charlotte looked down at the table, her face turning pink. "Yes, do you know of him?"

"I know he is quite handsome and has a well-turned calf."

"Mrs. Eff!"

"We are widows, Mrs. Collins. We are not dead, and we may certainly still appreciate male beauty, especially when it is housed in a gentleman of good family and substantial wealth."

Charlotte glanced at Edward, who did not appear to comprehend their conversation.

"He is handsome, but I confess that he sometimes makes me uneasy."

"Uneasy?"

Charlotte was sure that her face was as red as a poppy. "He flirts. At least, I think he flirts. But why would he flirt with me?"

"Why indeed. You have long been in need of a little flirtation."

"I am not certain that it is appropriate. Some of the things he says seem, well, risqué."

"That is flirtation! You are just unused to it."

"Perhaps you are right."

"Well, of course I am, dear."

The women lapsed into silence. Edward came and went, restocking the coal bin in preparation for their evening meal. At length, Charlotte stood and said, "I'll see to Maria now."

"I shall be here if you need me."

Charlotte found Maria pacing the sitting room. She did not appear to have benefitted from her time alone. Her hair was disheveled, and her hands grasped at the sides of her morning gown. "Maria, you must calm yourself."

Maria whirled around at her voice and threw her hands in the air, revealing the wrinkles she had put in her skirts. "I cannot possibly calm down, and you would not suggest such a thing if you knew what I have been through since you left."

Charlotte sat down on the chair by the fireplace and watched Maria take several more laps around the room. Finally, unable to track her along her dizzying path any longer, Charlotte arrested Maria's progress and demanded, "Do sit down and tell me what has happened."

Maria flopped onto a chair, ending sprawled in a very unladylike position, but Charlotte did not correct her.

"It is a disaster. It is worse than anything I could imagine."

Panic rose in Charlotte's throat.

"Has Lady Catherine been here?" Could she have heard of her dinner with Mr. Edgington so soon and disapproved so heartily? Would she require them to leave the cottage?

"No," Maria said, confusion on her face. "Why would she come here?"

Quickly, Charlotte asked, "Are mother and father ill?"

"No, indeed. What a silly question! This is about Mr. Card."

"Oh dear," Charlotte sighed and arranged herself more comfortably on the chair, preparing for a very long story indeed.

Tears quivered on Maria's blond lashes, and her blue eyes filled. "He has ruined everything. Absolutely everything."

Exasperated, Charlotte said, "For heaven's sake, tell me what has happened!"

"He arrived around eleven. I received him quite properly in the sitting room. You would have been proud. We were both exceedingly polite. Initially, I was happy to see him, for we have always been good friends. I remarked upon his attire. He looked quite fine today. He wore a particularly well-tailored green coat."

"He is always handsomely turned out."

"I have always liked that about him. In any case, we chatted, but as time progressed, Mr. Card seemed to become increasingly awkward. More awkward than usual, if you can imagine it."

"Oh dear."

"Yes, I was driven to ring for tea and biscuits just to have something to do, for he refused to leave."

"That was a kind decision."

"After our tea, Mr. Card began pacing the room, and I became very uncomfortable. I did not know what to say. And here he was just pacing back and forth. Then he began complimenting me. 'I have always admired you,' he said. And then I knew what was amiss."

"Did you?"

"He was going to propose, you see, and I did not want him to. Not at all. The only thing I could think of was finding a way to distract him. I suggested a walk in the garden. At first he seemed relieved, but he would not be dissuaded. He was quite determined."

"What happened?"

"Well, I got tired of walking. I just could not get away from him, no matter how fast I went. So I sat on the bench in the garden and steeled myself for the worst."

"Oh, Maria…"

"It was just as I suspected. He did propose. It was awful."

"I hope you were kind to him and considerate of his feelings."

"Kind to him?" Maria said in a high-pitched voice. "How could I possibly treat him kindly after he tortured me in such a manner. How could he not realize that I was trying to avoid the subject entirely?"

"Maria!"

"Oh! Do not chastise me, for I did not say anything too awful. I simply told him that I did not view him in such a way and that I never, ever would. Well, he would not accept that, so I told him that I loved another."

"Please tell me that you did not. Oh no. How did the poor boy react?"

"How should I know how he reacted? All I could think about was how to get myself out of this mess as quickly as possible."

"He must have been very upset. He has tender feelings for you."

"Do not look down your nose at me, Charlotte. You have no idea how to deal with such entanglements."

"I may not have had a number of lovers, but I do know that you should not have lied to Mr. Card."

"When did I lie to him?"

"You told him you loved another."

"Well, I do."

Charlotte was stunned.

"I am in love with Mr. Westfield."

Charlotte sat back in her chair, her spine straight as a piece of planed lumber. "But you hardly know him."

Maria looked offended. She stood in her own defense. "I know him well enough. He is everything a gentleman should be. He is clever, kind, and amusing. He is all that Mr. Card is not. And I told Mr. Card as much."

The situation was worse than Charlotte feared. Maria was not a delicate person, and she never seemed to comprehend the consequences of the things she said. Mr. Card would likely never forgive her.

"You should not have said such things to him. How must Mr. Card feel? He is a decent young man, handsome, charming, and rich. He has paid you the highest compliment by proposing, and how do you respond but by insulting him? You must apologize as soon as may be."

Maria crossed her arms. "I certainly will not. He will get over his hurt pride in short order and things will return to the way they have always been."

"Affairs of the heart are never that simple."

Maria groaned, left the room, and tromped up the stairs, leaving Charlotte to ponder the situation.

✆ Seven ✆

After her initial outburst subsided, Maria did not seem very much affected by the incident with Mr. Card. In fact, she seemed to have quite forgotten it. While ensconced in the cottage, she remained merry, spending much of her time daydreaming in the garden or reclining idly in the sitting room. Charlotte, however, knew that the storm clouds were gathering and that soon the deluge would begin.

A week later, an invitation to supper at the Farmington's arrived.

"You see, Charlotte." Maria waved the letter with an air of triumph. "This is proof that you have made far too much of my refusal of Mr. Card. We have been invited, you see, to join a supper party at Miss Farmington's house. I am certain that Mr. Card will also be there."

"For your sake, I am pleased to appear to be in the wrong." Charlotte remained unconvinced, but Maria beamed at her, unable to imagine any negative repercussions for her actions. Ah, if only imagination ruled reality. Charlotte would be beautiful and gentlemen would bring her carriages full of gold.

"I will write my reply straightaway." She crossed to the desk and selected a sheet of notepaper. She composed a lengthy reply, turning the paper and scribbling still more words, which Charlotte could only imagine conveyed untold silliness.

Meanwhile, Charlotte remained in the sitting room with her book in her lap. She attempted to read but soon abandoned the pursuit when her mind continued to wander. Despite all attempts to the contrary, Charlotte thought of gentlemen. What had become of her? She had not been this preoccupied even when she was in the prime of her youth. Perhaps it resulted from her sister's proclamation of love for Mr. Westfield. Or perhaps it stemmed from her conversation with Mr. Edgington. In any case, Charlotte continued to think of how much altered her life might have been had she experienced true love.

At first, this fictitious true love had no form or face. Then, much to her chagrin, she could not prevent herself from filling the void with the faces of men of her acquaintance.

First, she imagined her marriage with Mr. Collins. She recalled his manner and his words. She thought upon their days together and her feelings regarding him. Indeed, she would not call it love that they shared. It was rather more like strained companionship.

Next, the face of Mr. Basford entered her mind. She attempted not to think of him, knowing his poor reputation. She felt an embarrassed flush reach her cheeks merely at the thought of him. It was not proper for her to contemplate him. Any sort of amity with him would be insupportable.

Now, Mr. Edgington was a proper prospect for a woman such as her. He was widower of excellent family and reputation, and strangely enough he seemed to have an interest in her. Charlotte had always been rather plain, and she had not had the inducement of a large dowry to entice gentlemen. Though it was difficult to acknowledge, men had little reason to show her attention.

Mr. Edgington, however, had experienced marriage. He must have come to realize that there were aspects of greater import than a fresh face, family support, and deep pockets. Although deep pockets never hurt. Perhaps Mr. Edgington was the gentleman with whom to explore the possibilities of love that had escaped her.

Charlotte scoffed at the turn of her contemplation. Such nonsense for a woman of her age and experience, but for some reason she felt strangely buoyant.

But would Lady Catherine accept her?

Likely not.

The feeling of hopefulness did not last past the dinner at the Farmington's, however. The evening began well. Of course, most dinner parties have the advantage of expectation—of food and conversation and merriness. Only on rare occasions are these expectations met, and certainly, this was not one of those times.

While not as grand as the Cards' home, the Farmingtons' house was a large and welcoming residence. Miss Farmington greeted them at the door and escorted them into a well appointed drawing room. The furniture was upholstered in rich shades of jonquil yellow, and wax candles had been lit, causing the room to take on a dull yellow hue though it was past dusk.

The party conversed pleasantly until Mr. Card arrived. He entered the room, his posture erect and his hands clasped behind his back. He too was well appointed. His coat fit closely across his shoulders, giving him an aristocratic mien. His conduct and bearing were decidedly more aloof than ordinary. He surveyed the crowd, spotted Maria, and then walked purposefully in the opposite direction. No one, save Charlotte, took note.

Maria attempted to join the group with which he conversed. His bearing turned unambiguously cold, and although her sister appeared not to notice, it incited questioning glances from those who were assembled around them.

As the party moved toward the dining table, Miss Farmington arrested Maria, pulling her into an alcove in the hallway. Charlotte lingered behind them to listen to their conversation and wondered when she had lost her shame. "Maria, is something amiss between you and Mr. Card?" She need not have stood so close, for Miss Farmington's voice carried, and Charlotte hoped no one in the dining room had heard.

"I do not know to what you are referring, Miss Farmington." Although Charlotte could not see Maria, she felt fairly certain that her words were accompanied by a head flip.

"He is acting very strangely. How can this fact have escaped your notice?"

Charlotte waited as her sister contemplated a proper response. It took long moments. "If you believe him to be acting strangely perhaps it would be wise for you to question him, not me, for I am the same as I ever was."

Charlotte did not approve of that idea at all.

"Indeed I shall. It is fortunate, then, that Mr. Card is to be seated beside me."

Miss Farmington pulled Maria from the alcove and led the way to the dining room. Charlotte followed at length, found her appointed seat beside Mrs. Farmington, and was quickly engaged in conversation. Maria sat on the opposite side of the table between two of Miss Farmington's young friends, and the three of them chattered happily, completely ignorant of the others around them.

Out of the corner of her eye, Charlotte regarded Mr. Card and Miss Farmington. She could hear very little of their conversation, but she took notice of their continual glances in Maria's direction. Mr. Card's countenance was cold, and she was unaccustomed to seeing such an expression on so pleasant a gentleman.

The longer the two spoke the more shocked Miss Farmington appeared. She reached over and patted Mr. Card's arm comfortingly, and Charlotte was quite certain that she saw her call Maria an old fool.

In good conscience, Charlotte could not call her younger sister old, but unfortunately, she had to agree that she had behaved foolishly where Mr. Card was concerned. Perhaps she did deserve a measure of the censure that was certain to come her way.

For the remainder of the evening, Miss Farmington stayed at Mr. Card's side, fawning over him and making sure Maria was a witness to it all.

Indeed, Maria had seen, and she came to Charlotte in due course. "You see, the situation has not turned out as badly as you predicted. See there how Miss Farmington is enjoying his company, and what a charming couple they make. Mr. Card will soon forget his ridiculous proposal to me."

"I do not know—"

"—Oh, pooh. You just refuse to acknowledge pleasant things."

Maria flounced away, leaving Charlotte with a reprimand lingering on her tongue. Alone again, she sat down to observe the room. It was clear that the news of Maria and Mr. Card was now known by everyone present and would soon be the talk of Westerham. Based on the cold glare in the eyes of Mr. Card and

Miss Farmington—and the lack of conversation partners who had come Charlotte's way—she concluded that her sister—and herself by extension—would not appear in a positive light.

Oblivious to the entire situation, Maria spoke animatedly with the assembled company. Charlotte could hear her voice floating above the others. "I do not comprehend why everyone is so quiet this evening! Perhaps it is owing to too much of Mrs. Farmington's good wine." Her friends looked on with barely concealed disdain as she raised her glass to her lips and drank deeply.

Leave it to Maria to misread the situation so completely. It would not do to have her sister intoxicated; her conversation was questionable enough without the benefit of red wine. Charlotte resolved to stem the tide of the damage immediately. She stood and walked to the corner where Maria was in the process of questioning Mrs. Farmington about the vintage of the wine.

"Mrs. Farmington, thank you for an enjoyable evening," said Charlotte quietly, "but I beg you would excuse us."

Maria stared at her. "But it is so early."

"I do apologize, but I am feeling rather unwell and would like to be at home shortly."

"Oh dear," Mrs. Farmington said, "I will have a carriage brought round." She rang the bell and issued orders to the servant who arrived. Then she called her granddaughter to bid farewell to her guests. "Constance, do escort Mrs. Collins and Miss Lucas to the door."

"With pleasure." Miss Farmington did not attempt to conceal her rudeness. She offered her arm to Maria. "Shall we?"

Charlotte walked behind them, again listening to their conversation. Still no shame. "I am sorry to speak so in front of your sister, but how could you do such a thing to poor Mr. Card?"

They stopped abruptly at the door. Charlotte narrowly avoided a collision.

Maria took a confused step backward. "Do such a thing?"

"Your rejection of Mr. Card's proposal, of course, you ninny."

"Oh, that," Maria said lightly. "I had thought he would not mention it."

"Not only have you broken his heart, but you have done it for the stupidest reason imaginable."

"Wha—" Maria was flabbergasted.

Miss Farmington sighed in frustration. "You imagine yourself to be in love with Mr. Westfield, and I supposed you believe that he returns your feelings."

"I cannot speak for Mr.—"

Miss Farmington's eyes narrowed to mere slits on her freckled face. "Mr. Westfield is far above your station, and he certainly would never show interest in you."

Maria stared at her mutely, confusion etched in her face. Miss Farmington's visage had turned an unflattering shade of red, and her nose became so pinched that Charlotte wondered that she could continue to draw breath. "And worse, you have ruined your only hope for marriage. Can you not comprehend that? It is now certain that you will be as sad and lonely as your sister."

"That is quite enough." Charlotte spoke loudly as she stepped between the two young ladies. She touched her sister's hand. "Maria, shall we go?"

Maria managed to croak out a small "yes" and followed Charlotte weakly, her steps as careful as an elderly woman's.

Charlotte took her sister's arm and propelled her into the small, borrowed carriage as the tap of Miss Farmington's angry footsteps receded down the hall. Maria continued to look back at Miss Farmington's receding form. Her face had gone very pale and she turned to Charlotte and said, "I must speak with her."

Fearing that her sister would call out to Miss Farmington, or worse, burst in loud sobs, she said, "No. Do not say a word until we are home, Maria. Now is the time for discretion."

Maria stared uncomprehendingly. "How could Mr. Card do this to me?" Her lower lip wobbled.

"Not now. At home. The driver might overhear."

It appeared that Maria might protest her caution, but Charlotte kept her arm firmly around her sister's shoulders as they bumped along through the night. She absorbed the periodic trembling that rocked Maria's small form, and when they exited the carriage and descended into the night, Charlotte had to assist her into the cottage.

As soon as the candles were lit and the two sisters were alone in the sitting room before the peat fire that Edward had left burning for them, Maria's shock turned to anger, and she stormed to the fireplace. "How could Mr. Card do this?"

"Maria—"

"—He has ruined me. By tomorrow morning, the entire town will have turned against me. I shall have no friends. No prospects."

Charlotte remained silent.

Maria's voice rose, her face became ruddy in the candlelight. "And what will Mr. Westfield say?"

Charlotte took a place on the settee and waited for her sister to finish raging.

"Mr. Card said he loved me. Now he has done this. How could he? How could he possibly do this to someone he claimed to love, Charlotte? How?"

"He is angry and hurt, Maria. Only think of the things you said to him when he proposed."

"I said nothing terrible. I spoke the truth. There is nothing so inappropriate about the truth surely."

"You said yourself that you were cross with him. That you told him you would never love him. That you loved another. He has pined for you since your first meeting, Maria. You could have let him down more gently. How would you like to hear those things from the person you loved most in this world?"

"So I deserved all this censure?" Her voice cracked with emotion.

"No, certainly not. Mr. Card has made his share of mistakes in this matter as well. Not the least of which was confiding in that odious Constance Farmington."

Maria sighed. "What a disaster this has turned out to be."

"Yes, and now we are left to deal with it as we might."

Maria collapsed on the settee with tears streaming down her cheeks and cried silently with her sister's arms around her.

⁂

The next morning, Maria did not come downstairs, so Charlotte went to her bed chamber to summon her. She lay unmoving beneath the covers, despite the sound of her sister's movements as she threw open the drapes, allowing bright morning light to flood the room.

Maria groaned.

"Get up. We are going to town."

"I certainly am not. Everyone despises me by now."

"Listen, sister." Charlotte sat on the side of the bed. "It is best to deal with matters such as this directly. You must go out and meet your fate."

"Last night you told me it was the time for discretion," Maria said, her face still covered.

"That was last night. You were in no condition to deal with this situation rationally."

"Nor am I now."

"Today, you must be. You must not hide. You must acknowledge the wrong you did to Mr. Card and make amends. It is the only way you will regain your status in society."

"Urgh," Maria said. She threw the blankets back, giving Charlotte the first good look at her face. Her skin was pale, her hair matted, and there were swollen, dark circles under her eyes.

"Did you sleep at all?" Charlotte's tone was softer.

"How could I sleep?"

Charlotte stroked her hair. Her fingers caught in the knotted strands, and she dropped her hand.

"I did behave badly to Mr. Card, did I not?"

Charlotte paused, pleased to see that the morning sun had brought with it a measure of mental enlightenment. "Yes, I am sorry to say you did."

Maria sighed and turned her head toward the window. "I was so nervous, and I simply wanted him to leave. I focused only on avoiding the issue, so when he proposed, I had no idea what to say. I had no thought in my head at all but to avoid the matter entirely. So I blurted the first thing that came into my mind."

"It is always wise to consider for a time."

"I know, and that is why I simply cannot go into town. I have no defense against my behavior."

"I really think you should face the world as soon as possible. If you hide away here, people will only have more fodder for their gossip."

Maria pulled the covers back over her head. "Charlotte, please do not make me. I am far too embarrassed."

Charlotte looked down at the lump in the bed that was her sister. Her sister, who was giddy and sweet, thoughtless and silly, but who loved society above all else.

"I will not make you do anything, Maria, but I am going to the bakery for some cream cakes."

"Let me know if you see anyone."

"I shall."

"And do bring me a cream cake."

❦❧

Charlotte walked to town, vaguely saddened that her sister had elected to remain at the cottage, and she felt quite dreary in spirits although the sun shone brightly.

As she walked, she felt the stares of the others she encountered. Not a one spoke to her, although she could hear snippets of their conversations, which were focused on Maria's poor behavior. Torn between anger at her sister's stupidity, pity at the situation into which she had put herself, and fear at her own tenuous position in society, Charlotte picked up her pace, her sturdy boots crunching on the ground beneath them.

Turning the corner beside the Circulating Library, she found herself face to face with Jonas Card.

"Excuse me, Mrs. Collins." His voice was polite, his manner chilly. He tipped his hat and stepped aside so she could pass.

Charlotte responded automatically. "It is nothing, Mr. Card."

They looked at each other awkwardly until Mr. Card bowed and then turned to leave, but Charlotte stepped into his path. "Mr. Card, let us not behave this way."

He faced her once again and said with not a small measure of bitterness, "How then would you suggest I behave?"

Charlotte bowed her head at the anger she heard in his voice. He was justified in his sentiments if not in his behavior. "I can make no such suggestion."

"Then what is the purpose of this conversation?"

"I confess I am not certain," Charlotte ventured. "Perhaps, I simply wanted to reunite you and my sister as friends. You have always been friends, have you not?"

"No, I have never been her friend." His eyes blazed with anger. "I have never been content to be a mere acquaintance. You yourself knew of my feelings. My mother revealed her conversations with you on this matter." His voice dropped to a whisper. "You knew that I have always loved her. Every moment I have spent as her friend has been a torment."

"Oh, Mr. Card—"

"And as for her so-called friendship for me, I do not believe it exists. No friend would reject another friend in so rude a fashion."

"Her words were thoughtless, I agree, but I do not believe that it was her intention to wound you."

"Do you not? Then why would she possibly tell me that she found me unmanly and that I repulsed her? Why would she say these things unless she meant to hurt me?"

Maria had not confessed that she had said such things to poor Mr. Card. It was wrong indeed.

"I can make no excuses for her actions, Mr. Card, but I know she regrets the words she spoke to you that day. I do wish that you would speak with her, allow her to apologize."

"Speak with her! Certainly not. I am quite finished with her."

Charlotte chose her next words carefully. "But Mr. Card, you have not been entirely fair to her either."

His eyes widened, and his lips stretched into a sneer. "Have I not?"

"By speaking—undoubtedly in righteous anger—to Miss Farmington, you have made Maria the focus of vicious gossip."

"What did I say of her that was untrue? I spoke the unmitigated truth when I said that she insulted me and that she loved that dreadful American Mr. Westfield. Do you deny that I spoke only what Maria said herself?"

"No, I cannot deny it. I wish…" She paused. "I only wish that you would find it in your heart to forgive her—"

"—I have no heart left."

She pushed on. "And I also wish that you would help alleviate the gossip against her. She is a sensitive young woman, and she will certainly be crushed by what is being said about her."

"And I wish she had accepted my proposal, but we cannot always get what we desire, Mrs. Collins. Good day."

Mr. Card turned on his boot heel and stalked down the street, leaving Charlotte standing with her mouth agape.

She did not know how long she stood in such an undignified posture when she heard a voice behind her say, "Excuse me, Mrs. Collins."

Charlotte turned to find Mr. Edgington leaning against the corner of the building. He bowed to her politely, and she returned a curtsey.

"Good morning, Mr. Edgington." She wondered if he had witnessed her ordeal with Mr. Card.

"Forgive me, but I could not help overhearing."

Oh dear. So much for discretion.

"I suppose it does not matter. The damage has already been done."

"I confess that your sister has been the main topic of conversation about town all morning."

"That has been my unfortunate experience as well."

"Shall we walk?" He offered his arm, and Charlotte took it gratefully.

They continued along the sidewalk, and Charlotte found she rather enjoyed having someone in whom to confide. "My poor sister will not be able to bear this. She has always been such a social creature, and she had just found herself back in society."

"It is sad that she is so affected by what is said about her."

"I suppose that is the trouble with living amongst people. It would be so much pleasanter to be a hermit."

He laughed and then turned contemplative. "I am also sorry to see what effect this situation is having on you, but I hope it does not cause you to turn into a hermit.

"It has not affected me half so much as it has Maria."

"Oh, but it has."

"I am afraid I do not follow your logic, sir."

"I have noticed that no one has spoken to you all morning, and I have heard what they said about you after you pass by. Does not that concern you at all?"

"Of course it does, but I must think of Maria."

They walked along and Charlotte fancied that she could feel the stares of people on her.

"Have you considered taking a holiday?"

"A holiday?"

"Yes. Perhaps a trip to London for a few weeks will allow the storm clouds to pass."

"I do not know, Mr. Edgington. I do not relish the idea of retreating and retrenching."

"Nonsense. You know the nature of society. Your current trouble will dissipate upon the occurrence of the next event worthy of salacious gossip. I simply believe that there is no reason to witness the slander of your family firsthand."

Charlotte considered for a moment. She had advised her sister only this morning to go out and face her trouble, but having witnessed the magnitude of the situation for herself, having spoken to poor Mr. Card, she could well see the advantage of waiting out the storm in London.

"Do you have relatives or friends whom you could visit?"

"Yes, I do have some cousins in London whom I have not seen in quite some time."

"Well, perhaps now is the time to renew your acquaintance," he suggested. "And London has many pleasant distractions for ladies."

They lapsed into silence, and Charlotte spent the remainder of her walk with Mr. Edgington considering her options. She took her leave of him, completely forgetting to purchase cream cakes for which she had ventured out, and returned home to discover that Maria was not downstairs. As Charlotte ascended the steps, she began to hear the sounds of sobbing.

She knocked on the door to Maria's bed chamber and found her sister sitting in the middle of the bed dressed in her favorite gown of a white fabric patterned with blue stripes and medallions. Her hair had been done, but it had slipped its hold and now strands hung around her face. Her eyes looked defeated, and Charlotte immediately felt compassion for her.

"Oh, Charlotte."

She sat on the rumpled bed beside her. The same position she had taken that morning. "What has happened?"

Maria held up a letter. "This was delivered an hour ago. From Miss Farmington. She says…she says…here, read it for yourself."

Charlotte opened the letter, which was written in a looping, exaggerated hand, a silly choice of script.

> My dear Maria—
>
> I know that you must be having a difficult time at present and are probably not anxious to venture out amongst our acquaintance. However, I know you are too polite to rescind your acceptance to our picnic next week. I will save you the pain of disappointing us by telling you are no longer required to attend.

It was signed in exaggerated swirls that Charlotte imagined was her name.

The situation was utterly ridiculous, and Miss Farmington's behavior only served to convince Charlotte that she was not like her old red roan pony at all. She more closely resembled a mule.

"Is it not awful?"

"Yes, it is." She patted her sister's arm. "What would you think of a holiday?"

Maria's face lit. "Holiday?"

"Yes, to London to visit our cousins the Emersons for a time."

Hope lit Maria's eyes, then suspicion. "But you said I must face society and not run away."

"Forget what I said this morning. Perhaps this is the best way. What do you think? Shall we go?"

"Could we?"

"I believe we should."

Maria, whose eyes had brightened despite their red rims, smiled for the first time that morning. "I must admit that a holiday would be welcome. I will prepare my trunk straightaway…after I ring for tea. I could certainly do with a fresh cream cake."

๑๏ๅ Eight ๑๏ๅ

Westerham was twenty-five miles from London, an easy distance by most standards. Those standards had obviously been set by those who could afford to keep comfortable travelling coaches and horses of their own. Charlotte and Maria could afford only to purchase space on the stagecoach, and the accompanying horses, though large and undoubtedly powerful, looked like they deserved a respite in a grassy pasture.

They stopped briefly in Bromley to acquire fresh horses. The passengers disembarked while the new steeds, which looked only slightly more energetic than those they had left behind, were hitched to the coach.

Charlotte watched the slow, metered steps of the first team of horses as they were led to the paddock for rest, and she felt very much like them. Stiff and weary from travel. Though she had been sitting and not pulling, she had still been bruised by the jerking impacts of the coach's wheels through the rutted and hole-riddled roads. Travel, though necessary, had its own variety of unpleasantness.

Upon the coachman's call, Charlotte reluctantly took her seat, wishing she had brought a cushion, and continued the dusty journey toward London through the gathering warmth of spring.

Soon, the countryside was exchanged for the crush of the city. Buildings filled the horizon and the road became crowded with horses, wagons, and people on foot. The stage arrived at a coaching inn, which was fairly bustling with activity. Grooms dashed to care for the horses of the incoming stages, and passengers disembarked and milled about, searching for a hackney or seeing to their trunks.

Charlotte stepped into the busy yard and looked around. She wondered briefly if she and Maria would ever manage to find their cousin Harold Emerson amidst all the activity. Maria must have had similar thoughts, for she leaned to Charlotte and asked, "Will Mr. Emerson be able to find us, do you think? I am so weary and wish to be alone."

Charlotte patted her hand. She also wished to be alone. Maria had not been a pleasant traveling companion. She had complained nearly the entire duration of the journey. The coach was hot, the roads were dreadful, it was too crowded. All were valid complaints, but speaking them aloud would do no good.

Before Charlotte could reply, she spied Harold Emerson, who had appeared on the fringes of the crowd. Mr. Emerson was a pleasant gentleman of careful manners and curly auburn hair who had earned a substantial living in the practice of law, and he bowed before them. "Welcome, cousins."

The ladies curtseyed, and Charlotte spoke for them both. "Mr. Emerson, we feared we would never find you in such a throng of people. We are ever so glad that you have spotted us."

Maria nodded. "Yes, it is dreadfully crowded and hot."

He glanced between the sisters. Charlotte wondered if they appeared as dusty and bruised as they felt.

He said, "Allow me to see to your belongings, and we will be away as soon as is possible. I have already arranged for a hackney to take us to St. Paul's. Mrs. Emerson will be pleased to see you both."

Mr. Emerson disappeared briefly to look after their trunks and then he escorted Charlotte and Maria to the waiting conveyance. Charlotte was loath to sit once again, but she was eager to see her cousin Mary, and she took her place next to Maria and settled herself gingerly on the seat.

Mr. Emerson joined them forthwith and began a pleasant conversation. "How does your family do? Your parents, are they well?"

Charlotte responded to his polite inquiries while Maria sullenly studied the surrounding buildings.

Mr. Emerson then inquired after the comforts of their journey, a question to which Charlotte hoped Maria would not respond.

She did not.

And though it was not the precise truth, Charlotte said that their journey was most pleasant.

Here, Maria had uttered a sound of mild disagreement, which Charlotte attempted to conceal by asking, "And how does my cousin do?"

Mr. Emerson had been studying Maria, but he turned his attention back to Charlotte. "Mrs. Emerson has been anticipating your arrival most heartily. She is probably at the window even now, waiting for your appearance."

"My sister and I are eager to see her as well. How far are we from your home?"

"It is but a short drive."

"Oh, good!" Maria said, emitting the first genuine smile of the day. "I am quite ready to be situated in a solid structure that does not move or smell of horse."

Mr. Emerson seemed slightly taken aback by Maria's words, but his good nature would not allow him to think ill of her, and he assured her that their home neither moved nor smelled of horse.

For the remainder of their ride in the hackney, Mr. Emerson pointed out the sights, and soon, he gestured proudly toward his home. "We have arrived!"

While it was hardly the most fashionable London neighborhood, their home was clean and well-maintained, and it overlooked other similarly kept homes. Cousin Mary, a doe-eyed young woman with dark hair, greeted them at the door and ushered them immediately to the sitting room, while simultaneously managing to order some refreshments and see that their luggage was brought to their rooms.

Maria immediately made her excuses and disappeared into her chamber, but Charlotte stayed below stairs and enjoyed tea with the Emersons, who sat together on the settee. Charlotte observed the looks that passed between them with interest. It was clear that their marriage was founded on love, for Mary looked upon her husband with something akin to adoration, and Mr. Emerson, though much more reserved in his bearing, returned her affection with subtle glances of his own.

Though the couple had been married for very nearly five years, Charlotte could tell that they still enjoyed each other's company very much indeed, and she was quite certain that while not in company, they often sat much more closely.

Charlotte's observations were both encouraging and somewhat depressing, for she had never experienced such things. She had always sat as far from Mr. Collins as propriety would allow and looked on him as little as possible. Despite the jealousy that stung her as she watched her cousins, she was heartened to confirm once more that marital bliss was possible, and, quite likely, more common than she had thought.

"Thank you so much for opening your home to us. My sister was in very great need of an escape, and I confess that I too needed to leave Westerham for a time. As much as I love the country, it can become rather confining."

"We are happy to help you and poor Maria." Mary patted Mr. Emerson on the thigh, "Are we not, dear?"

"Indeed we are." Mr. Emerson sounded sincere but confused.

Charlotte shifted in her chair and appealed to Mr. Emerson. "I feel I must apologize for Maria's abrupt disappearance. She is still at sixes and sevens over the circumstances in Westerham."

"Do not trouble yourself." Mary waved her hand as if to dismiss the problem with a mere gesture. "We understand completely. As long as you are here, you must consider our home to be your home. Behave just as you would in Westerham. If Maria needs solitude, then she shall find it here."

"You are very kind."

"And you, my dear cousin, must get out and enjoy the atmosphere of London."

"Must I?"

Mr. Emerson cleared his throat and said, "Certainly. There is a great deal to be experienced, and now that you are here, you must experience it. It would not do for both of you to remain locked away in the tower, so to speak."

"Yes, allow Maria to heal in solitude. In the meantime, we will enjoy London, and when Maria is ready, she shall join us."

"I would not know which of the city's entertainments to select."

Mr. Emerson volunteered his services. "Allow me to arrange things. Shall we not begin with an evening at the theater?"

"Oh yes, dear, the theater."

"Then I shall arrange it."

∘⊙❧ ❧⊙∘

The very next night, the three of them left Maria to her bed and her biscuits and endured the changeable April weather to attend a performance of *The Inn-Keeper's Daughter* at the Theatre Royal at Drury Lane.

Mary's excitement over the evening's outing was infectious, and Charlotte was swept along in her tide of giddiness. The cousins spent the day preparing their outfits. Charlotte selected a short-sleeved dove gray gown, and when she saw Mary's gown of fine white muslin, for the first time, she regretted her own gown's black mourning trim.

Mary and Charlotte prepared for the theater together, and when the hour of their departure drew near, Mr. Emerson began to pace at the bottom of the stairs.

"Do not mind him, Charlotte," said Mary, as she held out two necklaces for Charlotte's opinion. "He would arrive a quarter hour early for every occasion if he could. It is up to us women to prevent the blunder of early arrival."

Though Charlotte was prepared to depart, she laughed at Mary, who was still a bit scattered. She pointed to the simple cross necklace. "I believe that will do your gown justice."

Mary hooked it around her neck and then regarded herself in the mirror. "Yes, I believe you are right. And now we may relieve Mr. Emerson's suffering."

They left the room and descended the stairs. Mr. Emerson paid them efficient compliments and then ushered them to the hackney.

Soon, the Theatre Royal at Drury Lane loomed before them. They had arrived a bit late, though Mr. Emerson said not a word of it as he escorted them quickly to their seats. Charlotte had hardly a moment to take in the edifice or the interior of the theater before she found herself seated in the balcony beside her cousin and her husband.

The production had already begun, but she easily slipped into the action of the play. Though she found herself enjoying the production, she felt rather like an interloper. The intimate ambiance of the balcony seats seemed to have relaxed Mr. Emerson, and the couple frequently glanced at each other throughout the performance and shared little comments and jokes that she could not hear. They passed Mr. Emerson's monocular opera glass between them, offering it occasionally to Charlotte, but she declined. She wanted to allow them privacy and interacted as little as possible, for they seemed to be enjoying each other so immensely. In fact, the Emersons soon seemed to forget her presence completely.

During the intermission, Charlotte took her leave of her cousins, descended the stone staircase, and strolled in solitude around the theater admiring the architecture and décor. She was well acquainted with the finer things. After all, she had been in Rosings, the great house of Lady Catherine de Bourgh, many times, but the sheer opulence of the theater filled her with awe. The sumptuous fabrics encouraged her to run her fingers across them, though she dared not, and the gilding made the room appear to glow golden. While Charlotte enjoyed a simpler style, the colors and textures of the rotunda caused her to fancy herself as a grand dame, whose closets were filled with gowns for every hour of the day, whose companions were always witty, and whose dance card was always filled.

"I thank you, but no," she would say to the wealthy baron, "I may not dance this set with you, for I am promised to the earl."

Charlotte smiled at her thoughts, knowing fully that she would never share them with anyone, for they were foolish and impractical, and they would never come to fruition. But what harm was it to imagine such *affaires de coeur*?

As she walked and dreamed, she became conscious of a familiar figure standing under an archway near one of the entrances to the rotunda. At first, she thought her mind was playing her for a fool and believed herself to be imagining the shock of red hair on his head, but as she ventured closer, she saw that it was indeed Mr. Edgington. Although not the baron or the earl of her daydreams,

Charlotte was pleased to see him, especially so handsomely attired in a fine black suit coat and breeches and an intricately tied white cravat. She stopped before him and watched as his eyes lit with recognition.

"Mr. Edgington, good evening."

"Mrs. Collins!" He stepped forward and grasped her hand in his. His gaze dropped admiringly at her gown, her best. "You are looking quite well, but I confess I am surprised to see you here."

"At the theater or in London?" She slowly withdrew her hand.

"Both actually." He allowed her to remove her hand from his grasp and then glanced furtively around the room, as if he had been caught in a compromising position. Perhaps he had held her hand a bit longer than protocol dictated. Charlotte too looked about her, but she recognized no one.

When she returned her attention to Mr. Edgington, he was looking at her expectantly, and she remembered that she ought to say something in response. "Well, you suggested that I bring Maria to London and it seemed a fine idea." Her halting speech embarrassed her. She took a deep breath, hoping it would loosen her tongue and dispel the awkwardness she felt. "The theater was my cousin Mr. Emerson's method of entertaining his poor country relation."

"Are you enjoying it?"

"To my surprise, I find that I am. I never fancied myself a fan of the theater. It always seemed so improper."

"Improper! I should think not." He laughed. "How does Maria do?"

"She is healing, thank you, Mr. Edgington." Again his eyes travelled the room, and Charlotte wondered at his distraction. He appeared to be searching the crowd. But for whom? Perhaps he was at the theater with friends. Perhaps he was escorting a young lady. Yes, he was most likely searching the assembly for his companion. But what sort of person was Mr. Edgington's companion? A woman, undoubtedly. Did he flirt with her as he had with Charlotte? Was she younger and more attractive? Did she have a claim on Mr. Edgington's heart?

People began filing back into the theater, and his eyes returned to Charlotte.

"It appears that the intermission is near its end."

"I should return to my cousins."

He stopped her as she began to turn away. His hand gripped her forearm.

She stared down at the hand on her arm.

"Mrs. Collins, forgive my impertinence." He released her. "Will you permit me to call upon you at your cousins' home?"

Ordinarily, Charlotte would have been inclined to deny such a request, if in fact she ever received one, but tonight—after witnessing the affection between Mr. and Mrs. Emerson and experiencing a twinge of jealousy at the thought that Mr. Edgington was at the theater with another lady—she said, "I would enjoy it very much."

She gave him directions to her cousins' home and then hurried back to her seat. She could barely focus on the performance for the remainder of the evening. Instead, she searched the audience for Mr. Edgington, hoping to glimpse his companion. His distinctive red hair should be easy to spot.

But it proved more difficult than Charlotte imagined, for the theater was quite overflowing with people.

"Mr. Emerson, may I accept your offer to use your opera glass?"

He removed the glass from his eye. "Certainly."

She issued her thanks and began to scan the crowd. Row after row, seat after seat, she searched. She began to feel very much like a foolish debutante, but envy, and natural curiosity, drove her to continue her search until she thought she espied Mr. Edgington.

She focused the lens on the gentleman. Yes, it was most certainly him.

He sat in the center of a row. On his left was a rather portly gentleman. Most likely not his companion.

But on his right sat a woman.

Charlotte squinted through her glass. She was not the lithe female she had envisioned but a slightly plump woman of questionable fashion sense. Charlotte could not discern the details of her gown, but her hair! Her hair could be seen from miles, she was certain. It was coiffed in ringlets and bound in a complicated wrap, and perched jauntily on the crown of her head was what appeared to be an entire bird's nest. Including the bird.

Perhaps a skylark or sparrow. Charlotte could not be certain from such a distance.

This woman must not be Mr. Edgington's consort, but his relation. Surely, he would have higher standards than to pursue a woman who would wear an aviary on her head. Perhaps he too was entertaining a poor country cousin. Charlotte smiled at the thought.

Mr. Edgington was available, and apparently, he was interested. Suddenly, a thrill ran through Charlotte. She felt jittery and a little sick. Did every woman feel this way when she was being courted by a gentleman? She had never imagined that love and nausea went hand in hand.

৩৫ Nine ৩৯৫

When Charlotte descended the stairs the following morning, she discovered Mr. Edgington breakfasting with her cousins.

She paused in the corridor at the first sound of his voice. What could he be doing here?

Charlotte's practical nature assured her that it probably signified nothing of greater import than the fact that he had come to call on the entire family, had interrupted their meal, and had been invited to dine with them.

It meant nothing. He had not come to call only on her.

Had he?

One never knew with gentlemen.

She checked her hair in the hall mirror and pinched her cheeks to lend them some color before entering the room.

"Good morning, Cousin Charlotte," said Mary over her muffin and tea. "I hope you do not mind, but Mr. Edgington arrived a few moments ago, and I invited him to share our late-morning meal with us."

Mr. Emerson and Mr. Edgington rose from their chairs and bowed to her. Mr. Emerson appeared to be studying their guest, as if to determine his worthiness to call upon his cousin, but Mr. Edgington's attention remained on her.

Surprised at Mr. Edgington's intensity, Charlotte spoke by rote. "Indeed, it was the proper thing to do."

She took a seat across the table from Mr. Edgington, and as the gentlemen returned to their chairs, she wondered if she would offend their guest if she filled her plate and then ate its entire contents, for she was really quite famished. She glanced at the dishes before her and decided she did not care much what he thought. She took a generous helping of ham, a boiled egg, and two slices of buttered toast and poured herself some tea.

Mr. Edgington was watching her, but he did not seem appalled by the amount of food on her plate. Apparently, he did not mind a woman who indulged herself occasionally.

"I had not intended on imposing upon your meal," he said, lifting his teacup from the saucer, "but I wanted to invite you on a walk this morning."

Mr. Edgington sipped. Charlotte looked to her cousins. Mr. Emerson produced a hesitant smile. And Mary shot Charlotte a conspiratorial look, which she hoped Mr. Edgington had not seen. "You have not imposed."

He replaced the cup gently on the saucer. "I am pleased to hear it, for I had no wish to disturb your morning routine." Then, he turned his charm on Charlotte. "Would you care to tour the shops with me, Mrs. Collins?"

She glanced at her cousins, almost asking permission with a look, which was foolish since she was an adult, a widow, and perfectly capable of choosing the company she would keep. Mary smiled again, and Mr. Emerson continued to eat.

She stiffened her spine. She did not require their permission. "That sounds lovely, Mr. Edgington, thank you."

Then, the conversation turned to the previous night's entertainment and later to other subjects. It was early afternoon before Charlotte and Mr. Edgington were finally preparing to depart on their ramble.

Mary accompanied Charlotte to her chamber to retrieve her bonnet and reticule. She dropped onto Charlotte's bed and whispered, "Mr. Edgington is very handsome, and he certainly seems to admire you."

Suddenly feeling like a young girl again, Charlotte sat on the bed too, grasping her bonnet in her hands. "Do you think so?"

"He called on you, did he not?"

"He called on the family."

Mary rolled her brown eyes. "Admit that he called on you."

Charlotte produced a reluctant "yes."

"And he invited you to walk with him?"

"Yes." She could not deny it.

"You see! I believe it has all the hallmarks of courtship," she said triumphantly, her eyes lighting with happiness.

Charlotte blushed.

"I see from your color that you return his interest."

"He seems to be a kind gentleman, and he has adequate resources. At this point, I have seen no reason to dislike him."

"Oh Charlotte, you must not always seek out the negative in people, and you must follow your heart for once, not your brain."

She considered her cousin's words. "You know very well that I have never been given to romance. I have always believed marriage to be a contract of mutual benefit between families. My parents encouraged that belief, and my observations seemed to prove it as well."

Mary sobered. "I know your thoughts on the matter very well, cousin. And I know that you disapproved of my marriage to Mr. Emerson—"

"—but I approve now—"

Charlotte had disapproved of her cousin's marriage to Mr. Emerson. At that time, he was but a law clerk who stood to inherit no fortune and had no family of name or rank. Any practical woman would have advised against the marriage.

Indeed, Charlotte had advised her against it. Most vehemently. For she had feared that Mary would end a bitter, lonely, old woman living at the mercy of her neighbors.

But Mr. Emerson had proved her wrong. He had earned his fortune and provided security for Mary. Charlotte was pleased to have been in the wrong.

Mary threw up her hands. "Do not trouble yourself. I know your opinion has changed." Mary patted Charlotte's arm. "I do not bring up the past to discomfit you, but to remind you that love and security are not as incompatible as you think."

Mary continued, "I dearly love Mr. Emerson, and I love you as well. I know that you were only concerned for my future and that you spoke to protect me. But it has all turned out for the best, you see. The risk you perceived was hardly risky at all."

Charlotte was still not quite prepared to wager her future on something as intangible as romantic love, but she was pleased for her cousin and she had no scruple of telling her so now. "I am happy for you, Mary, and in truth, I envy you. You are far braver a woman than I. I always seek safety. You followed your heart."

"You can follow yours as well. And there is a gentleman downstairs who seems to be ready to assist you in that."

And so Charlotte went below stairs to her gentleman.

They spent a pleasant afternoon in town touring Burlington's Arcade at Piccadilly, where Charlotte had been amused by the variety of goods for sale and by Mr. Edgington's commentary on the fashions and baubles offered for sale, and she felt vaguely disappointed when he walked her back to her cousin's home.

He too must not have wanted to depart, for he lingered at the doorstep for several minutes. When he took her fingers and bid her goodbye, she wondered if he had considered kissing her hand.

Strangely, she found herself glad that he had not, perhaps because of their location on the busy street. However, her relief at his decision did not prevent her from agreeing to join him on another walk when his business dealings permitted. He indicated that he would be busy for some days and would call on her at his first possible opportunity.

Charlotte could not help but admit to having been flattered by his attentions.

She had not had an unpleasant time, and Mr. Edgington had been very kind and amusing all day. She could only ascribe her feelings to her propensity to think on matters until her head ached. Perhaps her cousin was right when she suggested the idea of following her heart.

In her experience, Charlotte had seen few positive results when people in her acquaintance had followed their hearts. She had witnessed heartbreak and torment, and she had no wish to experience those things herself.

However, she had followed her mind and married Mr. Collins, and although she would not describe her life with him as either heart-breaking or tormented, she was not convinced that she had done right by neglecting her heart completely. Now, she was unsure how to find the median of the two. How does one use just enough heart and just enough mind?

Her friend Elizabeth Bennet, now Mrs. Fitzwilliam Darcy, had somehow managed to discover the balance. She had the good fortune to marry for love while not completely neglecting her duty to her family by securing a gentleman of good fortune.

She had chided Elizabeth about her passionate notions and had given many soliloquies on the subject of proper marriage strategies. Even after Elizabeth had married Mr. Darcy, Charlotte had only been able to see the monetary advantages of the match until later.

Once Charlotte had come to see the evidence of the true depth of emotion that existed between Elizabeth and Mr. Darcy, she had realized her mistake, though it took her many years to admit as much, even to herself.

She was embarrassed now at the memories and saddened at the rift that occurred in their friendship. Perhaps now was the proper moment to renew their acquaintance.

Sighing, Charlotte opened the door. She removed her bonnet as she walked toward the sitting room and pushed strands of her dark hair away from her face as she quickly appraised herself in the hall mirror. Her cheeks were bright from the exercise, and her eyes twinkled back at her.

Perhaps this was Mr. Edgington's effect on her. Or perhaps a result of a day in the sun. But if it were caused by the former and she appeared this youthful and attractive after just one outing with him, perhaps she should follow her heart.

But what message was her heart sending?

Charlotte could not bear to think of it any longer. She deposited her bonnet and parcel on the hall table and went into the sitting room where she found her cousins snuggled on the settee.

"Oh, pardon me." Embarrassed to have walked in on a tender moment, Charlotte prepared to withdraw.

"No, no, do come in and have tea with us," Mary said

"I do not want to intrude."

"Intrude? You are not intruding on us."

Charlotte hardly believed that.

"Perhaps we embarrass her, my dear," said her husband as he removed himself to a proper distance from his wife.

"Nonsense. Sit with us."

Charlotte poured herself a cup of tea and then took a seat across from them.

"Now tell us everything. Did you have a pleasant walk?"

"Pleasant enough. We ambled through the park and then enjoyed the shops at the Piccadilly."

"Did you purchase anything?"

"In a manner of speaking."

"Oh?"

"Mr. Edgington insisted on purchasing a pair of gloves I was admiring in the shop."

"Did he?" Mary asked with excitement in her voice.

"Yes. Is that inappropriate?"

Charlotte was certain that it was unsuitable for any young woman to accept gifts from a gentleman who was not her husband, but she had been less certain of the expectations of her position as a widow. The rules of propriety only became more clouded at the prospect of owning gloves so fine.

She and Mr. Edgington had become separated in the shop, and when he returned to her side, he had discovered her trying on a pair of delicate white gloves. She found them to be long enough, reaching just to the bend of her elbow, to be sufficiently fashionable, yet they remained practical enough to suit her tastes, for she despised garments that required continual adjustment and fuss to keep them presentable. Charlotte abhorred the current fashion of gloves so long that they necessitated the use of garters to maintain their position.

"Do you like them?" he had asked.

"Indeed. How could one not admire such fine craftsmanship?" She hurried to remove them and turned toward him, intending to leave the gloves on the display.

But Mr. Edgington picked them up. "Then you shall have them."

"I could not possibly afford them, Mr. Edgington."

"Then I shall make them a gift to you, for they suit your complexion very well indeed."

"I could not accept such a gift."

"Why ever not?"

"It simply is not seemly."

"It is not seemly for one to give a gift to his friend?" he asked incredulously.

Charlotte did not reply. He must know very well that his offer—generous though it was—skirted the boundaries of acceptable behavior. She was quite certain that his ignorance was feigned, but they were very nice gloves, and he seemed to be a very nice man.

"Please do me the honor of accepting them." His voice dropped lower, husky. "You may wear them at the next ball, and when you do so, I will know that you are thinking of me."

With that, Charlotte had allowed him to purchase them.

Now she was uncertain of her decision, but Mary looked at her with approval. "How kind! Of course, you should have accepted them, and you must allow me to stitch your initial in them for you. Embroidery is one of my secret pleasures. In limited doses, of course. Fortunately, the letter C is rather easy to stitch, and I shall have the task completed in no time at all."

Charlotte laughed at her cousin, who was an excellent seamstress. She retrieved the package from the hall table, unwrapped the gloves, and passed them to her cousin. Mary selected some pale blue embroidery threads and began to work, making small even stitches near the hem of the first glove.

"I find myself relieved that you approve of the gift."

Mary emitted a small, girlish giggle. "I think he is in love with you, Charlotte."

"Do you?" She was glad that Mary was concentrating on the gloves and did not notice the expression of confusion on her face.

"He has been very attentive to you. You must have noticed as much. Do you return his sentiments?"

Charlotte spun her teacup in the saucer, considering. "I do not know. There are instances when I am flattered by his attentions, but there are also moments when our association seems awkward and strange. I cannot explain it well."

Mr. Emerson cleared his throat. "It is not often that I intrude on women's affairs, but since I have been privy to the entire conversation, I will interject."

"Please do, dear." Mary winked at Charlotte. "It will be quite helpful to have a gentleman's opinion."

"You should relax and take time before you allow yourself to declare your feelings for any gentleman. Time is required for such an emotion to develop, for people to reveal their true selves. I knew my dear Mrs. Emerson for a full two years before I came to realize how devoted I was to her. Only then did I propose."

"But I fell in love with you immediately!" Mary protested, her eyes drawn for the first time from her work.

"You have proven the point I was preparing to make, my dear. People fall in love at their own pace, and circumstances are different in each person's life. Only think of the confusion that young Maria has experienced already. That is why I believe it is necessary to marry only when one is certain of their feelings and the true circumstances of the other party."

"There is probably a great deal of wisdom in your words," Charlotte said. "There was, however, a time when I would have disagreed with you wholeheartedly. I believed feelings were inconsequential."

Mary interjected. "Indeed, you must agree with him, for Mr. Emerson is the wisest man in all of England, and as there are few who may successfully argue against him, you may as well convert to his opinion. Besides, believing in love is ever so much more interesting than arguing against it."

Charlotte smiled at the faith Mary put into her husband. And that faith did not seem misplaced, for underneath his good nature and joviality, there seemed to be an active mind. She was certain that his courtroom adversaries often underestimated him. She certainly had.

Changing the subject in the intervening lull, she asked, "How does my sister do today? Has she been downstairs?"

A look of pity crossed Mary's face. "The poor dear. She came down in time for luncheon, and she tried to be pleasant, but it just was not in her."

"I am sorry that she has not been a good guest."

"Do not worry, dear," said Mr. Emerson. "We are her getaway. Her harbor in the storm."

Charlotte smiled sincerely.

"Would it be very wrong of us to tempt her downstairs with a cup of chocolate and some biscuits?" Mary asked.

"I do not believe so, for she has mourned long enough, and chocolate is perfect for all occasions, whether happy or sad."

Mary laughed at her cousin's words and then summoned her housekeeper. "Please bring us a plate of biscuits and a pot of chocolate and then summon Miss Maria from her room to join us."

The old housekeeper disappeared, delivered a large tray of sweets, and soon Maria appeared in the doorway. Charlotte was relieved to see a smile on her sister's face. Apparently, a week of mourning was all Maria could manage. "Come join us, Maria, for your cousins have offered us some delicious treats."

Maria descended on the tray of biscuits, popping two into her mouth in rapid succession. "You must have read my thoughts, for suddenly I am quite famished."

"You are feeling better then?"

"I am, for I realized today that I have done all I can to rectify my situation. I have apologized to Mr. Card."

"You apologized?" Charlotte was surprised that her very juvenile sister had thought to apologize to her friend. She felt rather proud.

"I did. I sent a letter almost the day we arrived here."

"Has he responded?"

"No, he has not, and I was very upset about his quietness. But I have done my best, and if he chooses not to accept my apology, then it is his affair, his wrong choice, not mine." Maria took a bite of biscuit. "Meanwhile, here I am in London, and I have not even left my bed chamber. I do not intend to waste the entire trip feeling sad or dreaming of Mr. Westfield. I want to see the city."

Mary clapped her hands together. "That is wonderful news. I had wished you would join us, for we have been so worried about you."

"My dear cousin, I appreciate your worry, and I believe London was the perfect escape for me. And I may enjoy the remainder of our stay here now that my conscience is free."

Maria plopped on the settee within easy reach of the tray of food. Apparently, she was always ready to enjoy the fruits of the household pantry as well.

"Mr. Emerson and I are pleased to hear it. It has been difficult for us to see you suffer so."

"I am happy to say that my suffering is now over. I will give no more thought to Mr. Card or Miss Farmington."

"And have you learned anything?"

"Yes, sister, I have. I will better guard my speech in the future."

Mary nodded. "That is wise."

Charlotte could not be more pleased that her sister appeared to have gained a new understanding of the ways of society. "Yes, our reputation is truly all we have, and we must guard it jealously and give no one cause to speak ill of us."

"There was a time I did not believe you, but indeed you are quite right, Charlotte. I have learned my lesson well. If I run afoul of society again, it will not be through any fault of my own."

After Maria had eaten her fill and chattered with her cousins, she went back upstairs to arrange her gowns for her coming trips into the city. Having had his fill of women's matters, Mr. Emerson disappeared into his library. With Mary occupied with her stitching, Charlotte began a letter to Elizabeth, telling her of her travels, Maria's troubles, and her meeting with Mr. Edgington at the theater.

At length, Charlotte completed her letter, sealing it carefully, and left the writing desk to join Mary on the settee.

"I am very glad that your sister's condition seems to be improving."

"I too am glad to see the improvement in her spirits. Maria is still rather young, and I want her to make a good match, but I do not relish seeing her in pain."

"Speaking of marriage, did I hear her correctly when she mentioned Mr. Westfield?"

"Yes, James Westfield is an acquaintance of ours from Westerham."

"Is he not a young relative of Colonel Armitage?"

"Yes, he is. He travels with his uncle Mr. Benjamin Basford of America. Are you acquainted with them, by chance?"

"I am. Before she went to the colonies, I was a friend of Mr. Westfield's mother. Evangeline and I were chums growing up and I was desolate when she married Mr. Westfield and went away.

However, they have fared well in the New World. Mr. Westfield has become a force in the shipping industry and has a fleet based quite far south along the coast, in Savannah. Mrs. Westfield often writes of gigantic oak trees dripping with moss, mosquitoes, and unquenchable heat. It sounds dreadful to me. I knew that she was sending her son to Europe, but I never imagined that you might be acquainted with him."

"Yes, we all met at a ball in Westerham last winter."

"His mother will be pleased to hear that they are faring well in our hostile country."

"Do you correspond with her still?"

"I do, but the post is so painfully slow that our letters are infrequent."

"What do you know of the younger Mr. Westfield?"

Mary considered for a moment, as if deciding how much information to divulge. "His mother tells me that he is very charming and that he only requires the benefits of society to help him mature."

"He has certainly impressed everyone at home. The young ladies, including Maria, are quite taken with him. He is young, to be sure, but I have seen no fault with him. However, his uncle has developed a rather shocking reputation in his short time in our country."

Mary's eyes widened, and her lips parted, closed, and they parted again. "I find that very surprising,"

"Do you? I have heard from reliable sources that he is infamous in America as well. They say he uses young women for his own pursuits."

The conversation lulled, and Mary appeared to wrestle with her thoughts.

"I do hate to correct you, but I fear you have been listening to the wrong people."

"Have I?" Charlotte remained unconvinced.

"Indeed, his sister includes a paragraph or two about Mr. Basford in each letter, and I have never read a negative word about him."

"Perhaps she is censoring herself for his benefit."

"I hardly believe that. Evangeline always speaks her mind and tells the absolute truth."

"Even about her own family?"

"Especially about them."

Mary saw Charlotte's look of disbelief. "She has confessed to me in the strictest of confidence that Mr. Westfield, her own son, is something of a flirt. That is why she has sent him to Europe under his uncle's care. She hopes that seeing a bit of the world will help him to settle down at home and that Mr. Basford will influence him to find a suitable wife."

"How would Mr. Basford know how to find a suitable wife? He too is unmarried, is he not?"

"He has never married. He tells Evangeline that he has yet to find a woman who would affect his heart and induce him to contemplate marriage." Then rather as an afterthought, she added, "I think his view is rather noble."

"Yes, I suppose it is noble, but I do not see how that qualifies him to be a good chaperone."

"Do you not? Mr. Basford has exhibited a great deal of patience, and certainly, he will not allow his nephew to make any rash decisions."

Charlotte conceded that it could be a good thing, but in the back of her mind, she doubted Mary's words. How could her impressions of Mr. Westfield and Mr. Basford be so skewed? She had always prided herself on being an excellent judge of character.

But after the episode with Maria and Mr. Card, Charlotte decided it might be best to reserve her judgment until she could observe them from a closer proximity. Whenever that might be. She had no notion of when they might return from their travels on the continent.

Mary handed her the newly monogrammed gloves. "Please do not say anything about Mr. Westfield. His mother would not wish it. She does not want him to gain the reputation of a flirt. And he may well have changed already."

Charlotte ran her fingers across the neat stitching. The pale blue letters stood in subtle relief against the material. She considered her reply.

Was it wise to withhold information from those of her acquaintance? Was Maria safe?

Although unsure of the wisdom of her words, she looked at Mary's concerned face and said, "Indeed, he may have changed. For Maria's sake, I do hope so."

❦ Ten ❧

For the remainder of their visit in London, Maria and Charlotte enjoyed the benefits of the city. Charlotte took Maria to Burlington's Arcade to admire the wares, but they could afford to purchase very little, which disappointed her greatly. She took some solace, however, in the purchase of some fine white muslin fabric, for shopping truly rivals chocolate in its ability to calm a harried mind.

The prospect of fine dresses had also tempted Charlotte beyond what she could bear. She could not force herself to remain in her out-of-fashion gowns when so many stylish women were walking the streets. Now with a dress of lovely pale striped muslin that had been sewn with the assistance of Mary, a length of Turkey red cotton, and a new straw bonnet and some fine ribbon to trim it, she was not only out of mourning for Mr. Collins, but she was in fashion. Her budget, however, would certainly suffer, and she would not have much meat on her table in the coming weeks.

Maria's spirits had been lifted by her activities in town, and Charlotte was pleased to see her joy, even if it derived from the more material benefits of the city. Her sister had begun to view life with the same youthful optimism as she had before the incident with Mr. Card.

Maria had also asked Mary to assist her in sewing a new gown, and in their unoccupied evenings, the two sat before the fire, surrounded by candles, and stitched the lightweight fabric into a gown. Unfortunately, Maria had not the temperament for such occupations, so Mary sewed alone amidst constant chatter.

Because Maria had missed their earlier foray to the theater, Mr. Emerson made arrangements for the party to attend a production of *Much Ado about Nothing* at Covent Garden. Charlotte was ashamed to admit how much time she spent readying herself for the evening, choosing her finest new gown and arranging her hair in ringlets, even though her stick-straight tresses resisted at every turn. She was even more ashamed to confess that she spent the entire first scene searching the audience for Mr. Edgington.

Of course, he was nowhere to be found, and Charlotte chided herself for her foolishness. It was a complete coincidence that she had met Mr. Edgington at the Theatre Royal. Coincidences, by definition, did not repeat themselves. And Charlotte accepted that hard reality by throwing herself into the action of *Much Ado about Nothing*, which she discovered was rather an easy task.

Suddenly, she was Beatrice, living in the exotic Italian countryside and involved in a merry war with the quick-witted Benedick. She was consoling the ill-fated Hero and demanding revenge against the evil villains who had forestalled her wedding to her beloved.

So much trouble and confusion caused by just a few blackguards, Charlotte thought. And how like her own life. Her current troubles too originated from this odd emotion called love. But would her strife end as easily? Would she be assured of gaining the heart of the handsome gentleman? Would Maria also be satisfactorily married? A play would resolve itself in five acts, but life held no such guarantees.

Leaving the theater, Charlotte, eager to discuss the play, turned to Maria. "How did you find the play?"

"It was dreadfully dull," Maria said, "but I did so enjoy being in society. Did you observe the quality of the gowns worn by the women in attendance? Oh, if only my gown could resemble those!"

"You did not enjoy the play?"

"I hardly paid it any mind. There was so much to see in the theater."

"Such as a play perhaps?"

Maria rolled her blue eyes. "Life is my play."

The sentence sounded pithy, but Charlotte knew her sister put no thought behind her words. She had been transfixed by the dresses and was probably plotting some alterations to her new gown, if only could convince Mary to help her.

And if life truly were a play, Charlotte's would be dull indeed, for she felt as though she were constantly waiting.

For Mr. Edgington.

She descended the stairs each day hoping to see him again at the breakfast table. When morning calls were paid, she hoped to hear his footsteps approaching the sitting room. But he never came.

Where was he? Charlotte wondered. Why would he have made her a gift of such lovely gloves and then disappear? She only intended to pine for a gentleman who was also pining for her. But was he pining for her?

Perhaps.

Perhaps not.

As the day of their return to Westerham drew near, Charlotte began to doubt her ever meeting Mr. Edgington again. Although she felt a twinge of loss at his continued absence, the pain tapered off quickly, and she found that she bore his disappearance very well indeed.

Maria was, however, beginning to feel the absence of Mr. Westfield rather keenly, and Charlotte began to wonder if her youthful infatuation was indeed something more.

As they strolled arm-in-arm through the park after a day of shopping, Maria admitted, "I have enjoyed my stay in London, but I am eager to be home, even if Mr. Card and Miss Farmington will not speak to me."

"I do miss our little cottage and the quiet of the country."

"Oh, I do not miss that at all. I miss the society!"

Charlotte thought of the shopping excursions and theater productions they had attended in the days since Maria had come out of her seclusion. "Did not London offer you enough in the way of society?"

Maria's eyes lit. "Do not misunderstand. I have enjoyed myself immensely. London offers a great deal of entertainment that

Westerham cannot. But there is one thing London cannot give to me."

"And what is that?"

"Mr. Westfield."

Charlotte almost expected her sister to sigh and flutter her eyelashes at the mere mention of his name. Fortunately, she restrained herself to a silly smile. "Westerham cannot produce him for you either, I am afraid, for he is on a tour of the continent, and who knows when he will return."

"Still, I hope we will see much of Mr. Westfield in the future. I know you do not much care for his uncle, but I wish you would learn to get along with him. If Mr. Westfield is going to pay court to me, as I believe he will, you will be forced into his company. Unless, of course, you prefer to leave us unchaperoned."

Charlotte cast her a wry look. "No, Mr. Basford and I have put away our animosities, and we will behave as proper acquaintances and suitable chaperones." She chose not to mention Mary's positive report about him, for it also contained a tentative review of Mr. Westfield. Speaking of the matter with Maria would do no good, and she had promised she would not.

"I thought I detected a softening toward Mr. Basford." She winked. "And I am glad to hear it, for if Mr. Westfield and I marry, you will be relations, and I will demand family harmony."

Maria glanced at her sister and seeing the look of reproof in her eyes, she cut her off. "Do not scold me, Charlotte. I know it is improper to speak of marriage when Mr. Westfield has not. But if I cannot share my dreams with my sister, then with whom may I share them?"

Charlotte took Maria's hand. "I want you to share them with me, for one of us must harbor some dreams yet. And it is best that it should be you. You are younger and more able to sustain them."

"Oh Charlotte, you are not yet in your dotage."

Charlotte felt no emotion, no sting of remorse at the future before her. "Still, no one will have me now, and neither do I want anyone."

"What about Mr. Edgington?"

"I confess that I was flattered by his attentions, but he has proven his lack of interest. I have not seen him for so long. I find that I do not miss him at all."

"Certainly, we will see him again in Westerham."

"Perhaps, but truly, I no longer desire his company as I once did." She found that her words were indeed true.

Again Maria searched her face. "Perhaps you are simply injured by his inattention."

Charlotte glanced at Maria as they walked along the sidewalk toward their cousins' home and found herself the object of her sister's careful study. People passed by in groups of multicolored material and plumage, but for once Maria seemed to take no notice. She studied Charlotte as if seeing her for the first time. What was she attempting to read in her countenance? Perhaps she was searching for some sign of sorrow, some depression over Mr. Edgington's loss. But she truly did not feel any such thing.

"I see that you are not hurt. You are far worse than hurt."

Charlotte looked away. "Am I?"

At length, Maria said, "Yes. You have lost hope, and that is a much more serious condition, as you have often told me. I felt hopeless until I wrote to Mr. Card. It was miserable to have no prospects and no future."

"I am comfortably set up in my cottage. I do not need prospects to have a future." She said these words, and she truly believed them. She could be content with these circumstances.

"No, indeed you do not, for you are a strong, independent sort of woman, but would you not enjoy sharing your future with someone worthy? Would prospects not be nice?"

"I suppose they would," Charlotte agreed reluctantly.

"I confess I am surprised—and pleased—to hear you admit it," Maria said. "You have always taken too much on yourself—marrying Mr. Collins to relieve the family of the burden of supporting you, agreeing to act as my chaperone when our parents could not, and even taking this trip to remove me from trouble of my own creation. You deserve more, and if there is anything I may ever do to ensure your future, I vow that I will do it."

∽ಿ❧ ❧ೊ∾

The morning of their departure for Westerham a letter arrived from Mr. Edgington. The maid brought it to Charlotte's room as she dressed. She studied the handwriting briefly and then set the letter aside.

The long-awaited contact had been made. Unfortunately, she no longer felt an excitement over the gentleman. In addition, he had shown his attentions in an entirely inappropriate manner. A gentleman simply did not compose and send letters to a woman to whom he was not engaged.

If Charlotte needed another bell to complete the death knell of her interest in Mr. Edgington, this was certainly it. She found that she did not feel sad or distressed by the realization. Her interest had simply vanished. She finished her morning ritual at a leisurely pace before dismissing the maid. Then she opened the letter with only mild curiosity.

> My dear Mrs. Collins,
> I hope you will forgive me for not calling on you as promised. My long absence was necessitated by business matters that required my undivided attention. I have now fulfilled my obligations and would like to turn my attentions to a much pleasanter subject: you. I hope you will not find my words too forward, for they convey my feelings for you adequately. Please allow me to call on you at your earliest convenience. You need only send a note to my hotel in London and I will be at your side.
>
> L. E.

Charlotte folded the letter and called one of Mrs. Emerson's servants to inform Mr. Edgington of their impending departure. She dropped his letter in her trunk and donned her traveling bonnet, determined to meet her future happily with or without a gentleman at her side.

ঙ Eleven ৩

When Charlotte and Maria arrived at their cottage in Westerham, no invitations awaited them, and Charlotte would not be understating matters to say that Maria was desolate. However, she soon learned that Mr. Westfield was in town, and her spirits lifted quite miraculously.

But Mr. Westfield did not come.

Charlotte began to wonder if there was a defect in the character of all males that caused them to show interest in ladies and then desert them altogether.

Soon, Maria's desolation returned, and desperate for consolation of company, she took to following Charlotte about the cottage. She followed her to the kitchen, the garden, and even to her bedchamber at night.

Charlotte was desperate for relief. She had briefly considered hauling Mr. Card and Miss Farmington to the cottage and demanding that they repair their friendship. She also considered finding Mr. Westfield and dragging him by his blond hair to pay a call on her sister. But it would not do to have him see Maria in such a state. She would certainly make a cake of herself by chattering Mr. Westfield into oblivion.

Charlotte could not have anyone else chattered into oblivion. It was too cruel a fate, as she well knew. Even now, Maria was talking, and she had not marked a word. She listened now.

"I find that yellow is the cheeriest color, do you not agree?" Maria did not even pause to allow a response. "But green is also a happy hue. Green suits me much better. You have always said so. And that is why I often wear the color. I do want to look my best, and green brings out my eyes. Well, actually my eyes are blue, but still, green compliments them very well. Blue and green match, I believe."

Charlotte stood. She did not care if blue and green matched or if Maria wanted to wear puce each day for the rest of her life.

"I am going for a walk."

"I shall join you."

"No!" Charlotte's voice had been harsh, and she moderated it. "I am going for a *long* walk."

"How long."

"Very, very long." She would walk to France if she could.

"Oh." Maria looked dejected, but then bounced in the direction of the kitchen. Poor Mrs. Eff. Charlotte hated to abandon her to Maria's conversation, but she had to preserve her own sanity.

Charlotte put on her sturdy boots and left the cottage before Maria could change her mind and accompany her. She shut the door quietly behind her. She could hear Maria's voice from the kitchen. She was saying something about goat cheese.

Poor, poor Mrs. Eff.

Charlotte hurried away from the cottage in the direction of the tree line. If Maria changed her mind—or if Mrs. Eff tossed her from the kitchen—she would not look for her in the dense undergrowth. She walked a few paces to the path and decided to take the direction of the pond, which bordered the Farmington's land. As she walked, her tension eased, and she became eager to explore the surrounding countryside.

At a bend in the path, she came upon a party of walkers from the direction of the Farmington's property.

Charlotte stood face to face with Miss Farmington, Mr. Card, Mr. Westfield, Mr. Basford, and a young lady Charlotte could not identify. Maria would be so disappointed not to have come, for she could have used this as an opportunity to regain her place in society.

Everyone stared mutely at each other for long moments, and then several of their party spoke at once.

Greetings were made, and introductions were given, but Charlotte was so surprised to have met them that she forgot the young lady's name as soon as it was given.

They all lapsed into silence. Charlotte did not know what to say. And given the extraneous circumstances, neither did the others.

Finally, Mr. Westfield spoke. "Mrs. Collins, we have been picnicking and are on our way to the trout pond."

"I was walking." It was quite obvious that she was walking. Charlotte felt like a fool.

Mr. Basford stepped forward. "Won't you join us?"

"Oh, yes, do join us," Miss Farmington's words did not sound sincere, but Charlotte decided to join them anyway. It was the right course of action.

Before Mr. Basford could offer Charlotte his arm, the nameless young woman reached for it and beamed. "I would not mind an escort over such treacherous terrain."

Mr. Basford allowed her to take his arm, but caught Charlotte's gaze and rolled his eyes. The treacherous terrain was a well-manicured path. Perhaps she feared that a wayward pebble might find its way into her walking boots. The horror!

Although Mr. Basford's expression conveyed Charlotte's own thoughts on the girl's behavior, it was audacious, and she sent him a look that she hoped communicated her disapproval.

He only smiled back. "Mrs. Collins, do you need assistance over the terrain as well?"

He offered his other arm.

Charlotte looked at the others who had already started down the trail. Mr. Card and Miss Farmington walked ahead with Mr. Westfield. Charlotte chose to walk alone. "I am used to navigating my way alone, thank you, Mr. Basford." She was truly content with the arrangement. She could hear the others chatting ahead of her, but she chose to enjoy the birdsong and wildflowers they encountered along the path. Before they arrived at their destination, the pond, the pace began to slow.

"I am exhausted," Miss Farmington complained.

The young woman on Mr. Basford's arm, whose name Charlotte continued to forget, agreed eagerly.

"This heat is oppressive indeed." Mr. Card said. He was sweating. But did it originate from the exercise or from Charlotte's presence? Charlotte hoped for the latter. Perhaps his discomfort would spur him to accept Maria's apologies and mend their friendship, and consequently restore her place in society.

"Shall we have a seat then?" Mr. Westfield pointed to a fallen log by the pathway. He leaned down to wipe the dirt from the bark and assisted Miss Farmington to sit.

Miss Farmington made much pretense of adjusting her dress. "What a charming spot! Mrs. Collins, will you sit as well?"

Doubting the sincerity of her invitation, Charlotte shook her head. "I take great pleasure in walking." She had developed the habit on the days when Mr. Collins remained inside the house to compose his sermons. "I think I should like to see the pond. You all relax here and I will be back as soon as my curiosity is assuaged."

"Allow me to accompany you," Mr. Basford offered.

"There is no need." Charlotte hoped to avoid being alone with him.

Miss Farmington waved a hand at her and spoke to her as if she were a simpleton. "You cannot go alone, Mrs. Collins. You could be attacked by some wild animal or a band of criminals. We will be fine resting here for a quarter of an hour."

Charlotte highly doubted that untamed animals or roving bandits occupied the Farmington's land, but she allowed Mr. Basford to guide her back to the path, and they walked for a while in silence. The woods deepened and soon the forest floor became a sea of lush green ferns accented by deep brown leaf cover. The temperature seemed to cool, and the air around them became moist and rich. Charlotte inhaled the scent and smiled. She could hear the sound of the stream as it meandered its way to the pond ahead. Charlotte was glad she decided to continue the walk, even if she was forced to be in Mr. Basford's company.

Thankfully, he remained silent and he proved to be a perfectly acceptable walking companion after all. He appeared to enjoy the atmosphere as much as she did.

Soon, the forest began to thin somewhat, and as they walked to the top of a rise, the pond came into view. Charlotte stopped and watched as some ducks took flight. The trees were reflected in the shimmering water, and someone had constructed a covered log dock.

"It's lovely."

Mr. Basford agreed. "Shall we walk to the dock?"

"Yes. I would like that very much."

They followed the path down to the wooden structure and walked to the railing. Charlotte leaned over, peering into the water to search out the fish that might be swimming below.

Beside her, Mr. Basford took a cloth from his pocket, unfolding it to display a heel of crusty bread. "I took the liberty of bringing this along. I thought I might see if the fish were biting."

Charlotte felt almost childlike joy at the prospect of something as simple as feeding fish. He broke the bread in half and gave a lump to her.

Together, they leaned over the railing and dropped crumbs while Mr. Basford occasionally told her the names of the different types of fish that appeared near the surface. Soon, they were surrounded by ducks who had regained their bravery and even some turtles had been drawn to the lure of food.

The bread was soon gone, but they lingered on the dock while the animals gradually took their leave.

Mr. Basford looked at her, and she flicked bread crumbs off her dress self-consciously. "I am sorry that you and Miss Lucas were not invited to the picnic."

"Do not trouble yourself…"

"It was wrong and I hope you know that you will not be excluded from the ball my uncle will be hosting soon."

She felt relief for her sister. There was an additional benefit: if Maria were allowed to rejoin her friends, Charlotte would be released from her constant conversation. "You are very kind."

He waved a dismissive hand, startling a duck. They stood silently for a time and then they returned to the path, walking slowly to the rest of Mr. Basford's party.

"I believe my nephew has an interest in your sister."

"Does he?" Maria would be thrilled. The day was improving indeed.

"I believe so." He seemed to study her reaction, and she hoped that she appeared disinterested. "I think it may be wise to arrange for him to call on her sometime soon."

"I—" Charlotte prepared to resist the idea of leaving her sister alone with Mr. Westfield, but Mr. Basford held up a hand.

"With proper chaperones of course. I'll be with him, and of course, you'll be there."

Charlotte turned away, uncertain whether she should be pleased for her sister or unnerved at being with Mr. Basford again, despite their pleasant walk. "I suppose you believe that my concerns are unfounded."

"I confess that I don't relish the idea of accompanying my nephew to call on a young woman, but I know it would mean a great deal to you if I did."

"Then you are doing this for me?" She tried to suppress the panic she felt rising in her. Why would he even admit to having such a notion? It was preposterous.

"I suppose I am." He kept his eyes focused ahead as they walked. She stared directly at him.

Eventually, he turned to her and smiled, and suddenly, Charlotte was compelled to look ahead. She did not care to contemplate why.

"But I am also doing it for my nephew and his mother and because it is my duty."

She worked up the courage to look at him again. His face was serious.

"I know you still do not think much of my brash ways." He straightened his cravat and brushed imaginary dust from his coat. "But despite appearances, I am an honorable man."

Charlotte could not disagree with him and she felt properly chastised. Again, she could not bring herself to meet his gaze.

They did not speak again until they returned to the log where they had left the others. Mr. Basford rejoined his simpering nameless companion and Charlotte continued to walk alone.

৩৪ Twelve ৩৪

Time passed rather slowly as time is wont to do when one is anticipating an event. The days prior to Colonel Armitage's ball seemed to stretch out endlessly with little entertainment or distraction. Charlotte and Maria had spent their time at the cottage, receiving only a few callers, returning those calls, and occasionally writing letters to their parents, who were keeping to themselves in their small drawing room in Hertfordshire, and to Elizabeth and Mary, who demanded to be kept apprised of all occurrences of a romantic nature.

Charlotte had received a response from her missive to Elizabeth, and she was well pleased. Elizabeth had written a lengthy reply full of good natured questions and stories about her two children, Jane, who was six, and Cassandra, who was four. Their friendship, it seemed, was back on course, and Charlotte found herself divulging her interactions with both Mr. Edgington and Mr. Basford in her return letter. Although she valued the companionship and commiseration that Maria provided, there was something vitally important about having a best friend with whom to mull over such situations.

Despite Mr. Basford's words during their impromptu walk, neither he nor Mr. Westfield had called on them. Because she had not been privy to the discussion and because Charlotte had not divulged the contents of her conversation with Mr. Basford to her, Maria was not expecting him to call, and therefore, happily, she remained unaffected, but Charlotte was disappointed for her sister and angry at the entire male sex. Were all men apt to promise to call and then disappear? In her mind, she had relegated Mr. Edgington, Mr. Westfield, and Mr. Basford—and indeed most men in general—to the lowest circle of Dante's Inferno.

In her desperation for society, Maria focused on the gossip she could glean from Mrs. Eff after her trips into town. She insisted that Charlotte listen as she recounted each one.

Apparently, Mrs. Holloway was still engaged in an affair, but the gentleman had not yet been discovered. Mr. Holloway still had his pig and claimed that he would never slaughter so fine an animal, even if it meant doing without pork for a year.

Story after nonsensical story poured forth from Maria, but Charlotte could not bring herself to pay much attention, so she soon focused her efforts on embellishing bonnets and dresses with bits of ribbon or simply moped about the cottage.

When the official invitation to the ball had arrived, the serene mood was shattered by Maria's overwhelming joy.

The letter arrived on a particularly dreary morning when Charlotte had been forced to neglect her garden. She and Maria had lingered over a breakfast of toast and tea and discussed how dreadfully depressing the weather had become. Even the usually cheery kitchen with its patterned wallpaper and bright trim seemed dull.

Maria sighed dramatically. "I do not know what I shall do with myself for an entire day if this weather keeps up. I so long to be in town or to call on friends."

"This weather will not last forever." Charlotte too longed to be elsewhere.

"Indeed, it shall," Maria proclaimed, plunking down her teacup definitively. "This weather will persist just to spite me. The gods of weather know I have my heart set on Mr. Westfield, but they do not want me even to see him."

Charlotte laughed at her sister's dramatics. "I doubt very much that the weather gods, as you called them, have any interest whatsoever in your love life."

"Indeed, I suppose you are right, for I have no love life. I cannot have such a thing as long as I am trapped in this cottage."

"Have another cup of tea. It will make you feel much better."

The second helping of tea did not do as much for Maria as the invitation that was delivered soon thereafter.

Mrs. Eff entered the room and was in the process of removing soiled dishes from the table when she almost off-handedly said, "This arrived by messenger, Mrs. Collins. I did not want to disturb your eating."

She handed the letter to Charlotte, and Maria bounded out of her chair to look over her sister's shoulder. Charlotte opened and carefully unfolded the paper.

"Faster, faster!" Maria demanded. "I believe that is Mrs. Armitage's hand!"

Before Charlotte could even set an eye on the contents of the letter, Maria shrieked. "A ball!"

Mrs. Eff jumped, and the teacups clattered in her grasp.

"The ball Colonel Armitage promised to give in honor of his relations. Thank you, weather gods!"

"Maria, do be quiet and at least pretend to be civilized."

Maria scowled, plucked the paper from her hands, and returned to her seat.

"Finally, some entertainment! And I have yet to tell you the best news, Charlotte."

"Can there be something better than a ball?"

"Indeed. Mr. Westfield has already secured me for the first two dances."

"How can that be possible if you only learned of the ball two minutes ago?"

Maria blushed, her cheeks turning a deep red, her lashes downcast. "I hope you will not think it too forward, but he asked for the first two dances at the next ball—whenever it was to be held—when we last spoke all those weeks ago."

Charlotte was not entirely sure she approved of such forward behavior, but she said, "The only thing better than a ball, I suppose, is to have a gentleman with whom to dance."

"Well, of course, silly, for that is the entire purpose of a ball."

"Then I may as well stay at home, for I do not intend to dance."

"No, you may not just stay home, for I would not be allowed to attend." Her voice contained a note of panic.

"Do not trouble yourself. I know how much this means to you, and although I rarely dance, I quite enjoy balls myself. But I have other things to think of besides men."

"Well, I think you should not waste your figure. It will not last forever, you know."

Charlotte rolled her eyes and glanced down at herself. Her figure was probably her most alluring feature. Her face had always been plain, and she had accepted that, but she said, "You really ought to show more respect for your elder sister."

"And you really ought to live a little. Who knows. Perhaps Mr. Edgington will return to town for the ball and sweep you into a state of loving bliss."

"I seriously doubt that will occur at this ball or any other."

Maria tilted her blond head and said, "Only because you will not allow it."

✦ ✦ ✦

The ball was held at Colonel Armitage's home, and Charlotte, who generally preferred the smaller, private balls, found herself almost as eager to arrive as her sister. She had to prevent herself from rushing into the carriage, which the colonel sent to retrieve them. Charlotte fidgeted with her dress and adjusted her wrap. She had worn her best gown and the monogrammed gloves that Mr. Edgington had given her before she had left London. She felt odd wearing a gift from a gentleman, but the gloves were very fine, and she found she could not prevent herself from slipping them on. And they looked very well with her gown.

Maria spent the entire carriage ride chattering loudly. Her sister's enthusiasm was infectious, and by the time they arrived and alighted from the carriage, she was very nearly convinced that it was a magical night.

Charlotte dearly loved her sister's optimism, but she rarely allowed it to affect her own opinions. She preferred to avoid disappointment at all costs, and she had found that looking forward to an event and building it up in her mind was the best way to ensure that the evening would be a complete disaster. She hoped that would not be the case.

The ballroom was quite large and more than adequate to host a large ball. Located on the back side of the house, it had the advantage of an entire wall of windows with two doors at opposite ends of the ballroom that opened onto a gracious balcony overlooking the courtyard behind the building. The doors were thrown wide open, allowing sweet-smelling air to cool the dancers and freshen the room. Adjacent to the ballroom, there was a smaller room for refreshments where many older gentlemen—who were already secure in their matrimonial bonds or who no longer cared for that sort of bondage—tended to gather and consume mass quantities of food and drink.

Charlotte began the evening by standing by the opened windows. The breeze blew her skirts around her ankles as she watched the first dances. Maria fairly glowed in Mr. Westfield's arms, and although her concern for her sister's reputation continued, Charlotte could not help but rejoice in her happiness. It appeared that Miss Farmington would at least be civil, and Mr. Card had yet to make an appearance, so all might be well.

Across the room, Mr. Basford seemed pleased as well. Charlotte had yet to speak with him that evening, but the expression on his face appeared open and readable.

She was considering Mr. Basford when she felt a presence at her side. She turned to find Mr. Edgington looking at her intensely.

"Mr. Edgington, I did not expect to see you here. When did you return to Westerham?"

"Mrs. Collins," he said, bowing, "I returned only a fortnight ago."

Charlotte was surprised. The comings and goings of eligible men were not usually neglected in Westerham. She ought to have heard of his return.

"I am pleased that you had a safe journey."

He appraised her appearance. "I am more pleased to see you. I noticed that you are wearing the gloves I gave you."

Charlotte blushed. He grinned back wolfishly.

She looked down at them. "Yes, they suit my dress very nicely."

He smirked, and his red hair appeared to flame in the candlelight. He was dressed in fashionable formal attire. His deep blue coat and tan breeches fit snugly, revealing a strong, square silhouette. His boots shone, and he smelled of strong, musky cologne. He was almost overpowering.

He stepped slightly closer. "Will you do me the honor of a dance?"

She employed her standard reply. "I am afraid I did not come with the intention of dancing."

He challenged her. "You are no longer in mourning, and unless you have an objection to your potential partner, I see no reason to decline."

Charlotte shifted her weight. "I suppose it could do no harm. I only hope that you can forgive any missteps. It has been a long time since I have danced."

"Believe me, your dancing abilities are the least of my concerns." He led her to the floor.

The dance began, and Charlotte focused solely on the steps. She did not intend to ruin the dance for the other couples on the floor by her own poor skills, and even more, she did not want to make a spectacle of herself as she always had been when paired with Mr. Collins.

After the first section of the dance, Charlotte began to feel more at ease, and she was able to glance at her partner for the first time. Immediately, she wished she had not done so.

Mr. Edgington was looking at her ever so intensely. His eyes fairly burned through her. She blushed deeply and looked away. As the dance continued in silence, Charlotte could feel his stare, and the flattery initially caused by his intensity began to transform into concern and embarrassment.

She attempted several conversations, but she was unable to keep up a steady stream of distracting chatter. If only she possessed Maria's oratorical gifts! Finally, she abandoned the pretense of talking altogether.

All around them people watched and no doubt assumed that there was an attraction, at the very least, or an attachment—at most—between them. At that precise moment, Charlotte was neither attracted nor attached to Mr. Edgington, and she longed for the musicians to play the final chords of the dance, releasing her from the obligation of his stare.

She considered trying to strike up another conversation, but she disregarded the possibility quickly. Any interest she showed in Mr. Edgington would only serve to convince the people around them of an attachment that certainly did not exist.

The dance ended without another word passing between them and without Mr. Edgington looking away from Charlotte. Taking her gloved hand, he escorted her back to where Maria stood near the exit to the balcony.

He released her with a look of exaggerated remorse. "Thank you for the pleasant dance, Mrs. Collins."

Charlotte attempted to conceal her displeasure and thanked him quickly in return.

He smiled, his eyes still too intense, and said, "I hope that we will speak again before the evening ends."

Mr. Edgington then turned on his heel and disappeared into the crowd.

Charlotte turned to her sister and said through gritted teeth, "I do not know what to think of that man."

She giggled. "Well, after a dance like that, there is no doubt about what he thinks of you."

"Oh no!" Charlotte cried. "Pray, do not say such a thing!"

"Why are you so upset? What is wrong with having a gentleman interested in you?"

Charlotte was beginning to doubt that Mr. Edgington was a gentleman, but she would not say as much to her sister, and certainly not in a public place.

"After all, balls are for the express purpose of making matches. I have been working toward that end all evening."

"Lower your voice, Maria," Charlotte warned in a ragged whisper.

Maria gave Charlotte a cross look, but when she spoke again it was with a softer voice. "I have had two dances with Mr. Westfield, and he has proclaimed that were it possible to do so, he would dance every dance with me."

"I am pleased for you, but you must not be so public about your feelings."

"Maybe I am not the problem. Maybe you should be more overt about yours. Poor Mr. Edgington probably thinks you do not like him."

"Well, I…"

"You do not like him?" Maria asked, confused. "I believed you did."

"Let us not speak of this here." Charlotte glanced at those around them. Then in a louder tone, she asked, "Does not everyone look well tonight?"

"Most people do look lovely, although I find some questionable hairstyles. I believe one woman has a bird's nest in her coiffure this evening."

Charlotte was preparing to remind Maria that it was impolite to criticize other people's fashions in public, but something niggled at her mind. A bird's nest? She had seen a bird's nest used as an accessory of late. But where?

She thought for a moment and then the memory came to her. The theater. At Drury Lane in London! She had seen a woman with such an audacious affectation in her hair from the balcony of the theater. The woman whom Mr. Edgington had escorted. The plump one she had believed to be his poor country relation. Could it possibly be the same woman? Charlotte hardly thought so, but she leaned to her sister anyway. "Who is wearing the bird's nest?"

"Oh, I can never recollect her name. A plump woman. There was some gossip about her recently. Why can I not recall her name?" Maria scanned the room. "There!" She inclined her head toward a group of people beside the fireplace.

Charlotte did not instantly see the bird's nest, but when the group shifted, she saw a woman wearing elaborate wrap. Her hair dripped in bouncy ringlets. But was it the same wrap and the same ringlets that she had seen at the theater? Charlotte could not be sure until she saw the bird.

The mystery woman shifted slightly, revealing more of her hairstyle. Charlotte's heart began to flutter as the bird emerged. It was definitely the same one she had seen in the theater. It had to be. There could not be many women who would wear a bird in their hair in that very style. It must be the same woman she had seen with Mr. Edgington. She had the same build, and, now that

Charlotte considered it, she thought it could be the same gown, although she was not certain.

Who was this woman? She strained, but still she could not see her face. Was she accompanying Mr. Edgington this evening? If so, why ever would he have danced with her? Had his companion observed their dance? She certainly would not have been pleased to see the rapt attention he paid Charlotte. She would be jealous indeed.

The woman turned, and Charlotte stifled a gasp. It was Mrs. Holloway!

Mrs. Holloway, who was rumored to be having an affair with an unknown gentleman. She had been with Mr. Edgington in London. She was engaged in adultery! With Mr. Edgington.

Clearly, Mr. Holloway was right to focus his attentions on a pig, for his wife was an undeserving creature.

And even more clearly, Mr. Edgington was the worst of men.

While Charlotte was deep in contemplation, Mrs. Farmington joined them with her granddaughter in tow. "Mrs. Collins, Miss Lucas, how lovely you look tonight."

Charlotte wondered how she could possibly look lovely. In all likelihood her realization about Mr. Edgington had robbed the color from her cheeks. But it would not do to behave as though something ill had occurred, and she schooled her features accordingly.

Would not Mrs. Farmington, and indeed all of Westerham, relish this news? But she certainly did not care to reveal her knowledge of this illicit affair. She wished she knew nothing of it.

Charlotte turned her attention to the older woman. She wore feathers in her colorless hair, but no bird. Her frost-colored curls bobbled as she walked and the plumage on her head waved back and forth. Miss Farmington was more attractively attired in a softly patterned blue dress with white trim. Her chestnut hair—also styled without a bird—glowed in the candlelight, and her eyes gleamed with malice as she looked a Maria. The harridan!

"And how popular you both are!" Miss Farmington looked slyly at Charlotte.

Oh! If this ninny had marked Mr. Edgington's attentions, then everyone had. Of course, no one knew that he was Mrs. Holloway's lover and was, therefore, a disreputable fellow. So she seemed safe.

"Yes, we could not help but notice how much attention Mr. Edgington paid you, Mrs. Collins," old Mrs. Farmington agreed.

Charlotte clasped her hands into fists and felt the material of her gloves wrinkle in her palms. "I can assure you that I have done nothing to invite his attentions, if indeed he paid them to me."

"He had eyes only for you." Miss Farmington sneered and made Charlotte want to clap her hand over her mouth. Fortunately, her next words changed the course of the conversation in a different, thought not entirely pleasant, direction. "And it seems that Mr. Westfield has eyes only for you, dear Maria. If I did not like you half so much, I believe I would be jealous."

Maria seemed taken aback by Miss Farmington's abrupt tone. She thought a beat. "You have no reason to be jealous. Mr. Westfield is very kind, but we have no attachment."

"He selected you for the first two dances."

"Yes, but he has danced twice with you, has he not?"

"I suppose he has."

"He is a delightful dancer."

"Yes."

"You see." Mrs. Farmington leaned in closely and inclined her head toward Mr. Edgington's group. "I was right. You two are indeed popular tonight."

"You are too kind," Charlotte murmured, still barely able to latch on to a coherent thought.

Mrs. Farmington spoke. "Are you certain you do not wish to tell us of an impending engagement to Mr. Edgington?"

"No, indeed, for we have no understanding. We had only one dance, and one dance does not a betrothal make. It does not even signify a friendship." But a bird's nest in the hair did signify an affair. "It barely even signifies an acquaintance."

"Well, you may mark my words, Mrs. Collins. Mr. Edgington will make a proposal to you very soon."

Charlotte certainly hoped not.

She was spared a reply when Mr. Basford spoke. He had appeared beside them without drawing Charlotte's immediate notice. The ladies curtseyed and greeted him. "Good evening, Mrs.

Farmington, Mrs. Collins, Miss Lucas, Miss Farmington. Are you enjoying this evening's entertainments?"

Charlotte certainly noticed him now. His attire, while still somewhat informal and his cravat rumpled, was striking. His dark green coat drew her attention to his eyes, which beamed openness and honesty. Her tongue clung to the roof of her mouth, and all thoughts of Mr. Edgington and Mrs. Holloway and the bird vanished. They were none of her concern anyway.

"Indeed we are, Mr. Basford," Maria replied for her.

Old Mrs. Farmington and Miss Farmington gave their agreement.

"I am only sorry that my uncle could not be a little more in spirits tonight. He enjoys society and balls."

"Oh, is Colonel Armitage ill?" Mrs. Farmington asked, with concern in her voice. The elderly did not relish hearing of sickness, for fear that the words would somehow pass the condition on to them.

"Don't trouble yourself, Mrs. Farmington. He is quite well. It is just a touch of gout. He will be himself in no time. Until then he will have to be content to sit on the side of the action and enjoy his wine."

"We must be certain to give him our regards. Now come along, dear, I am in need of some refreshment." Miss Farmington and her grandmother bid them good evening and headed toward the door to the refreshment room.

Mr. Basford turned his attention to Maria. "I know my nephew enjoyed the favor of your dances together."

"You may tell him that I enjoyed them as well."

"It was nice to see you dancing as well, Mrs. Collins."

"I was just saying as much to her myself."

He turned to Charlotte and smiled. "Would you dance with me? We arranged it at the winter ball, if you'll remember."

Charlotte had forgotten his offer. She had not accepted it, had she? There was no obvious way of refusing him this time, so she accepted. As he led her to the floor, he subtly leaned closer to her ear. "Thank you for not embarrassing me with another rejection."

Surprised, she smiled. Standing at such close proximity, she could smell him. He smelled like the woods they had walked in several weeks ago. Without thinking, she inhaled deeply.

He continued as he led her into the dance, "I know you do not like public displays, so I'll be a proper gentleman, I assure you."

"Thank you."

"I saw you dancing with Mr. Edgington."

"Did you?" She still hoped she had imagined the attention they had attracted.

"He was very intense."

"I suppose he was."

He gave her a look of disbelief and said, "You are too kind to tell the truth."

"But I am not kind enough to think well of inappropriate behavior."

They walked forward with the other dancers, and conversation paused.

"You have reminded me of the importance of appropriate behavior several times."

Her back prickled, but there was no reprimand in his eyes.

She attempted a joke. "Perhaps you needed reminding."

He was silent for a moment, and she feared she had offended him, but then she looked into his face. His grin was somehow a mix of honesty and humor, and Charlotte smiled back. "Perhaps I ought to pass your reminder on to Mr. Edgington."

Charlotte could not repress her laughter, but she sobered at the intensely kind expression that suddenly lit Mr. Basford's eyes.

They finished the dance in companionable silence. Charlotte contemplated Mr. Basford. She had chastised his behavior almost from the moment she made his acquaintance, but it was now evident that he was a true gentleman. And more disconcertingly, it appeared that her own good judgment, which she prized, was flawed.

It did not matter now. She knew the truth. She would be kind to Mr. Basford, and she would never again hold two minutes' discourse with Mr. Edgington. It was as simple as that.

⋞⋟ Thirteen ⋞⋟

Mr. Basford proved to be an excellent partner, and it felt natural to move with him around the floor. Charlotte found herself forgetting about the steps and the onlookers—including Mr. Edgington and Mrs. Holloway—and simply enjoyed being on the dance floor.

When the dance ended, he led her from the floor, and she was reluctant to go. When he returned her to her place near the balcony door, he gave her hand a squeeze before releasing it. "Thank you, my friend."

She suddenly felt flushed and rather weak. A warm rush moved through her body at the sincerity in his voice.

Charlotte watched as Mr. Basford disappeared into the crowd. She realized that she was holding her hands in front of her as if to retain the feel of his hand on hers. Abruptly she relaxed her arms, letting them come to her sides and skim her skirt. She should not feel anything for him, of course, but there was warmth that still radiated through her body, and she did not know how to explain it. Thinking the fresh air might cool the heat that Mr. Basford had caused, she stepped onto the moonlit balcony.

The breeze did little to cool her cheeks, but there was no one else on the balcony and Charlotte was glad for the solitude. Mr. Basford persisted in her mind, however, and as she reviewed her interaction with him, she indulged in a bit of girlish fancy.

Mentally shaking herself, she pulled off her gloves and clutched them in her left hand. She should not be thinking of any man, not

Mr. Collins, Mr. Edgington—the swine—or even Mr. Basford. She should be thinking of Maria and chaperoning her, as was her duty.

Charlotte turned to go back inside the ballroom and find her sister, but she stopped abruptly at the sight of Mr. Edgington behind her. His face was in shadow, and a shaft of light coming through the ballroom windows illuminated his fine dress clothes.

She glanced quickly around her. The far edges of the balcony were in deep shadow, but it appeared that they were alone.

"Mr. Edgington, I did not hear you arrive." Charlotte attempted to sound stern. Instead, she sounded as squeaky as a mouse cornered by a hungry cat.

"I did not mean to startle you, Mrs. Collins. My apologies."

Charlotte was on the verge of following her original intention of never again speaking to Mr. Edgington and returning to the ballroom, but he moved toward the railing, blocking her way. His face came into the light. He was smiling. He took his place near her and leaned his hands casually against the railing. "It is a pleasant evening, is it not?"

"For some, I suppose it is. But it is a very welcome relief from the rain."

"Yes, travel was quite difficult on the muddy roads."

"I imagine it was."

Charlotte leaned against the corner of the railing and looked at him sidelong. She must find a way to return to the ballroom. It would not do to be alone with this ogre.

Mr. Edgington moved slightly closer, his eyes intent on her profile. "I am pleased that I chose to return to Westerham when I did, despite the poor traveling conditions."

He was facing her squarely now, his hip leaning against the railing.

"Are you?" She kept her gaze resolutely forward and attempted to keep the malice from her voice.

"Very glad," he whispered.

Mr. Edgington appeared to be reaching for her hand, which was resting on the rail, but then he reconsidered, and he was left standing very close to her, leaving her no means of escape. She could feel his breath on her nape, causing wisps of hair to stir along the neckline of her dress. She wanted to gag at his overbearing presence, and all she could think of was fleeing him.

"I must return inside."

She expected him to move away, to allow her to pass, but instead, he said, "You are always leaving, Mrs. Collins."

"I fear I must."

Again, he did not move. "I missed you when you departed London."

"I do not think it is possible to miss someone with whom you barely associated."

"On the contrary, we saw quite a bit of each other, although not as much as I would have liked."

"It is polite of you to say, sir, but—"

"It is the truth, Mrs. Collins. I find myself thinking of you often."

Charlotte shrank back at his words. He only came forward to fill the vacated inches between them.

She looked up at him firmly. "That is very flattering, sir, but it is probably best that you do not think of me at all."

"I do not see how I can stop myself."

"I am certain that it will be an easier task than you anticipate. I am not a particularly memorable or exciting woman."

"On the contrary, Mrs. Collins, to me you are both memorable and exciting."

She glanced around. Still no one had appeared on the balcony. "Pray, do not say such things."

He leaned even closer. "I cannot help myself. I must say these things."

"One always has the capability of helping oneself when one so chooses."

He smiled and laughed at Charlotte as though she were a child who just said something very foolish. She looked sideways, searching again for an escape route, but Mr. Edgington had effectively blocked her in the corner with his large body. She began to fidget with the gloves in her hands. She wished she had not worn them. Perhaps they were unduly encouraging him. She would burn them as soon as she returned home. If she could ever get off this wretched balcony.

He glanced at the gloves, too, and reached down and took the fingertips of one glove in his and stroked them, but he did not touch her directly.

"Mrs. Collins, I would like to court you," he said with his head bowed over her hands.

"I...I..."

"I have admired you from the first, and I would like to know you better. Much better."

"Mr. Edgington..."

"Please, call me Lewis."

"No," she said sharply.

Her eyes met his, and he gave her a wry grin. "My proper Mrs. Collins."

Charlotte recoiled at the sarcastic tone of his voice. "I am not your Mrs. Collins."

His eyes turned hard, and she immediately dropped the glove that he held in his hand, releasing it to his custody. The other glove remained clutched in her fingers.

He moved back half a step, giving Charlotte a modicum of personal space. She could not see his eyes clearly now that his face had gone into the shadow. But he seemed intent on the glove that now dangled from his fingers. He transferred it to his other hand and began to follow its contours with his index finger. Charlotte watched as his fingertip reached the top of the glove that had so recently rested in the crook of her elbow. He began to trace the monogram he found there.

"I am glad you wore the gloves I gave you." His voice sounded cold.

Charlotte could not respond, but only watched him continue to examine her glove.

"They mark you as mine."

"Yours?"

"Mine."

He raised his eyes to her. "Did you not know that accepting gifts from men is often a sign of a deeper relationship?"

"That is certainly not the case here," she said in a desperate whisper.

"Is it not?" He slapped the glove gently against his opposite hand and then let it slide slowly across his palm.

Charlotte's eyes flew to his. His face was very close again, and for a moment she feared he would breech propriety and kiss her, but he did not. He simply continued to look at her with the same hard intensity.

"We have no relationship." She spoke with as much dignity as she could muster. She turned with the intention of sweeping back into the ballroom, but he shifted, effectively blocking her movement.

Acting as if he had not purposefully and rudely blocked her, he said nonchalantly, "Yes, but we could have."

Charlotte stiffened her resolve in preparation to reply in the most negative manner possible when he interrupted her.

"Before you refuse, consider, imagine, the possibilities. We have both experienced the world. We know that love is an illusion, and marriage is good for nothing other than securing a fortune or creating children."

"I certainly would not marry you," Charlotte spat.

He looked angry, but when he spoke again, his tone was even and quiet. "I will not be offended by your unkind words because I did not propose, nor do I intend to do so. My proposition, Mrs. Collins, is completely different."

He spoke her name now as though it were a slight.

"Unless your proposition is that we return to the ballroom and join the others before someone gets the wrong impression, you may be assured that I will say no."

"Dear Mrs. Collins, always so concerned about the opinions of others. My proposition is very simple. As two mature adults, we are ideally suited to take care of each other's physical needs, are we not? Widows often have arrangements with men such as myself."

Charlotte recoiled as he reached to stroke her cheek.

He smiled at her evasion. "We who are unfettered by the bonds of marriage can truly enjoy each other."

"No! Indeed we shall not, and it is indelicate and offensive of you to make such a suggestion." The pitch of Charlotte's voice was high with panic, but she tried to maintain a whisper.

He leaned closer, and Charlotte could feel the heat from his body. "What is it the poets say, 'Gather ye rosebuds while ye may'?"

"I do not trust poets, and I certainly will not let pretty words change my decision."

"All the same, you might want to reconsider." He tucked her glove into the pocket of his coat with careful deliberation. "After all, it may appear to some people that we are already so engaged. We have been alone here for quite a long while, and I have a memento of our time together. A memento that, I believe, was also a rather intimate gift."

Charlotte was stunned into utter silence.

"You may cling to your high moral principles, but you will have to content yourself with them. Your morality may be questioned by society when they see such damning evidence of your behavior."

The realization that he was threatening Charlotte, blackmailing her into an indecent relationship, registered despite her shock. Was this how he had begun with Mrs. Holloway? Was she not so much his lover but his victim?

Regardless of how he had engaged the services of Mrs. Holloway, Charlotte was ruined no matter what decision she made. She would either be a woman defiled or she would appear to be one to the rest of the world. She would devastate her family and lose her friends, or she would lose her self-respect. How could she—a woman who prided herself on common sense and propriety—have been so foolish?

"Return my glove this instant," she demanded with more confidence than she felt.

He smirked. "Indeed, I will not."

She stared, still unable to believe the baseness of his character.

"It would behoove you to reconsider my offer, Mrs. Collins."

Though her reputation was already as good as ruined, Charlotte still could not consider his proposition. "Mr. Edgington, do you find joy in blackmailing women in this manner?"

He glared. Moments crawled by. "You misunderstand, my dear Mrs. Collins. For a gentleman such as myself, it has nothing to do with the joy of mere words. I desire an entirely different sort of joy. Perhaps I ought to use the word euphoria. With this token," he said as he patted the pocket where her glove was concealed, "I have the opportunity to experience the sort of joy I desire."

Charlotte struggled to breathe. He was a monster. "Why are you so intent on torturing me? I have done nothing to merit it."

"Done nothing?" His voice became thick with barely restrained anger, "You reject me. No other man in England would have you, a cold, joyless woman, and still you reject me. I would have you."

Charlotte suddenly had the urge to throttle him, and instead of launching herself at him bodily, she struck him across the face with her other glove. Then, shocked at her physical outburst, she stared as his hand went to his cheek.

"You old fool!" he said between clenched teeth. "Do you realize what I may do to your reputation? Do you not comprehend? My connections in Westerham society, to Lady Catherine, will assure your ruin. One well-placed word from me about how you offered this glove as an inducement to an affair, and the dear old bat will see that you lose everything. Including your very home!"

Charlotte stepped backward. She knew that Lady Catherine would not hesitate to remove her from the cottage if she merely suspected her to be a part of the demimonde. Her cottage. It was her only real security. She could not lose it. But what could she do?

Her eyes darted around the balcony as if the answer would be written on the wall. But no such response appeared. After a long hesitation, Charlotte resigned herself to her fate. "Do what you will, but my conscience is clean and the truth will set me free."

He sneered. "I thought you many things, my dear Mrs. Collins, but never naïve. Truth is found in perception, and we have already been perceived," he said, gesturing to a movement on the opposite side of the balcony.

Charlotte squinted into the shadows. She could see a hint of motion, but she could not discern who had joined them.

Mr. Edgington took her hand in his rough grip and kissed her knuckles. Charlotte pulled her hand away, wiping it on her gown to remove the sensation he had imparted on her skin. Her fingers and her spirit felt bruised by his roughness. Mr. Edgington walked back into the ballroom, leaving her at the mercy of whomever had come onto the balcony.

ഛ Fourteen ഛ

Charlotte's mind whirled, yet her thoughts were disconnected, and she could not latch on to one before another overtook it. She felt hot and cold at the same time, and she began to fear that she might faint. She had never fainted in her life, and she refused to begin now. Not over that swine Mr. Edgington. She grasped the hard wood of the railing until her knuckles turned white, and her eyes ached with barely restrained tears.

What should she do? What could be done? She had blundered far worse than Maria ever had.

She was ruined. Irrevocably ruined.

Suddenly, she heard a voice behind her. "Charlotte?" She jumped and spun quickly to find that Mr. Basford looked concerned. "Are you well?"

She responded without thinking. She could not think. At least not rationally. "I am quite well." It was, of course, a lie. A polite lie, but a lie nonetheless.

He studied her in the dim light. "I can see, despite your words to the contrary, that something is amiss."

Charlotte bit back a sob. "No, I assure you…"

He took her hands in his, a soft, reassuring touch, but the contact of his gloved hand on her naked skin only served to remind her of her missing glove.

"What has happened?"

Aghast, she pulled her hands away and stepped back two full steps. "I cannot say."

When Mr. Edgington's slander became public, the last thing she needed was for anyone to have seen her alone in the company of Mr. Basford as well. She would be labeled as an irrevocably fallen woman and the results would do no favors for herself or her future happiness. She stared at the ground while attempting to compose herself.

"Please, I may be able to help."

She looked up at him sharply. "I am afraid no one can help. I am quite beyond it."

Mr. Basford answered her with a skeptical look and stepped back to lean his hip against the railing. His posture was much like that of Mr. Edgington, but his bearing was completely opposite. He made the position seem more amicable than antagonistic He studied her silently for several moments while she tried to gather her wits about her.

He did not move, but the concern in his eyes conveyed as much as any physical comfort he could have offered. "I saw you here with Mr. Edgington. Has he done something to upset you?"

She was shocked at how easily her façade cracked under his kindness. Tears welled again in her eyes, and she only shook her head.

He turned abruptly, searching the ballroom intensely. "I can see that he has. I'll speak to him."

"No!" She laid a bare hand on his arm to restrain him. "You must not." She desperately wanted to tell him everything, to share her burden. In fact, she could not prevent herself. "Please, I am already ruined."

At her words, he turned back to her, and her hand fell to her side. His face was drawn into a confused expression. His forehead was a furrowed as a farmer's field, and Charlotte had the strange inclination to smooth it with her bare hand. "Ruined? Impossible. You are the most upright woman I've ever met."

"It does not matter. He will tell people, and they will believe him."

"Tell people what? No one who has ever met you will believe any negative remarks about you."

"They will believe him when he shows them the evidence."

He noticed the single glove clutched in her hand, and gently, he took it from her. The cloth seemed to burn her hand as it slipped through her fingers.

She hung her head as she saw understanding begin to come over him.

"He has the other glove?"

"Yes."

"Why would he take it?" He looked at it as though it would reveal its secrets.

Charlotte shook her head, unable to speak the truth, wiping at her eyes to keep the tears from falling.

His voice came out in a harsh whisper, his eyes hard. "He is trying to intimidate you into some sort of illicit affair with him!"

Charlotte nodded but did not meet his eyes. "He will ruin me if I do not give in to his demands, and I will be ruined if I do as he wishes. Either way, my reputation in society will be completely and utterly destroyed."

Saying the words out loud caused Charlotte to comprehend the full extent of her situation. "Not only will I be ruined, but so will my family. And poor Maria will have no hope of ever marrying well. Oh Lord.... And my house. I shall lose that as well once he goes to Lady Catherine."

Charlotte covered her face, her hand shaking, but she did not even think to be embarrassed by her exhibition of feminine frailty. She cried quietly for a moment and then took a deep, fortifying breath. Now was not the time for hysterics. She must try to think of a solution.

Unfortunately, she knew very well that nothing could be done, but she reviewed possible courses of action anyway. Perhaps she could somehow retrieve the glove during the evening, but how? Impossible. In all likelihood, he had already sent for his carriage and would soon be away. Perhaps she could destroy the remaining glove and deny the matter entirely. Also impossible, for the glove bore her own initials. She could go to Lady Catherine and tell her what had happened, but why would she believe her over her own relation? Indeed, nothing could be done to save her.

"He will show them my glove, which was a gift from him many months ago. A gift that bears my initials. And that dance...." She winced. "I have been here alone with him all this time. People will believe him. They will have no choice in the face of such evidence."

She expected Mr. Basford to leave her now, to save himself from sharing in her ruin. But he did not move. He stood like a rock before her.

Seeing his implacable features, Charlotte turned to leave, to spare him if he would not spare himself. "I must find Maria and procure a carriage. I must leave here immediately! Please order the carriage for us, if you please."

"No."

He was refusing his carriage! Feeling trapped, she began to panic. How would she and Maria get home? Would they have to walk home in shame through the dark streets of Westerham?

"You must not leave, and you must not cry. What you do now will have a large impact on your future." Mr. Basford's voice sounded authoritative and calm.

Even amid her distress, the truth of his words penetrated. She must minimize the damage. She turned back to him and watched in horror as he removed his own gloves and placed one in his jacket pocket. "What are you doing?"

"You must have gloves for the rest of the evening. I understand that going without them is simply not done. People will take notice and ask you about them, and you're certainly in no frame of mind to deal with the situation directly, at least not yet." He handed one glove to her. "Put on your glove and carry this other with you. People may notice that you're only wearing one, but they will see that you carry its mate. If anyone asks, tell them that the fabric has irritated your skin and that you regret that you must carry it."

She stared at him, unsure of what to do or think. Her mind was muddled, her thinking unclear. Would it benefit her to allow Mr. Basford to come to her aid? Could she trust him? Did she have any choice?

She did as he suggested and slid her glove back on her hand. She took his glove, which she folded to disguise its masculine cut, and held it in her hand.

"But you will be without gloves."

He rolled his eyes subtly. "I'm an uncouth American. It will be expected that I would break with custom in this way."

"But—"

"Do not concern yourself with my reputation, Mrs. Collins." He offered his arm, but Charlotte only stared at it, uncomprehending, as though he were the first gentleman ever to offer her such a courtesy. All proficiency of etiquette seemed to have deserted her. "You must go inside, speak to people, and behave as if nothing has happened."

"I do not think I can." Her hands shook, and her stomach was tight. The world seemed to tilt around her, and she leaned against the wall for support.

He stood squarely in front of her. His body was very broad and strong, but his carriage was not at all intimidating. He waited until her eyes met his. His voice was firm when he spoke. "You can and you shall. You must begin to fight his lies even now. You have done nothing wrong."

She nodded mutely, taking another bracing breath as a faint glimmer of courage shone inside her heart. She knew what she must do and turned to Mr. Basford, took a deep breath. "You must dance with me."

Charlotte almost expected him to make a jest about her forward behavior, but, thankfully, he appeared to give the idea serious consideration. "Yes, I think it wise for you to dance with me, and also with any other gentleman who asks. Talk with your friends. You and Maria will depart in our carriage at the end of the evening as planned."

He offered his arm again. Slowly, she reached for it. He took her ungloved hand, tucking it in the crook of his arm, and led her toward the door.

As they walked toward the ballroom door, Charlotte tried to think through her situation. Was she behaving wisely or would she exacerbate the problem? Every emotion told her to flee, to leave the ball and continue to run, but her mind said that flight was the easy course of action. And Charlotte had often found that the easiest solution did not yield the most desirable results. The difficult road was usually the one that ought to be travelled.

They reached the doors, and Charlotte took a shuddering breath. Mr. Basford gave her a stern look. The furrows were back in his brow. "Just don't cry."

She looked at him crossly. She may be a little rattled, but did he think her so weak that she might burst into tears in public? Perhaps she had cried on the balcony, but she would never do so in the ballroom! She was stronger than that. She detested debutantes who allowed their emotions to rule their behavior, or worse, who used their tears to manipulate others. She would see herself through the evening, and she would behave with her usual grace and good sense.

She hoped.

Charlotte kept her focus ahead of her as they entered. The room was alive with movement and sound. Couples danced in dizzying patterns, and voices seemed to swirl around her. What had seemed so pleasant only ten minutes prior now overwhelmed her, and she wondered suddenly if she was capable of maintaining her poise.

Her hand tightened on Mr. Basford's arm.

He whispered, "You've spent your whole life performing for others. You can certainly continue to perform for the rest of the evening."

Again, anger cut through her embarrassment, and she glared up at Mr. Basford. Did he think her merely a performer?

He only smiled back. Pleasantly. Charlotte wanted to remove that smirk from his face, but she forced her attention to the people around her. She had a fleeting recognition of her longtime friends as they moved around the ballroom. Would any of these people ever speak to her again after Mr. Edgington's news came out? Mrs. Card and Mrs. Farmington were seated in a corner, leaning toward each other to share gossip. Maria stood nearby watching as Mr. Westfield finished a dance with Miss Farmington. Would any of these people ever deign to speak with her again?

When the next dance began, Charlotte found herself being led to the floor by Mr. Basford. The steps came automatically, and she scanned the room for Mr. Edgington. She found him leaning insolently against the far wall. Mrs. Holloway stood nearby, conversing with two women. She looked frequently at Mr. Edgington and was obviously attempting to draw him into their conversation. Charlotte wondered where Mr. Holloway was. Perhaps he was taking some refreshment or had stayed at home with his pig. It was most certainly better company than his wife.

Mrs. Holloway's ridiculous bird adornment bobbled as she spoke, still glancing at Mr. Edgington, but he paid her little heed. He was watching Charlotte. Heat rose along the skin of her neck, and angry tears jumped to her eyes.

Mr. Basford spoke to her softly. "It is a nice ball, is it not, Mrs. Collins?"

She tore her gaze away from her enemy and looked at her partner, and his gaze was intense, calling her to focus and forget Mr. Edgington. "It is indeed, Mr. Basford."

"Of course, since it was given by my uncle, it would be rude of you not to agree."

Charlotte laughed, but even to her own ears, it sounded odd, forced and unnatural.

"I find that I enjoy your English country dances more than I expected." Mr. Basford was attempting to be companionable. "We have many similar dances in Savannah."

Charlotte made her best effort to focus on the topic of conversation. "It is nice to hear you say something positive about our land."

He smiled down at her sincerely. The furrows were gone, and smooth skin took their place. He looked so attractive, even to her overwhelmed mind. His steps were confident, and each time his bare hands met her bare one she could feel his strength enter her body.

As their hands met again, he gave her fingertips a gentle, warm squeeze. "There are many things I like about England, although I may not have shared as much as I should have."

"And I find that Americans may not be as ill mannered as I originally believed."

He grinned widely, and somehow Charlotte knew that her secret was quite safe in his possession.

They made polite small talk for the remainder of the dance, and Charlotte almost managed to forget her situation under Mr. Basford's compliments and distracting comments. When the dance was completed, he offered to escort her to acquire some lemonade, which she accepted, drinking gratefully, not realizing how thirsty she had been. After lingering a few moments over the cold meats and cheeses, Mr. Basford led her to an empty place alongside the dance floor. She expected him to excuse himself, but he did not. Instead, he took his place beside her, seeming almost proprietary in his stance. Acquaintances came to chat, and still Mr. Basford remained at her side. She wondered if she ought to speak to him, tell him he could go, but she found she liked having him there.

And so conversation flowed freely, and soon, the crowd began to dwindle. Alone with Charlotte again, Mr. Basford leaned down near her ear and said, "Relief is on the way. I see that Maria is making her way across the room. It is undoubtedly time for you to return home."

She spotted Maria and Mr. Westfield as they slowly made their way around the small group of dancers who kept to the floor, talking and laughing along the way. It was good to see Maria among her friends again even if all her wounds had not yet healed. She wondered if any of her companions would remain when Mr. Edgington's slander became public.

"You have done well." Thank heaven for Mr. Basford and his ability to distract her from her thoughts. However, Charlotte knew she did not deserve such a compliment. During the last few hours, she had been relying on his strength a great deal, but when Mr. Edgington used his weapon, she would be completely alone and unaided.

She began to say as much to Mr. Basford, but he interrupted her. "Do not contemplate the future just yet. We will deal with that as it comes."

"We? This is not your dilemma. It is mine alone."

Mr. Basford looked away quickly, but she saw irritated lines cross his brow. She was surprised to realize that she might have angered him, and eager to soothe him, she turned her full gaze on him. "I appreciate all that you have done for me tonight, but you are not required to suffer for my folly."

"What folly? You have done nothing to deserve this." His voice sounded harsh, and Charlotte wondered at his tone. She studied his profile. His teeth were clenched and his lips were stretched into a tight line. He was not angry, she realized, but injured.

Her tone was gentle, as if to calm him. "Have I not? I trusted an undeserving man."

Maria and Mr. Westfield were very close now, so Mr. Basford leaned down slightly to say, "I hope that will not cause you to distrust all men. Some of us are worthy."

Before she could think of a response, her sister arrived at her side with Mr. Westfield as her escort. "Has it not been a lovely evening, Charlotte? I am sorry that it has to end already. Everyone behaved charmingly, even Miss Farmington and Mr. Card," she added in a discreet whisper. "No one suffered from the want of a partner. Such wonderful music, delicious food, and..." Maria glanced at Mr. Westfield. "...such agreeable companions."

Although she could not concur with the hearty compliments her sister lavished on the ball, she said, "I am glad you had such a pleasant time."

"Indeed, it has been a most enjoyable evening. It is a shame to see it end." Mr. Westfield's eyes were intent on Maria, and Charlotte felt hope for her sister. Perhaps he was in love with her, and she only prayed that his love was strong so that Mr. Edgington's slander would not dissolve it.

Mr. Basford, who had been watching his nephew, turned to Charlotte. "Perhaps we'll call on Mrs. Collins and Miss Lucas this week."

"Oh, yes, that would be pleasing indeed, Uncle."

Charlotte nodded her assent, grateful for the excuse to speak with Mr. Basford again soon, but she did not meet his eyes.

Mr. Basford stepped away to order the carriage while Mr. Westfield bid Maria a fond farewell, causing her to giggle, as he escorted her out the door. Charlotte remained behind.

When Mr. Basford returned, Charlotte saw that they were quite alone in the vestibule and offered his glove to him. "Thank you for this evening."

He only shook his head, and she dropped her hand. "I hope you do not object to us calling on you later this week."

Knowing that she should act demurely, she could not. She looked at Mr. Basford squarely. "No, indeed. I quite look forward to it."

He inclined his dark head toward hers. His voice was soft but firm when he said, "Until then, do not worry. We will simply tell the truth. All will be well."

ஸ்ஃ Fifteen ஸ்ஃ

The Armitage's carriage rumbled up the cottage drive. Candlelight flickered in the sitting room window, and Charlotte knew that Mrs. Eff and Edward had awaited their return. For the first time, she wished they had not. Mrs. Eff would not be as easily fooled by her veneer of nonchalance as Maria.

The coachman assisted Charlotte and Maria from the carriage and then the conveyance disappeared with a loud growl of wheels on stones. Mrs. Eff opened the cottage door as they approached. "Welcome home. May I take your things?"

Maria removed her wrap and gloves and piled them in Mrs. Eff's arms while recounting each minute of the ball. Charlotte removed her pelisse and handed it to Edward, but she retained her gloves. She hoped no one had noticed.

Mrs. Eff handed the heap of Maria's garments to Edward. "See that these are properly stored." He disappeared down the hall, and Mrs. Eff looked at the sisters. "A fire is still burning in the sitting room. I thought you might enjoy some tea before bed."

Charlotte clutched the mismatched gloves behind her skirt, wringing the fabric back and forth. She did not want tea. She wanted privacy. Why would not everyone just go to sleep?

Maria yawned. "I do not think I could stay awake long enough for the water to boil."

Thank heavens. Now Charlotte could engineer a few moments of peace to dispose of the evidence of the night's crimes.

"Mrs. Collins?"

"Thank you for your kindness, Mrs. Eff. I think I will sit in solitude by the fire for a few moments, but I do not require any tea."

"Are you certain?"

"Yes, you and Edward have had a long day. You ought to retire."

Mrs. Eff eyed her and then nodded. "Sleep well, Mrs. Collins. I do look forward to hearing about the ball tomorrow morning."

Charlotte tried to smile and wondered if she had managed to do so. Mrs. Eff said nothing, looked at her oddly, and then disappeared to her chamber.

The door to the sitting room was ajar, and Charlotte pushed it open. She walked into the chamber as though she were moving in water. Her steps were slow, and as her arms swung at her sides, the fabric of the gloves brushed against her skirt in long, slow strokes. Whoosh, whoosh, whoosh. It was the only sound she could hear. When had the house become so quiet? Could Mrs. Eff hear the hum of fabric on fabric? Would she hear the crackles of the glove as it burned?

Charlotte stood before the mantel, and the peat fire smoldered before her. If only destroying the glove would destroy Mr. Edgington's slander. But as long as its mate existed, Charlotte was ruined.

Still, she would do what was within her power. And that was to destroy the offending article. She flung her glove on top of the smoldering peat and watched as flames began to grow and consume the fabric.

Holding Mr. Basford's glove in both hands, she stood in front of the fire and watched as it died slowly, the embers glowing and banking. In and out. In and out.

The embers should have been peaceful, and she had expected to feel relief when the glove had turned to ash, but she felt neither peace nor relief. Realizing that her back and legs ached, Charlotte turned to go to her bed chamber and discovered Edward watching her through the open door. She quickly hid Mr. Basford's glove behind her back.

"Are you well, Mrs. Collins?"

She cleared her throat. Why was she suddenly nervous? Edward was her sweet but muddle-minded servant and probably comprehended little of the intricacies of society. "Yes, why do you ask?"

"I called your name over and over."

"Oh." How could she not have heard him? She wondered how long he had been observing her. Had he seen her burn that glove? Had he seen Mr. Basford's glove?

"I am fine. Go to bed, Edward."

He studied her with steady eyes, and she thought he might speak again, but he only nodded and left the chamber.

Charlotte also went to her bed chamber, where she tucked away Mr. Basford's glove in the small wooden box that housed her hair ornaments and jewelry—some inexpensive earrings, a string of pearls from her father, and a cross pendant—and placed it in the cupboard. She would return it to him at an opportune moment.

Satisfied that Mr. Basford's glove would remain safely hidden, she removed her gown and draped it over a chair. She had barely prevented herself from throwing it onto the floor in disgust. It was a good gown, and she would not allow the memories of Mr. Edgington ruin it for her.

When she had finally laid down to rest, sleep had eluded her, and when it did claim her, she found herself dreaming of gloves and fires and dances and Mr. Basford. Sounds began to drift in and out of Charlotte's dreams, and they became even more confused. She heard Mrs. Eff and Edward about their morning chores: the sounds of fresh coals hitting the kitchen grate and the clatter of breakfast dishes. Could it be morning already? Usually, Charlotte went down to greet them and discuss the news from town with Mrs. Eff, but instead, she turned onto her left side and pulled the covers over her head to block out the sounds from below.

Hours later—or perhaps only minutes, Charlotte could not be certain—she heard Maria moving about below stairs and snippets of her voice as she told Mrs. Eff about the ball. Charlotte knew they would be expecting her, but still, she could not manage to arise and face the day. At any moment the news of her scandal would become public, and the happy sounds of her household would disappear. She would be ostracized from her friends and family, leaving her with little choice but to take in a dozen stray cats for company.

More bewildering than the taunting sounds of normalcy that could not last was the fact that Charlotte's mind continued to stray to Mr. Basford. Each time she closed her eyes, she was on the balcony again. Mr. Edgington was gone, and Charlotte would turn and watch as Mr. Basford emerged tall and strong from the darkness. She saw the concern in his eyes and her heart began to flutter just as it had the night before.

Charlotte threw her arm over her head, trying to block out her thoughts but seeing only Mr. Basford in the crook of her elbow. He had promised to help her, but he could not possibly be able to do so. What could be done after all? Mr. Edgington had her glove, and he would not hesitate to use it against her now that she had rejected his vile offer. There was nothing to be done but wait for the inevitable to occur.

Charlotte closed her eyes and managed to doze for several more hours, experiencing dark nightmares of Mr. Edgington. His red hair had turned to flames, and he advanced on her, but Charlotte could not run. Just as he reached for her gloved hands, she would awake with a start.

Once awake, she contemplated Mr. Basford. A much pleasanter topic, but inappropriate nonetheless.

She knew that she could not stay in bed forever, and even if she were to attempt such a feat, her blankets would not shield her from the coldness of society once the scandal became known. She pushed away the linens and threw her legs over the side of the bed. The planks of the wooden floor felt cool beneath her bare feet as she washed at the washstand, did her morning ablutions, and put on her plainest morning gown. She then gathered her courage and went downstairs.

Mrs. Eff was dusting the small table in the hallway, and she looked up from her work and concern crossed her once delicate face. "I was beginning to worry about you, my dear, are you well?" She dropped the dust cloth onto the table and assisted Charlotte down the remaining steps.

Charlotte attempted a reassuring smile but failed miserably.

Mrs. Eff patted her hand. "Do I need to consult the apothecary?"

Charlotte walked with ginger steps toward the sitting room. "I do feel rather weak, but I think a cup of tea will be all I require."

"Rosehip tea then, my dear, made from your own garden. It is just the thing for an aching head. Why do you not go to the sitting room and rest a bit more?" With a kind smile, she led her to the settee. "Back in my dancing days, before our family lost its holdings, such as they were, I never felt worse than the day after a spectacular ball."

Charlotte sat down and tucked her legs under her in a comfortable yet thoroughly undignified fashion. She might as well be comfortable if she could not be proper.

Mrs. Eff arranged cushions around her. "I suppose you do not feel like talking just yet. Let me bring you some tea and toast."

Charlotte nodded at Mrs. Eff, grateful that she had suggested food. She had not realized how hungry she had become, and it was much later in the day than she had anticipated. From her seat, she craned her head to look out the open window. The sun was high in the sky, beaming on Edward who toiled in the garden. His face was content but smeared with dirt. Charlotte envied him. He truly had a simple life and took pleasure in small things. He did not have to worry over the words and deeds of unscrupulous people. He only had to tend to the rosemary.

She turned away from the pastoral scene, and her mind began to bounce from one thought to another like a young debutante in a room full of potential beaux. The news must soon become public. She must formulate a rebuttal. She must see to Maria. She must protect her assets. If only she had the energy.

A sound in the hallway caused her to jump in the anticipation that it would be a neighbor coming to confirm Mr. Edgington's story. She sat bolt upright when a knock sounded at the sitting room door. Her nerves hummed as she rearranged her skirt. "Come in."

It was Mrs. Eff. God bless Mrs. Eff, for she carried a pot of tea and a plate of toast and jam, and not the ill news she expected. The smells of food surrounded her, making her stomach clench in anticipation. Mrs. Eff offered her a cup of rosehip tea, and Charlotte sipped it, letting the warmth and sweetness of the liquid give her strength.

"Miss Maria asked me to tell you that she has gone for a turn about the garden. She was all a-twitter this morning. I suppose balls take more out of us as we age."

Charlotte wished that age were the cause of her morning depression. She said nothing, took up her plate, and selected a piece of toast. Mrs. Eff chatted about some matters of the cottage and their upcoming meals and then launched into the news from town. With the introduction of each new tidbit of information, Charlotte became anxious and then felt relief wash over her when it became apparent that she was not the focus of the gossip. Why had she ever found gossip to be an agreeable pastime?

Fortunately, there was no mention of Mr. Edgington, only of the general pleasure everyone experienced at the ball. General pleasure. Ha! Charlotte thought. It had caused her acute pain. And strangely, Mr. Basford had provided acute joy. How, she wondered, could joy and pain coexist in the same evening?

But why did not Mrs. Eff speak of Mr. Edgington and the glove? Perhaps she had heard but was too timid to speak of it. No. That could not be the case, for Mrs. Eff was always very forthcoming. Perhaps the news had not yet gotten out. Perhaps Mr. Edgington had been killed in a tragic hunting accident early this morning before he could ruin her reputation. Perhaps a wild boar had mauled him. Were boars even in season? She doubted a pheasant could do sufficient damage. A sudden mauling was too good—and too horrid—a circumstance to contemplate.

Still, Charlotte was beginning to feel a bit of relief and had almost finished eating an entire piece of toast when Mrs. Eff produced a letter from her apron pocket. Her relief was instantly shattered into splinters of fear. "This arrived this morning while you were still in your chamber. Now that you've had some nourishment, I expect you are ready for a word from the outside world."

She held out the paper to her, and Charlotte stared at it, still chewing on her last bite of toast. Was this ill news? Had the knowledge of the glove become known? She stared at the direction, but she did not recognize the handwriting. Slowly, she put down her plate and took the letter from Mrs. Eff's hands. "Thank you."

"Is there anything else I can do for you?"

"No, thank you, Mrs. Eff. You have been a great help already."

"I shall leave you to your letter then."

Charlotte watched as Mrs. Eff exited the sitting room, her skirt trailing behind her. She looked down at the letter again, and drawing in a deep breath, she opened the seal. Quickly, she checked the signature first.

Mr. Basford.

Relief raced through her and a silly smile reached her lips. She was too pleased that it was not a threat from Mr. Edgington that she did not contemplate the breach of etiquette he had committed in writing her. But the smile fell from her lips. Perhaps he had come to his senses and was writing to withdraw his support. She took a deep breath and began to read.

> My dear Mrs. Collins,
>
> I hope you will not think this letter is inappropriate, for I'm writing it with the best of intentions. Before you begin to panic, let me to assuage your fear. Don't trouble yourself. Nothing has occurred to ruin you. I'm merely writing on behalf of Mr. Westfield and myself to solidify our appointment with you and Miss Lucas. My nephew is eager to speak to your sister. I hope it will be acceptable for us to call on you both tomorrow afternoon. In the meantime, Mrs. Collins, do not trouble yourself. All will be well.
>
> B. B.

Charlotte carefully refolded the letter and set it in her lap. She stared down at it, occasionally repositioning it on the fabric of her dress. Her heart was torn with hope and doubt. Why was he so kind? How could he possibly benefit from helping her?

Certainly he had already proven himself to be an upstanding man and very much unlike what she had expected upon their first meeting. His letter had soothed her in a manner that nothing— neither the rosehip tea and toast nor Mrs. Eff's conversation—had managed.

·ോ ഉ·ം

Maria returned inside and sank ungracefully onto the settee beside Charlotte. She looked fresh and excited, her blue eyes shining. Charlotte felt like a storm cloud—a woman of dark and changeable moods—and probably resembled one as well.

"Did you enjoy your walk?"

"I would have much rather talked to you, but you refused to get out of bed at a reasonable hour. I suppose you felt ill?"

"I had a dreadful headache this morning, but I am feeling better now."

"I am glad to hear it." Maria took Charlotte's hand. "I do not say it often enough, but I do not know what I would do without you. You have given me a home and a chance to enjoy society. If it had not been for you, I would never have met Mr. Westfield."

Guilt raced through Charlotte. Maria's happiness was indeed attached to hers. And how tenuous was Charlotte's happiness! Unsure of whether she should break the bad news to her sister, she hugged Maria tight, looking down at her blond head where it rested against her shoulder. The poor girl had already been the target of the sharp arrows of gossip, but still she managed to retain her innocence and optimism. Her good nature had seen her through the loss of her friendship with Miss Farmington and Mr. Card. Perhaps Charlotte ought to rank optimism a little higher in her list of virtues.

Charlotte sighed. She feared that her brush with the slings of society would not leave her as innocent. The horrid tale would become public eventually, and it would be better to tell Maria beforehand. But Charlotte could not bear to ruin her sister's elevated mood, and there was Mr. Westfield's impending visit to consider.

Perhaps tomorrow he would propose, and engaged to the man she loved, Maria would be safe from partaking in Charlotte's ruin.

·ോ ഉ·ം

Mr. Basford and Mr. Westfield arrived at the cottage the next day in the early afternoon. In the sitting room, Maria sat in a chair appearing completely composed while Charlotte fidgeted on the settee.

"Mr. Basford and Mr. Westfield." Mrs. Eff announced them at the door. Charlotte imagined that her voice held a note of finality.

The sisters stood and turned to greet them.

"Good day," Charlotte said. She tried not to seek reassurance from Mr. Basford that the news had not yet spread, but she could not help herself. Her eyes sought his.

He smiled, his lips drawing into a subtle U-shape, and she knew her secret remained safe.

She released the breath she had been holding. His smile deepened, revealing a row of nicely formed teeth. Charlotte dragged her gaze away from him and focused on Maria, who was blushing prettily as Mr. Westfield greeted her.

Charlotte forced herself to remember her role as hostess. "Please, do sit down."

"That is very kind of you, Mrs. Collins," Mr. Westfield said, "but I was hoping to have the pleasure of taking a turn about the garden with Miss Lucas. Would you grant us your permission?"

If it were possible to shout inwardly, Charlotte did so. Outwardly, she remained composed. There could be no doubt but that Mr. Westfield was going to propose! Charlotte would convey her parent's blessing forthwith, and perhaps the marriage would occur before Mr. Edgington's news could do damage. At the very least, her sister would be securely engaged when the dreadful news became available to the public.

"Certainly, Mr. Westfield. It is a fine day for walking." Charlotte had to restrain herself from pushing them out the door. Instead, she kept her seat as Mr. Westfield escorted Maria from the room, but she did wink at her sister when she turned back in the doorway and smiled hugely.

Once the door had been shut behind them, Mr. Basford said, "That was a very cheeky gesture for so refined a woman."

Charlotte elected to reply in a similarly cheeky manner. She actually felt a bit cheeky just now. "You forget, Mr. Basford, that I am—or very soon will be—a woman with a reputation. It is expected that I would behave in such a shocking fashion."

He sobered. "You don't believe that, do you?" he asked, leaning forward in his seat.

"What? That soon society in general will believe me to be only slightly better than a harlot and that they will expect me to behave accordingly? I cannot help but believe it."

"Surely no one will believe you capable of what Mr. Edgington will assert."

"I wish that were true." She looked down at her skirt. "But in my experience, people are eager to believe the worst in others."

A pause.

"What about you, Charlotte, are you inclined to believe the worst in others?"

Charlotte considered. She had believed the worst of Mr. Basford, and in reality, he was the best of men, but she had believed the best of Mr. Edgington, and he had turned out to be a pig. A serpent. A demon! She stopped her litany of insults. "It appears that I always believe the opposite of what is true. I find that I cannot read the character of others at all."

"First impressions can be deceiving."

"Indeed."

Although the conversation dwindled, the two sat comfortably together for a time. Then, Mr. Basford shifted in his chair. "My nephew is proposing to Maria."

Charlotte's head snapped up. More inward rejoicing. "I am so pleased, and I know my sister will be pleased as well. She has developed deep feelings for your nephew."

"James is quite fond of her too. He needed only a little encouragement from me to make his proposal."

"Encouragement was required?"

"Oh, no, do not misunderstand. The boy wanted to propose. He told me so himself. He simply needed a little nudge to overcome his initial hesitancy."

She was somewhat relieved. "I see. And you merely nudged him."

"I thought the timing was right."

He meant, of course, that the timing would prevent his young charge from caving in to societal pressure once Charlotte's disparaging story was known. She dropped her eyes, ashamed that she had the potential to affect her sister's life negatively. But if it resulted in an engagement, the circumstance could not be entirely bad.

"I did not tell him your situation."

"I greatly appreciate that."

He stood, crossed the room, and joined Charlotte on the settee. He sat at a respectable distance, but Charlotte slid further toward the armrest. She made a great pretense of rearranging her skirt. And then, realizing that she was preening like Maria in a room of eligible gentlemen, she took a fortifying breath and looked at Mr. Basford.

He was lounging against the back of the settee, looking calm and relaxed indeed. How could he manage to be so calm when she felt so nervous? His legs were stretched in front of him in a very inelegant position that somehow managed to suit him quite well.

Her eyes moved up past his deep blue frock coat, his loosely tied white cravat, and his neck to his face. Slowly, she met his eyes, and the events that had concerned her only moments ago seemed to disappear into insignificance. What cared she about Maria and Mr. Westfield when she felt such a pull toward Mr. Basford?

Charlotte did not know exactly what to do next, but she could not force herself to remove her gaze from his. She clasped and unclasped her hands in her lap several times before she realized she was fidgeting. How inexperienced she must appear. She dropped her hands beside her, allowing them to rest on the settee. Finally, she sat, unmoving.

Mr. Basford, however, was not so immobile. Gradually, gently, his hand moved from where it had laid across his chest. It slid ever so slowly across the brocade fabric of the settee. Charlotte saw the movement in the periphery of her vision, but she continued to meet his eyes. Her heart beat faster as his hand approached hers. Slowly, slowly, his hand continued to move toward her, and time seemed to stop as she waited for their fingers to meet.

His hand was so near to hers that she could feel the heat from his skin. A shiver of anticipation rushed through her. Her whole being was focused on Mr. Basford, and she was shocked to discover how desperately she wanted his touch and wished to experience his ever-present warmth.

The door burst open in the moment before Mr. Basford's hand met hers. His hand retracted politely to his lap as Maria and Mr. Westfield dashed in, smiling and laughing. The moment dissipated like dew on morning grass, leaving Charlotte's face as warm as if she had been standing in the sunshine.

Charlotte was thankful that her sister was unobservant, for she did not notice the blush on her cheeks, and she did not feel the tension between her and Mr. Basford. She simply hurried into the room and said, "Charlotte, Mr. Westfield would like to speak with you."

Composing herself, Charlotte adjusted her position on the settee, sitting straighter and turning her gaze to Mr. Westfield. She attempted an authoritarian demeanor, but she feared her red cheeks would hinder the facade. "Should we step into the next room?"

Mr. Westfield came forward, clearing his throat. Maria stood behind him, her face flushed with excitement. "No, Mrs. Collins, I believe everyone here will share in our joy."

He paused, glanced down at the floor, and cleared his throat again. Charlotte wondered if he had lost his nerve. Finally, he said, "I have asked Maria to become my wife—"

"I said yes!"

"Yes. Indeed, she gave her consent, but now I must ask the permission of her family—"

"And is it not true, Charlotte, that Mama and Papa have given you the power to agree to a match?"

Charlotte glanced between them. Mr. Westfield was still staring at the floor and periodically clearing his throat, and Maria was looking at her with wide, hopeful eyes.

"Yes. Mama and Papa have given me the option of granting their permission in their absence."

Maria stepped forward and grasped Mr. Westfield's elbow. "And will you grant it?"

"That depends." She glanced again at Mr. Westfield. "Sir, do you promise to make my sister happy? To provide for her? And, most importantly, to love her knowing that she has no dowry to speak of?"

Mr. Westfield met Charlotte's direct gaze. "I will do my best, Mrs. Collins, with or without a dowry."

"Then, I do grant permission."

Maria squealed with glee. She abandoned her betrothed and ran to throw her arms around Charlotte while Mr. Basford rose to clap his nephew on the shoulder.

Maria bounced up and down in Charlotte's embrace. "We must begin planning the wedding immediately!"

"Maria wants to be married as soon as possible," Mr. Westfield explained. He paused. Another cough. "As do I, naturally."

"We will see to the license while the ladies plan the ceremony," Mr. Basford assured him with a glance at Charlotte. She felt heat rise in her cheeks, and she focused instead on her sister.

"First, we must see to a dress…."

The good news of Maria's engagement to Mr. Westfield spread around Westerham, and soon there were many callers wishing to congratulate them. Mr. Basford and Mr. Westfield had procured the license and the ceremony was set to take place in three weeks' time. The gentlemen were frequent callers at the cottage, and the sisters always looked forward to their arrival.

In her happiness, Charlotte had almost forgotten about Mr. Edgington's intended blackmail, but the threat had not yet passed.

৩৩ Sixteen ৩৩

It is said that bad news spreads quickly, but whoever first uttered those words probably did not realize that there was something that spread faster: pernicious gossip.

No one was quite certain how the story began, but everyone knew without a doubt that it was true. *Someone* had seen the glove. No one was quite sure who.

The only thing that was certain was that Charlotte Collins was a fallen woman.

The news came to Charlotte in this way: she was in the kitchen stitching new ribbons onto the dress Maria intended to wear on her wedding day when Mrs. Eff, who had been with Edward in town procuring foodstuffs for the household, arrived at the cottage looking very grim. She entered and immediately sent Edward to their chambers, which were adjacent to the kitchen, instead of requiring his help with the provisions. He disappeared through the open door, and Charlotte heard him moving about.

She looked at Mrs. Eff, whose face appeared pale. Immediately, she was concerned. "Mrs. Eff, are you ill?" For once she hoped for illness because the alternative was her own downfall.

"No, Mrs. Collins. Not ill. Just sick at heart."

Oh dear.

Charlotte pushed the ribbons and cloth aside and gestured for Mrs. Eff to sit at the table. "Do tell me what is the matter." She did not really want to hear what she knew must be forthcoming.

"Edward and I have heard the most dreadful news in town."

"Has someone died?" Now Charlotte hoped for a death. Please, a death.

Mrs. Eff sucked in a deep breath. "No one has died, but a reputation has perished."

Charlotte's fingers curled around the edge of the table. The story had begun to spread. She knew it with perfect certainty, but she asked anyway, "What do you mean?"

"Word has got out that," Mrs. Eff hesitated, looking down at the floor and then back at Charlotte, "well, that you committed an indiscretion with that awful Mr. Edgington. Someone said you gave him a glove as a memento."

Charlotte's hand tightened again on the table, and her knuckles turned white. Her eyes dropped to her lap, and she knew that her face flamed with anger and embarrassment.

"It is not true, is it, Mrs. Collins?" she paused for a quick breath, and then continued, "Well, it could not be true. I told Mrs. Sinclair that myself when she told me. I told her there was no possibility that an upstanding lady like you would do such a thing."

Charlotte shook her head, but could not speak, and to her horror, tears began sliding down her cheeks. What a weak and pitiful woman she was! She could not even bear up under the scrutiny of Mrs. Eff. Imagine how she might humiliate herself in public. She would have to become a recluse. There was no doubt.

Mrs. Eff leaned forward with a look of pity on her face. "Oh, my dear. Tell me what has happened."

Charlotte took a few moments to compose herself. The kitchen was silent, and Edward had stopped knocking about in his chamber. Everyone, it seemed, was awaiting an explanation that would vindicate her. She took a bracing breath, but still her voice shook. "I was completely deceived by Mr. Edgington. Completely and utterly deceived! I believed him to be a man of good character. But he is not."

Mrs. Eff's frown deepened as Charlotte relayed the entire story, including the stolen glove and Mr. Basford's role in the debacle. When she finished speaking, Mrs. Eff leaned back in her chair, and Charlotte let her head fall into her hands.

"Well, this is quite a fix indeed."

Charlotte massaged her temples, trying to relieve the pressure that bore down on her. "There is nothing to be done, I am afraid. Nothing. Now that the slander has become public, I am ruined."

"That is not true, Mrs. Collins. Everyone in Westerham knows your good character."

"Yes, but they will have no choice but to believe Mr. Edgington. In fact, they already believe it. You have said so yourself."

Mrs. Eff let out a frustrated breath. "I cannot believe that the rumor will persist when people begin to think logically about your character. None who knows you will believe such a thing for long."

"Will they not? You know as well as I that people do not think logically about gossip. What is heard is believed. It is as simple as that." Tears continued to fall down her cheeks and she swiped them away. "Everywhere I go, his lies will haunt me. Even if I leave Westerham, I will always look behind me."

"Surely you do not think he would follow you?"

"I do not believe so, but he is well traveled. Will he happen upon me in Hertfordshire and expose me there? If I go to Bath, will the story follow there as well? Can I go anywhere to be completely safe?"

Mrs. Eff considered for a moment, and then said, almost to herself, "As long as he has that glove, he might be able to convince others, but without that proof, his power is gone."

"If only I had not accepted those gloves in the first place..."

"You cannot go into the past and undo it now, but perhaps if we could get that glove back.... Do you have its mate?"

Charlotte hung her head. "No, I destroyed it the night of the ball."

"There must be some means by which to retrieve that glove," Mrs. Eff said. "Can you not think of a way?"

Charlotte had thought and thought of how to get that glove. Each of her schemes had ranged from the far-fetched—sneaking into his home and stealing the glove—to the utterly immoral—setting his home ablaze, and the glove with it.

"There is no way."

Mrs. Eff looked a bit deflated and pondered the situation for some minutes before asking, "Did anyone see you alone with Mr. Edgington at the ball?"

"I cannot be certain, but I believe only Mr. Basford observed us. Though anyone could have looked out onto the balcony without my notice."

"I do believe that Mr. Basford is a gentleman who can be trusted."

Charlotte looked up, her chin in her hands. "I hope so. I do not know anymore. The people I think I should trust seem to turn out to be unsavory, and those I mistrust at first meeting seem to be the true gentlemen."

"Is not that always the way?"

ॐ ॐ

Later that day, Maria returned from paying a call at the Armitage house and dropped her bonnet on the kitchen table where Charlotte was distracting herself by arranging a vase of flowers cut from her garden. Maria fluttered around the room, searching for a biscuit to assuage her appetite, and recounted the events of her afternoon. Her conversation barely registered in Charlotte's ears. It was quite plain to her that Maria had not heard the vicious gossip. Charlotte was relieved that word had not yet reached her, but she knew she would have to confide the whole sordid, embarrassing story to her.

Charlotte interrupted her sister's soliloquy regarding her impending nuptials. "Maria, sit down. I must tell you some news."

Oblivious to her sister's grim tone, Maria perched on one of the kitchen chairs and began idly touching the flowers before her. "I do hope it is delicious news, for I have had a delightful day. Is it news of a tender nature? Has a new couple formed an attachment?"

"No, indeed. It is not news of an attachment. In fact, it is the opposite."

"Oh, then do not tell me, for I am in no mood for ill news." Maria dropped a flower back into the vase.

"I am afraid you must hear this." Charlotte pushed the vase out of the way. "For it affects you."

"How can that be? I have done nothing to warrant the gossip of others. At least not recently."

Charlotte quieted Maria with a serious gaze. "I am afraid that I am the subject."

Charlotte recounted the story, attempting to conceal the seriousness of the issue from her younger sister, but Maria comprehended the situation fully. She listened in shock, her blue eyes large and watery on her sister's behalf, and then she lapsed into anger. Her porcelain-colored skin flushed red. She leapt from her chair and rushed to her sister's side and wrapped her arms around her.

"He is a monster! What kind of man would do such a thing?"

Charlotte's eyes filled with tears as she listened to her sister's outrage and felt her comforting arms around her. She was so quick to jump to her defense and had not even considered the repercussions to her own life.

Maria rocked Charlotte back and forth in her arms, repeating, "Poor, poor, Charlotte. You do not deserve this."

Charlotte pulled away gently, wiping the tears from her eyes. "Listen to me, Maria." She held her at arm's length so she could see her face. "This situation could affect you as well."

"What? How?" A look of genuine confusion crossed her face.

"Gossip is already spreading through town. Mrs. Eff and Edward heard this morning. It is but a matter of time before our friends and neighbors are acquainted with the terrible story. I am rather surprised that you did not hear of it while you were with the Armitages today."

"Oh dear, I had not thought...."

"And you know how things like this are wont to go. The gossip never affects just one person. It affects the entire family, I am sorry to say."

"What are you saying? How can this affect me?"

Charlotte, searching for delicate words, hesitated and then said, "People might believe that you engage in the same type of behaviors of which I am accused. Or at the very least, they will look down upon you because you are related to me. You may lose more friends over this."

"Lose friends? Over nothing? How could anyone believe this of you? Even if he does have that glove!"

"I do not want this to spoil your wedding. You deserve a perfect day."

A wistful expression crossed Maria's features. "I am safely engaged to Mr. Westfield and nothing will ruin my wedding. We are so blissfully happy. Until then, I will just ignore any gossip I hear."

Charlotte mustered a smile at her sister's bravery, or her foolishness, whichever it was.

The next week proceeded in the way Charlotte had expected. The story circulated through Westerham, and soon there was no one who had not heard of her supposed downfall. Visitors called on her, demanding to hear the truth of the matter. Some supported her, but a majority seemed to reject her. Still others shunned her, choosing to believe Mr. Edgington's story without first seeking her version of the event.

Soon the visits began to dwindle, and Charlotte could not decide whether to be relieved by the fact that she was no longer forced to defend herself to inconsiderate neighbors or to be upset because many of her acquaintances had chosen to believe Mr. Edgington's slander.

As the cottage became quiet, Charlotte became depressed. But when the next visitor arrived, she realized how utterly unprepared and completely naïve she herself had been.

Maria was on a drive with Mr. Westfield when a closed carriage, complete with gilded family crest and team of four perfectly matched steeds, rumbled ceremoniously into the drive. The sound attracted Charlotte to the window, and she drew away immediately at the sight, as though a view alone could injure her. And injure her it had, for she recognized the carriage as one belonging to Lady Catherine de Bourgh.

Charlotte withdrew further from the window and debated which room to choose to meet her inevitable doom. Perhaps she ought to go out and meet the carriage. Face her destruction head on. She took two steps toward the door and stopped.

No, she would not go like a lamb to the slaughter. Lady Catherine would come to her. It was the only power she retained: the power to inconvenience.

Charlotte arranged herself in the sitting room. She selected the high-backed chair by the fireplace, for it seemed the most regal, and she waited. She had hardly allowed herself to consider how Mr. Collins's former patroness and the proprietor of her rented cottage would react to the slander. Certainly, the encounter would not end well.

Mrs. Eff announced Lady Catherine, and the great lady swept into the room, skirts swirling in her wake. Charlotte contemplated keeping her seat, but then she stood. Her heart fluttered in her chest and her palms began to sweat, and suddenly, the world seemed to shrink as her vision closed in on her guest.

She closed her eyes, to regain her composure, and spoke. "Lady Catherine." The name held power, and Charlotte felt certain that merely speaking it aloud would unleash the plagues of the Day of Judgment.

When she dared to open her eyes, she saw no swarm of locusts or apocalyptic horsemen. The world was as it had been moments before, quiet and calm, only now a woman in severely fashionable attire stood before her.

"Mrs. Collins." Her voice was as severe as her attire.

"Will you sit?"

"No, I shall not! I do not hold pleasant discourse with women such as you."

Charlotte sat. She might as well be comfortable when the ill news was delivered.

"A report of an alarming nature has reached me."

"Has it?" Charlotte attempted indifference. "I find it surprising that you would come to me with gossip."

Lady Catherine's eyes narrowed, and her face hardened into planes and steep ridges. "It has come to my attention that the state of your morality has declined drastically."

"I am afraid that your information is incorrect, for my morality is as it has always been."

"The unmitigated gall!" Lady Catherine strode across the room and stopped only just before her skirts brushed Charlotte's knees.

"I have researched the matter fully. My relation has shared with me the evidence—a glove bearing your very initials."

Here Charlotte attempted a protest, but words failed and Lady Catherine continued.

"This debauched behavior is completely unacceptable in anyone associated with the family of de Bourgh. You have left me with no choice but to sever all ties with you and your relations and to request your removal from this cottage." She looked around her as if Charlotte's supposed ill deeds had sullied the very walls around them. "Vacate my property before a month has passed."

Lady Catherine turned with the intention of sweeping from the room, but Charlotte stood. "You do not offer me the benefit of a reply?"

The older lady spun on her heel. "Certainly not. Mr. Edgington is of the house of de Bourgh and has no reason to speak falsely. I trust him." Again, she attempted a dramatic exit.

"Folly indeed."

Lady Catherine stopped. Charlotte stopped. The world stopped.

"Mrs. Collins, I am sorry that the situation has come to this." She sounded anything but apologetic. "I hope you will find your way back to the straight and narrow path of which your husband, the Reverend Collins, often preached."

To this message Charlotte had no reply.

It was the apocalypse of Lady Catherine, and unlike God, she had no mercy.

✤ Seventeen ✤

As Maria prepared for her wedding, Charlotte quietly prepared to depart from the cottage and return to Lucas Lodge a fallen and humiliated old widow. Her reputation was completely and utterly ruined in Westerham, and finding comfortable and affordable lodgings in town was unlikely, especially with the poor reference of Lady Catherine. Indeed, she had no desire to remain in a place that was hostile toward her, despite her need to vindicate herself.

She informed Mrs. Eff and Edward that she would have to do without their services and began to pack her few and precious books into a trunk. She did not want to remain at her parents' home forever. She had become accustomed to her independence and she could not bring herself to abandon it, even if it meant that she would live in a small abode, with no servants, and little meat. Doing without was preferable to being a burden and a source of shame to her family.

Maria came upon Charlotte as she was putting the last of her books in the trunk. "Whatever are you doing, Charlotte?"

She looked up from her task, startled. Maria was watching her with confused, concerned eyes.

"Packing my books."

"Well, that is quite obvious, but why?"

Charlotte closed the lid of the trunk, inhaling as the scent of paper and printer's ink wafted into the air. She found it impossible to explain the full truth of her financial situation to her sister, and moreover, she was unwilling to burden her with her troubles right before her wedding. So she simply said, "I hope you will not think me a weak person when I tell you this, but I have decided to return to Hertfordshire. I cannot live with the specter of Mr. Edgington's slander."

"Oh, Charlotte…" Pity was evident in her voice, and Charlotte interrupted her.

"Do not feel sorry for me. I am content with this decision. I will be near Mama and Papa, and I will be in the company of longtime friends. And with a good measure of luck, Mr. Edgington will never visit."

Maria's eyes were wide with concern, and she thought for a long moment before speaking again. "Although I am sad that you have made this decision, I must say that I approve. I would worry about you here alone. Lord knows what Mr. Edgington is capable of doing."

"Do not worry about me, Maria, wherever I am. I am a resilient person, and I will recover and rise above each new problem." Charlotte hoped her words would convince both her sister and herself.

"If anyone can survive, I know it is you. You are the strongest woman I know."

Charlotte gave her sister an encouraging smile, although she did not believe her, for at that precise moment, she felt herself to be the weakest of the weak and the poorest of the poor. She felt incapable of carrying her trunks down the stairs much less being able to carry the burdens her new life must impart.

But Charlotte forced a smile. "I am only sorry that I will not have the pleasure of receiving you and your new husband when you call on me here."

"We will call on you wherever you are. No matter where Mr. Westfield and I live, even if it is the farthest reaches of America, I will always write. Every day."

"As will I."

A bit teary, Maria took her leave, and Charlotte continued to pack her things alone. She moved through the tasks without much conscious thought, for such serious contemplation only led to sorrow.

✦❧ ❧✦

Days passed and Charlotte hardly seemed to notice. She received no visitors and was loathe to go into Westerham, so she was pleased when Mr. Basford called on her.

In fact, she almost burst into tears when she saw him riding toward her cottage with Mr. Westfield. He looked so strong and gentlemanly astride his tall bay horse. He was dressed in the same rather unfashionable attire as usual, and beside the dapper Mr. Westfield, he looked rather rough, but Charlotte saw him with new eyes.

She and Maria received them in the sitting room, which was now somewhat more bare thanks to Charlotte's packing efforts. The gentlemen did not mark the lack of accessories. Charlotte counted herself fortunate that gentlemen rarely take note of such things. A lady would have recognized the lack and commented immediately.

The conversation, mostly on the subject of the fine weather and the upcoming wedding, was strained as the four pretended that nothing was amiss.

Mr. Basford chatted amiably, keeping the conversation on the lighter side. The four laughed, but behind it was a sort of anxious restraint. Neither Mr. Westfield nor Mr. Basford ever mentioned the ugly gossip, and Charlotte was thankful. She could not bear to speak of it to one more person, and she certainly could not discuss it in front of her sister's betrothed.

When the gentlemen prepared to mount their horses and take their leave, Mr. Basford took Charlotte's hand in his, giving it a gentle squeeze. When she met his eyes, his gaze was warm and sincere, and she felt that warmth and sincerity to her core. She felt his unspoken support and was very thankful indeed.

Maria and Charlotte stood at the window and watched Mr. Basford and Mr. Westfield ride away. The sisters stood so close that their elbows touched, their silence companionable and relaxed. Despite the tension that had existed during their time together, Charlotte was sorry to see them go. She regretted not being able to have a private moment with Mr. Basford, but his visit had managed to give her a measure of strength. Still, she wondered at Mr.

Westfield's relative quiet during the conversation. Usually an avid conversationalist, he had been polite, but not as talkative as usual.

"That was rather awkward at first, was it not?"

"Do not trouble yourself. All is well," Maria watched the gentlemen's progress down the path.

"Mr. Westfield, in particular, remained rather quiet, do not you think?"

"Perhaps he spoke a bit less than usual, but I see no cause for concern."

"I cannot help but worry. My situation has caused so much strife already, and I would hate to think that it would ruin—"

"Do not even say it!" Maria faced Charlotte, "Mr. Westfield is simply tired from the wedding preparations. That is all."

"But I still worry."

"If Mr. Westfield truly loves me, then nothing—not a thousand Mr. Edgingtons—would prevent our marriage. So you see, nothing you have done—or not done—can hinder our marriage."

Charlotte hoped Mr. Westfield's love was as strong as he had led Maria to believe, but only a week before their nuptials, the reasons for his awkwardness became known.

Charlotte was working the garden, gleaning the late summer flowers and preparing the garden for the autumn. It was foolish, Charlotte knew, to tend her plants when she would be vacating the property in only two weeks' time. But still, she could not stop herself. Chopping flowers off their stalks and hacking in the dirt provided a somewhat ladylike method for relieving her tension and venting her frustrations. She had just beheaded a rather pretty rose when she heard footsteps approaching at a rapid pace. Charlotte turned, the rose still in hand, and saw Mrs. Eff hurrying down the path with Edward following behind. Her bonnet had fallen from its place on her head and hung on only by its ribbon, and between her swirling skirts and the dust kicked up by her boots, Edward was almost obscured.

Charlotte stood, her knees protesting at her sudden movement, and she dropped the rose in the direction of her basket. It fell instead onto the ground, but she took no notice. "Mrs. Eff!" she called out in surprise. "What is the matter?"

Mrs. Eff stopped before her, unable to speak for want of breath. She held up her hand to halt Charlotte's questioning momentarily. Charlotte looked to Edward, who was breathing less heavily. The lines on his young face conveyed his concern.

"Maria…" he said. "So sad."

Charlotte's eyes flew to Mrs. Eff, who quickly shushed Edward. "Where is Miss Maria?" she asked in a strained voice.

Charlotte looked around her. "Still in the kitchen, I suppose. I left her working on her wedding attire. What has happened?"

Mrs. Eff raised a shaking hand to her forehead. "Oh Lord…. I hate to be the bearer of ill news."

"What is it?" she whispered, as though Maria might be able to hear her through the walls. Somehow, though, Charlotte already knew. There could be little doubt that Mr. Edgington's slander had caused more damage. And to Maria this time. But what was the nature of this damage? Please, God, do not let it be the wedding.

"Mr. Westfield and Miss Farmington disappeared sometime last night," Mrs. Eff said.

"What?" Charlotte asked, momentarily confused.

"They have eloped. At least that is the appearance."

Charlotte knew that the potential for disaster had existed in their circumstances, but this was an eventuality she had not expected. Mr. Westfield had eloped. With Miss Farmington. It was inconceivable.

But as Charlotte considered their state of affairs, everything became clear. Events crystallized in her mind. This explained Mr. Westfield's odd behavior when he and Mr. Basford had last called. Even then, he had no intention of following through with his engagement to Maria. The cur! And he could not very well call off their engagement, for such a thing was not done. Instead he chose to flee, leaving Maria again in shame and embarrassment.

And it was all Charlotte's fault. Mr. Edgington's scheme was ruining her life and now her sister's as well.

"Oh dear." Charlotte could think of nothing else to say. "Oh dear, oh dear, oh dear."

Edward repeated, "Oh dear, oh dear."

"Mr. Basford left at first light to attempt to recover them."

Charlotte could not even offer one more lame "oh dear," for her voice was now gone.

"It all seems so sudden, but it must have been brewing for quite a while," Mrs. Eff said. "Mr. Westfield had us all fooled, even his uncle, it seems."

Mrs. Eff was waiting for a reply, and all Charlotte could think to say was "Poor, poor Maria."

"I am so sorry. She will be inconsolable."

They stood in silence for a long moment. Charlotte attempted to gather her thoughts. What was she to do? How was she to break such news to her sister? Maria loved Mr. Westfield. It would break her poor heart.

Perhaps it was all a mistake. "How did you come to find this out?" Charlotte asked.

"You are well aware of the manner in which news travels in Westerham, through servants especially. I had to hurry so that Maria would hear it from you instead of from someone on the street. The vultures are gathering." She took a deep breath. "Miss Eames at the Farmington's said she saw the young lady enter Mr. Westfield's carriage very late last night. She saw it with her own eyes."

It was doubtful, then, that it was a mistake. Servants may exaggerate the goings-on in their households, but if Mrs. Eff believed this Miss Eames, then it must be true.

"Thank you for coming here to warn us." Charlotte paused. "Do you know why…why he left Maria?"

"You mean, does it have anything to do with Mr. Edgington's falsehoods?"

Charlotte nodded, fear clutching her heart at the knowledge that she had ruined her sister's chance at love. Mrs. Eff's face conveyed the truth though she did not speak a word. Charlotte groaned. Everyone found the ground fascinating for several moments.

Charlotte tried to be sensible. "Even the best of men might be persuaded to leave a good woman in the face of such a scandal in the family."

Mrs. Eff's face became a mixture of sorrow and pity, and struggling with her emotions, Charlotte only nodded. The fault was indeed hers.

No! The fault lay with the depraved Mr. Edgington, and as guilty as Charlotte felt, she must force herself to remember that fact. She had done nothing worse than trusting the wrong gentleman. Many a woman had made such a mistake, yet they did not suffer such public humiliation.

Mrs. Eff finally found her voice. "I cannot say for certain the cause of Mr. Westfield's actions. Some people say that he simply got his head turned by Miss Farmington, and some say that Mr. Edgington's story caused him to begin to doubt Miss Maria's morality."

"I do not like Mr. Edgington," Edward said. "He is unkind. And Miss Maria is sweet."

Edward was correct. Maria did not deserve such ill treatment. Charlotte winced at the pain she would suffer. Mrs. Eff hastened to say, "But that is all just conjecture. Who is to know what a man such as him could be thinking? The truth is that only Mr. Westfield knows for certain. It is impossible to know his reasons for such treachery without consulting the villain himself, and at the moment, he is nowhere to be found."

"Perhaps Mr. Basford will find him," Charlotte speculated, "but the damage is already done. She will be heartbroken."

Maria rounded the corner of the house and entered the garden. "Who will be heartbroken?"

Charlotte, Mrs. Eff, and Edward stared at her dumbly for a moment.

Mrs. Eff took Edward's hand. "Perhaps we should go."

Maria stopped them. "Oh no. Do not leave on my account. Now that you are no longer in our service, you must stay and chat with Charlotte and me. We are lonely here without you!"

Mrs. Eff looked to Charlotte, who nodded slightly, granting permission to stay, needing her support.

"Now tell me the gossip from town." Maria picked up the rose Charlotte had dropped and twirled it between her fingertips. "It will be a relief to hear something other than these heinous lies about Charlotte."

Mrs. Eff grimaced. "My dear, I am finding that gossip does no good for anyone. It is getting so that no news brings me pleasure anymore."

"What do you mean?"

Charlotte took Maria's hand, halting the twirling of the flower. "The news that Mrs. Eff has just related to me concerns Mr. Westfield."

"Oh?" A hint of worry colored her voice.

Charlotte was unsure of exactly how to divulge such sensitive information. "It seems that he has left Westerham."

"Perhaps he has gone on his uncle's business in London." Maria tried to be sensible. It saddened Charlotte all the more.

"I am afraid not," Charlotte paused and took a deep breath. "It seems that he has disappeared and taken Miss Farmington with him."

"What?" Maria shook her blond head.

Thankfully, Mrs. Eff spoke. "It is believed that they have eloped." Her voice was soft and gentle, and Charlotte was glad that she had been the one to bring the truth to light. She could not seem to find the words that would break her sister's heart.

Maria's fingers tightened around the stem of the rose and the blossom trembled slightly in her grasp. "No, I do not believe that. Mr. Westfield and Miss Farmington? The very idea is preposterous. Mr. Westfield loves me. He is engaged to me." Maria looked from Mrs. Eff to Charlotte. "He loves me. He does."

Charlotte grasped her hand in both of hers. "We know nothing for certain. That is only what Mrs. Eff heard in Westerham." Her words were meant to soothe, but Charlotte doubted their veracity. "She thought you should hear it from us first and not from someone else."

"It is no matter. It is not true." The stem of the rose bent in her grasp. "I will not believe it until I have proof of it from Mr. Westfield himself. Until then, we must assume that the wedding will proceed on schedule."

Maria lifted her chin resolutely and began to walk toward the front of the house, but then turned around. "I will believe nothing ill of Mr. Westfield. He loves me."

Charlotte wondered just whom she attempted to convince.

Mrs. Eff, Edward, and Charlotte stood in silence, listening to the swish of Maria's footsteps along the path.

"I hope she's correct in her faith in him," Mrs. Eff said.

Charlotte nodded. "As do I."

But neither of them held out any true hope.

❧❧ ❧❧

For the next few days, the cottage was rather quiet, and Maria's behavior could only be described as stoic. Charlotte was as impressed by Maria's fortitude as she was concerned about her refusal to acknowledge her true circumstances. Maria appeared to move through her days as usual, without tears, and always speaking well of Mr. Westfield. She was unusually helpful around the cottage. She assisted Charlotte's packing efforts and took long walks in the garden and surrounding woodlands, but she did not go into town.

Then, a letter arrived from Mr. Westfield.

Charlotte watched as Maria took it to her room, her face impassive. She did not return for several hours, and Charlotte thought it best to give her time to digest whatever news the missive contained.

She could very well guess its contents.

It was full dark when Maria entered the sitting room and took the chair opposite her sister. Her face showed the effects of tears, but she was no longer crying.

They sat in silence for many moments, and Charlotte was loath to speak, fearing what she would hear once the conversation began.

Finally, Maria spoke. Her voice was very soft, but it did not crack with emotion as Charlotte had expected. "I am no longer engaged to Mr. Westfield." Charlotte blinked at the detachment of Maria's voice. The sad words were simply stated as though she had just said, "Dinner is at seven," or "The weather is quite fine today."

Charlotte approached Maria's chair, not sure what to do or say. Kneeling before her, she took her hand. "I am so sorry, Maria."

Maria began to stroke the back of Charlotte's hand as she spoke. "So am I. But there is nothing to be done. He and Miss Farmington have eloped."

"Oh my dear…" Charlotte dropped her head into Maria's lap. Everything was ruined. They were both doomed to return in disgrace to their parents' home in Hertfordshire. Worse, neither of them would find love or security now that Mr. Edgington's damage had been done.

"His letter was very kind."

"Oh, well, at least he was kind."

Charlotte felt Maria stiffen and then relax. She said, "Do not be cruel, Charlotte. I do not believe Mr. Westfield meant any harm. He just went about things the wrong way."

How could she forgive him? she asked herself. Then Charlotte realized the reason. Any anger must be shared between her suitor and her sister, for she had been the cause of the problem. "The fault is mine." She raised her head to look into her sister's eyes. They were calm and almost peaceful, but she read the truth of the matter there.

"Do not blame yourself, Charlotte—"

Charlotte could not fathom the idea that the two events were unconnected. There were just too many mitigating circumstances for her to continue to believe the best of Mr. Westfield. It was far too coincidental that Mr. Edgington's lies would become public and shortly thereafter Mr. Westfield would break their engagement.

"I cannot help but blame myself. All the facts support my supposition. Had Mr. Edgington never come into my life, you would not be in this situation."

Maria pushed stray hairs from her sister's forehead. "I will tell you the truth. In his letter, he did say that he preferred not to join himself to such a scandal."

Tears fell down Charlotte's cheeks. Her sister's future happiness was ruined along with her own. Together, they would be ostracized from society. "I am so terribly sorry. So sorry."

Maria lifted Charlotte's chin. "Listen to me, Charlotte. Do you know what I think? I think Mr. Westfield is just using Mr. Edgington's slander as an excuse."

Charlotte studied her with confused, teary eyes. "What could you possibly mean?"

"I do not believe he ever loved me."

Charlotte stared, perplexed. Why would he have proposed if he had not loved her? She did not have a large dowry or a lofty title. "Of course, he loved you."

"As depressing a thought as it is, I believe it is true." Her voice was breezy. "I do not think he ever loved me. When I first read the letter, I was outraged. I cried and wanted to kill him and Miss Farmington, but then I began to recall all our past interactions. Suddenly, I felt calm. I could see what had been before me all along. It was such a strange sensation. I do not believe that I have ever thought so clearly." She seemed to ponder that for a moment. "I realized that he was always very attentive to Miss Farmington and that he only called upon me when Mr. Basford called upon you as well."

"What nonsense. Mr. Westfield wanted to call on you. Mr. Basford was merely a chaperone."

"Oh, I think Mr. Westfield had some interest in me at first, but he soon gravitated toward Miss Farmington. And why wouldn't he? She has a far bigger dowry, and she is a determined flirt."

Yes, Charlotte could well believe that. She had witnessed Miss Farmington's flirtatious behavior, although she wondered why any man would have an interest in a woman with such horse-like features. Even with the inducement of a dowry. "Then why did he propose to you?"

Maria paused, considering. "I do not know, but I am glad that we are no longer engaged. I certainly do not want to marry someone who does not love me."

Charlotte tried to recall what she had observed in Mr. Westfield, but her mind did not seem to be functioning. There was too much information to process. One thing only nagged at her. "You do not blame me then?"

"How could I possibly blame you? You have done nothing wrong."

"I trusted an untrustworthy man, and as a result you may have lost Mr. Westfield and I have lost my home."

Maria started. "What? Lost your home? What do you mean? You told me that you had elected to leave Westerham. Voluntarily."

Charlotte had not meant to break the news in so clumsy a fashion, but the words had simply slipped out. She hesitated, trying to think of a way to cover her error.

"Tell me," Maria demanded. "The truth. I am so weary of lies."

"Lady Catherine heard Mr. Edgington's gossip, and she revoked the lease on this cottage."

"That old bat!" Her voice was indignant and high-pitched.

Charlotte considered reprimanding her for not showing respect for those higher in society, but she refrained. Lady Catherine was an old bat.

"It is very unfair of her to punish you for something you would never do."

Charlotte attempted a practical reply. "It was within her rights to withdraw from our agreement. I cannot blame her."

"Bah! I shall blame her on your behalf."

"And I shall blame Mr. Westfield on your behalf."

Maria laughed softly, and Charlotte was pleased to hear the sound. "I think that is an even exchange."

They sat silently for a while. Charlotte's heart ached for her sister and for her own predicament. She and Maria had no recourse now but to slink home in disgrace.

As if reading her mind, Maria asked, "Is Lady Catherine's regrettable decision the true reason that you are returning home to Hertfordshire?"

"While I did not relish staying here to fight the gossip that surrounds me, Westerham has become my home. I have lived here for years, and I had no wish to leave it. Unfortunately, Lady Catherine has left me no choice. I can no longer live here and it will be some time before I am able to discover such agreeable accommodations on my small income."

Maria's brow furrowed. "But you will never be satisfied living at Lucas Lodge."

"No…"

"Neither would I." Maria paused. "What are we going to do? Surely, you do not intend to seek out another Mr. Collins."

"No indeed." The thought of an expeditious marriage had briefly—oh so briefly—crossed her mind. Ever since the news of Mr. Westfield's elopement had reached her, Charlotte knew that she must do more than simply disappear into Hertfordshire. She must help provide for them both since their parents' income had become so limited. "Must we discuss this now?"

"Yes, we absolutely must! Now, tell me what you are planning. I can tell there is more, and I can tell it is dreadful."

"I may have no choice but to seek employment." Charlotte observed the shock in her sister's wide eyes. "Perhaps an elderly lady in Hertfordshire requires a companion."

Charlotte knew that her parents had not the inclination to house two grown daughters, and she had no desire to become a burden to them, or to allow Maria to become so, especially since the dissolution of her engagement had been solely Charlotte's fault. She must support herself and her sister. It was her duty.

But it was impossible on her income. Lady Catherine's discounted lease fee had allowed her to live in such relative luxury. In any other circumstances, she would have been living in a tiny home with no servants at all.

Though she hated to acknowledge the fact, it was becoming painfully clear that employment was the solution. The idea was not as unbearable as the idea of a loveless marriage, for Charlotte was not afraid of toil. But what type of employment ought she seek? There were so few professions available to a woman like her. Governess, companion, or tutor: those were her choices. And they were not entirely objectionable. Now if only she could find someone willing to hire her, she could be somewhat content.

But Maria did not share her resignation to employment. A stern look crossed Maria's soft features. "You cannot be serious."

"It is a perfectly acceptable form of employment for someone of my position."

"Indeed it is, but Charlotte, you deserve so much more."

"Do I?"

"Of course you do! You deserve to have a proper husband, whom you love. A proper house and a companion of your own, if you like."

"You are only saying these things because we are related. I am no more special than anyone else."

"To me, you are special. Perhaps my reason lies in the fact that you are my sister, but I say this also because you are a worthy woman."

Charlotte smiled at her sister's vehement defense of her. "Thank you. You are very kind. But there is nothing to be done about it now."

Maria's look became quite determined.

"Indeed there is something to be done about it, and if you refuse to acknowledge that fact, then I suppose it will be up to someone else."

ஒ Eighteen ஒ

"Good afternoon, Mr. Basford." Charlotte stood and brushed the dirt from her hands. It was the Tuesday after Maria's wedding was to have taken place and less than a week before they had to vacate the cottage at Lady Catherine's request.

He bowed. "Mrs. Collins." Was she imagining it, or did his posture show contrition?

Charlotte had not expected him, nor had she expected the anticipation that rose in her as she had looked over her shoulder and seen him coming down the path toward her. From a distance, he had looked quite well put together in a deep brown coat and tan breeches, but as he drew nearer, she saw that he looked somewhat disheveled. More disheveled than usual. His face seemed drawn, and tired lines surrounded his eyes.

For a moment, he stood facing her. Then he turned abruptly and paced a few steps away. She watched and wondered what his odd behavior could possibly signify. She was already aware of the situation with Mr. Westfield and Miss Farmington—Mrs. Westfield, she corrected herself. "If you are here to inform me of a relationship between your nephew and Miss Farmington, I have already heard. Do not trouble yourself. All is well."

"Mmm..." Mr. Basford turned on his heel and looked at Charlotte. "I know this does not conform to proper English etiquette, but I would like very much to sit down." He laughed. "And I could really do with a cup of tea."

"I believe, as the fallen woman I am reputed to be, I am well past the need for meaningless etiquette at the moment, Mr. Basford. Do come inside."

He followed her into the cottage. They walked past the trunks and bandboxes in the hallway, and Charlotte hoped that he was too distracted to notice. She did not desire to explain the cheerless turn her life had taken. After they walked by the sad evidence in the hall, she gestured to the sitting room, offering him a seat and telling him that she would go fetch the tea.

When she returned with the tea tray balanced in her hands, Mr. Basford was standing with his back to the room. His attention was focused out the window, and he did not realize that Charlotte had entered until she set the tray down on the table with a gentle thud. He turned around and looked at her, his gaze softening.

"Tea?"

Charlotte poured his tea, handed it to him, and watched as he took a sip.

A look of satisfaction crossed his handsome features, and she was tempted to joke that England had affected him more than he cared to admit. Instead, she gestured to a chair, and he sat. "When did you develop such an affinity for tea?"

He smiled, put his teacup back on the saucer, and tipped the chair on its back legs. "As you once reminded me, Americans enjoy tea as well."

"Ah, but you claimed that you did not."

"Perhaps since being in England I have begun to appreciate it more." He echoed her previous thoughts.

They sipped in silence and a sort of uncomfortable feeling descended upon the room. Mr. Basford, too, looked rather unsettled.

Finally, Charlotte set down her cup and decided to plunge into the conversation they had been avoiding. She cleared her throat. "How does Mr. Westfield do? I understand that he is now happily married."

Chair legs hit the ground with a thunk, and Mr. Basford placed his cup on the table. He looked abashed.

She sought to reassure him. "Pray, do not concern yourself about what has happened between my sister and your nephew."

"How can I not concern myself?" His countenance was sad.

"You have done your part to rectify the matter. Did you not search for him after he and Miss Farmington disappeared?"

"Indeed, I did. It was the only thing I could do."

He stood and began pacing the room again. The furniture fairly shook under his heavy strides. Charlotte wished she could command him to sit, if only to save the floorboards. But they were Lady Catherine's floorboards, she thought with a dash of spite, so she allowed him to pace and hoped he would wear a path in the wood.

"And did you discover them?"

"Yes. I am sorry to say that they had eloped to Gretna Green. A dreadful process and so far below what was expected of him." He looked at her briefly. His brown eyes, altered by the discontent they held, seemed darker. "His mother is going to be so disappointed."

Charlotte sat back on the settee. She had secretly hoped that it had all been an unattractive rumor. But it was not, and the last vestiges of pointless hope, which she had held out for Maria's sake, drained away. "Oh."

He returned to his seat, tipped it back. "They returned to Westerham with me last night."

Charlotte did not know quite what to say. She was pleased that they had returned safely for his family's sake, but she felt pain for her sister. She managed to say only "Mmmm."

"They intend to travel to Savannah in the coming weeks."

"Will they make their home there?" She hoped for Maria's sake that they would.

"No, my nephew is quite enamored with England, and Miss Farmington." He paused, realizing that he had not used her proper name, but he didn't correct himself. "She says she cannot bear to part from her family. They will make their home here."

"I see." She hoped she sounded noncommittal and wondered what would become of Mr. Basford. His duties as chaperone had been completed. Would he too return to America? Would he ever venture back to English soil?

Before she could inquire, he stood abruptly and began pacing again. "I am so sorry, Mrs. Collins. I am sorry for what I have done to you and your sister."

His words surprised her. "What have you to be sorry for?"

He ran his hands through his hair. "I am responsible for the entire situation."

Confused, Charlotte began to twist the fabric of her skirt in her hands and tried to work out what to say next. "You cannot be responsible for Mr. Westfield's decisions."

"No, but I believe I had undue influence over his choice to propose to Maria."

She endeavored to read his face, but he had turned aside, giving her only a view of his tight profile. "What do you mean?"

Mr. Basford walked a few more paces and then faced her. The light from the window streamed around his body. "I mean that after that…" His voice tapered off as he no doubt searched for the proper epithet to use in company. "…fool Edgington began spreading those lies about you, I felt…." He paused again and ran his hand through his hair, leaving it even messier. "Well, I felt the need to take action. I knew you'd be very upset about the gossip, and after seeing people's reaction when Maria turned down Mr. Card, I had an idea of how the town would respond. I also knew that you were more concerned for your sister than for yourself. I wanted to help. I thought it would be helpful."

"I am afraid I do not understand."

"I encouraged James to propose to Maria."

"You mentioned that when we last spoke."

"No. I *encouraged* him." He said the word as if it were poison.

"What?"

"I sensed his reluctance." He paused in his speech but continued pacing. He faced the settee again. "But I genuinely thought he was in love with her."

Charlotte stood. What was he trying to say? "Did you force Mr. Westfield to propose to Maria?"

"No, I did not force him, but I did encourage him."

Sorrow and confusion rose in her, and Charlotte warred against them. There was no sense in allowing her feelings to overcome her. Emotional behavior would do her no good, and it certainly would not improve her reputation. But she thought of Maria and the valiant way she was accepting her situation. Perhaps she would not have been so upset if Maria had been upstairs crying, but the serene way she accepted the circumstances absolutely broke her heart. Maria had lost hope, and that was the worst of all possible outcomes.

Charlotte knew not how best to respond.

"I was thinking of you." His gaze was direct and unwavering, causing Charlotte's breath to catch. "I knew how concerned you were about how the gossip would affect your sister."

"I was naturally anxious given the circumstances in which I found myself," Charlotte managed to say, "but I certainly did not want anyone forced to marry Maria."

"I did not intend to force him to propose. I did not think myself to be doing so. I believed him to be in love with her. Confess. You believed it to be so as well. Did you not?"

Charlotte could not lie. "I hoped he loved her."

"I believed it was a match of mutual love. Otherwise I would not have acted as I did."

Charlotte believed him. The pain in his expression was genuine. She had just cause to be angry and hurt, but she found that she could be neither. Her common sense would not allow it. "Mr. Basford, you have always shown yourself to be an honorable gentleman of the highest morals, and I believe that the actions you took in this situation were the result of your good intentions. I am sorry that my sister was injured, but, pray, do not hold yourself accountable. Mr. Westfield is solely to blame."

They stood a moment in silence, and Mr. Basford seemed to relax. The tension left his shoulders, and his hands unclenched and fell loosely at his sides. He returned to his seat and picked up his teacup like a civilized gentleman and not the barbarian who had stalked the room moments ago, and Charlotte followed his lead, picking up her teacup and sipping daintily. The tea was cool.

"Miss Lucas's heart will mend, although it may not seem likely now."

Charlotte was not sure if he sought to reassure her or himself.

"It is not her heart that concerns me but her hope. She has lost hope, I think."

Mr. Basford's expression changed to one of pity. "I am sorry for that."

"As am I."

They sat a moment, drinking tepid tea, while Charlotte considered her next words carefully. "I do not know how to say this without giving the appearance of rudeness, so I will be frank. I believe it would be best if you were not here when Maria returns." He began to protest, but she interrupted him. "She may not appreciate a reminder of Mr. Westfield so soon."

He nodded. "I do understand. Perhaps I may call on you again, while Maria is absent of course."

Charlotte thought for a moment. She knew what she must do. She must raise herself above suspicion, and to do that she would be forced to sever their friendship, though in merely contemplating the decision, she felt as though she were severing a vital part of herself. Refusing to meet his eyes, she spoke. "Despite my great appreciation for the kindness you have shown me and for the friendship that has grown between us, my reputation is fragile. I hope you will understand when I say that it might be for the best if we do not meet privately again."

He set down his cup. Upon hearing it hit the table, she looked up. His face displayed his disappointment. For a moment, they sat, frozen. Neither moving or speaking. Charlotte wondered if he too wanted to make their final moments, though uncomfortable, last longer. Then, he stood slowly, his body tight again and his hands clenched. "I am sorry to hear that."

Charlotte desperately wanted to snatch her words back, to invite him to call as soon as was convenient. But she could not. She was leaving Westerham, and even if she could remain, it would be inappropriate for them to meet again. She remained silent, and he took his leave of her with a nod and perfunctory words of parting.

Apparently, he did not understand.

Charlotte listened as his crisp footsteps retreated, paused, and then returned.

She rose as he reentered the room. "Mr. Basford?"

He ignored her questioning tone completely and asked a question of his own. "What are all these trunks?"

"They are not your concern." She looked away momentarily, but he pushed onward, walking toward her. His facial expression was hard and then softened.

When he spoke again, his voice was quiet, and it brought color to Charlotte's cheeks. "Tell me. You're not leaving Westerham, are you?"

"I must."

"And that is why you brought the tea and not Mrs. Eff. She is already gone, isn't she?"

"I had no other option, but to dismiss Mrs. Eff and Edward."

"Of course, you do. I know Edgington's lies have done some damage, but leaving now and dismissing your servants will only confirm people's suspicions."

"Truly, I have no other choice."

"You always have a choice."

Charlotte clenched her hands and stared at him, uncertain of how much to confess. She chose to confess all. What could it hurt? She had nothing left. "Mr. Edgington's slander has reached my proprietress, Lady Catherine de Bourgh. After Mr. Collins died, she graciously provided this cottage for me at a reduced rate, but she prefers not to house a fallen woman."

Mr. Basford rocked back on his heels.

"I can no longer afford to employ Mrs. Eff and Edward. They have not been here in weeks. I miss them," she added wistfully, then sobered. "I must vacate this lovely cottage soon."

Mr. Basford's eyes were focused on the floor. "Where will you go?"

The kindness of his voice made Charlotte resent her pitiful situation. "I must go to my parents' home to Hertfordshire and take Maria with me. She certainly cannot stay in Westerham alone." Charlotte again debated how much she should divulge, but his kind eyes drew her onward. "I will seek employment. Eventually, perhaps I will be able to lease my own home, but I will always mourn my cottage here."

"I am sorry. I did not realize…." Mr. Basford's voice trailed off into quiet.

Charlotte continued, now eager to share her feelings once she had begun: "I was so pleased when Mr. Westfield proposed, for it meant that Maria would be spared my indignity. Now, she must return home with me."

"Surely the situation is not so dire."

Charlotte sighed. "Not dire. But Maria will live far below what she deserves."

"And so will you."

He appeared genuinely sad.

"Pray do not concern yourself with me. I shall be fine." She attempted to steel herself against the need she felt for his kindness and compassion. She would soon depart, and in all probability, she would not see him again. She must learn to do without his friendship.

"And this is why I am not invited to call on you? Because you're leaving?" His eyes were wide, searching hers for the truth.

Charlotte lowered hers.

She wished that her departure was the only reason she should reject his visits, but it was not. She would not lie to him, but she did not desire to injure him. She said nothing, and eventually she gathered the courage to look at him.

Their eyes met and held for what seemed like many minutes, and then, with a nod, he turned and walked out of the room.

She did not want to feel remorse at his departure, but she went to the window and watched Mr. Basford—his back straight, his stride long and ground-covering—walking away from her cottage. She would not see him again, and the thought did not appeal to her.

She had liked him.

She had liked him very much indeed.

◈ Nineteen ◈

Charlotte and Maria walked in the garden together. Both ladies had needed the time out of doors and a bit of physical activity to refresh their depressed spirits. Maria had been very quiet during the duration of their stroll and seemed not to be affected at all by the sunlight or surroundings, and Charlotte spent the time attempting to memorize the cottage and its garden. She committed each flower to memory, each leaf and color. Charlotte had installed most of the plants and cultivated them with her own hands. She learned by heart each stone of the cottage walls. She felt sure that the smooth brown stones would go with her in her memory no matter where her life led her.

Charlotte cast a sidelong glance at Maria. Her blond hair blew around her face and her dress wrapped itself around her ankles, making her gait seem labored. Her expression remained tense, with tiny frown lines around her mouth. Concerned that the fresh air had done nothing for her sister's spirits, Charlotte felt certain that Maria would benefit from a cup of tea and some biscuits to lighten her mood. She was about to suggest that they return inside when she heard the sound of a carriage approaching.

They turned to see it enter the drive, a dust cloud trailing behind.

A team of gray horses trotted in front of a familiar barouche, their large, well-muscled bodies easily pulling it along. The sound of their hooves was rhythmic and somehow soothing, and some of Charlotte's anxiety was carried away by the cadence.

Charlotte looked at Maria, who stared at the carriage as it drew ever closer. Her body seemed to go lax. She whispered, "It is Mr. Card's carriage."

"I think you must be right." But what did it signify?

Mr. Card alighted from the carriage almost before it drew to a halt and certainly before the coachman could assist him. Suddenly, he stopped and looked at the ground, his hand still clinging to the side of the carriage as if his courage and bravado had disappeared the moment his feet touched the earth. Maria, however, approached him rather boldly, and Charlotte followed close behind.

Maria's voice was somehow a mixture of courage and hesitancy. "Good day, Mr. Card."

Mr. Card looked at her and removed his hand from the carriage. "Good day, Mrs. Collins, Miss Lucas."

"Good day," Charlotte repeated. She was preparing to invite him inside when he spoke again.

"I know relations between our families have been strained of late, but you must excuse my plain speech." His face was a study in consternation. He rushed on. "I have heard of your trouble. Quite frankly, I do not believe a word of it."

Embarrassed, Charlotte found herself to be the one who was looking at the ground. "Thank you for your kindness, Mr. Card. I certainly am not guilty of that which I have been accused."

"I knew it!" He raised a fist in victory and then lowered it. "I knew it simply could not be true. But Mama tells me that you are leaving Westerham."

Charlotte nodded quickly but wondered how Mrs. Card had heard about her departure. She had hoped to leave Westerham quietly, to disappear and be forgotten. She had not believed her plans to be common knowledge, but apparently, her arrangements had been discovered. She would not concern herself with the details now.

Mr. Card's voice grew uncharacteristically strong. "There is no cause for such a drastic move."

"I am afraid it cannot be helped," Charlotte said. "We leave at the week's end."

"So soon?"

"I am sorry to say it is so."

Mr. Card glanced at Maria and then back to Charlotte. "Would you grant me the privilege of speaking with Miss Lucas?"

"Certainly," she said, though she was sure that her voice conveyed her uncertainty. "It would be very wrong for me to deny you a moment to say your goodbyes."

Mr. Card said a quiet thank you. Then, he offered his arm to Maria, and she shyly accepted.

Wondering at the portents of their conversation, Charlotte watched Mr. Card escort her sister to the back garden, and then she turned to go inside the cottage. Perhaps they would repair their friendship. At least something good would come of the sad situation.

She busied herself with the novel she had been reading and managed to get through one or two paragraphs at a time without her mind wandering to what might be occurring in the garden. At length, she heard the hoof beats recede as the carriage pulled away from the cottage.

When Maria entered the sitting room, Charlotte was prepared for a torrent of tears. It was not easy to say goodbye to friends, and despite what had occurred between them in the recent past, they were friends.

Maria, however, seemed strangely serene, her spirits much improved. She entered the chamber and remained quiet, pacing slowly across the room. Charlotte watched as her sister walked to the window.

"Tea?" Charlotte offered although no teapot was present.

"No, thank you."

Maria did not turn away from her place at the window. Her blue dress was washed in sunlight, and her blonde hair glowed. "Charlotte, there is something I must tell you."

Charlotte stiffened. This did not bode well. "I do not believe I can take more bad news."

Maria turned away from the window. "It is not bad news. It is the best news."

Charlotte paused, waiting. Her body was on edge, as if poised to flee at a moment's notice.

"Mr. Card has proposed again, and—"

"Oh no!" This was certainly far worse than she had expected. Their friendship would not be repaired and Maria would leave Westerham with only unpleasant memories to console her.

"—and I have accepted."

Charlotte leapt to her feet, and her book landed on the floor with a thunk.

"What? Proposed? Accepted?" Charlotte repeated stupidly. What could Maria be thinking?

"Mr. Card has proposed again, and I have accepted," Maria spoke as though to a young child as she crossed the room to where Charlotte stood frozen in shock by the settee.

"He has struck during a moment of weakness."

"No. He has waited until I understood the truth of marriage."

"But you do not love him!"

Maria took Charlotte's hand in hers. Her grasp felt strangely steady but not at all reassuring. "I do not consult my emotions in this case." Charlotte shook her head, but Maria continued. "We are to be married."

Charlotte stepped back. She comprehended the situation perfectly. Mr. Card's proposition had come at the moment of their greatest need, and Maria fancied herself to be her savior. "Please do not make the same mistake that I made with Mr. Collins. I know our situation seems bleak now, but things will work out for our good."

Maria ignored Charlotte's protest altogether, "We will not have to leave Westerham after all. We will both be living in Mr. Card's grand house, you see."

Fear crept into Charlotte's heart, and she clutched Maria's hands even tighter. "No. Maria, do not trade your chance at love for security. No amount of money is worth a loveless marriage."

"It may not be as loveless as you predict. Perhaps I shall grow to love him."

"How can you possibly say that?"

"Have not many other happy couples begun their marriages in this way?"

"How ridiculous. You cannot be so naïve after witnessing my own failed marriage." Maria knew how absurd it was to believe that love would come after marriage, especially a marriage of convenience. "You do not love him. You love Mr. Westfield."

"No. I was mistaken in my belief. I thought love to be something shocking, like a lightning bolt or a runaway carriage, and that it would knock me over. But now I realize that love might be something else entirely. Perhaps love for Mr. Card will sneak into my heart."

"Maria—"

"Charlotte, do not argue with me." She dropped her sister's hand abruptly. Her voice was strong, almost harsh. "It has been decided. I am marrying Mr. Card, and you are living with us."

The sisters faced each other in defiance. "I know you are doing this because you are afraid for your future."

"I am afraid for our future—yours and mine—but I do feel a fondness for Mr. Card. Is that not a foundation on which to base a marriage? Yours was formed on a great deal less."

Charlotte stared in disbelief. She could make a thousand different, accurate retorts. She could remind her of the pain of her marriage to Mr. Collins. She could tell her that her notion of love was a sham, that it would never come after marriage. She could tell her that all love was a sham, for that was how she felt at that precise moment. Instead, she asked, "What about our parents' permission? I do not believe I can act in their stead and give my permission to a marriage of convenience that could bring you sorrow."

"We do not require your permission, Charlotte, though I hope in time you will come to understand my decision."

"Has he sought Papa's permission?"

"He did so when he first proposed all those months ago. So it is all settled."

"I see." There was nothing Charlotte could do. The bargain had been struck without her. She stared down at her hands. "Do not do this. I beg you would not."

"Do not look for Mr. Collins in Mr. Card. He is not there."

Maria was correct. Mr. Card was not like Mr. Collins at all, but she was no more in love with Mr. Card than Charlotte had been with Mr. Collins. "How could I ignore the similarities of our circumstances? You are not in love with Mr. Card."

"I like him, and that is a kinder feeling than you ever experienced with Mr. Collins." Maria's face was set, as though sculpted in granite. "And Mr. Card can help us."

Yes, he could help them, but the cost was quite dear. Her sister bought and sold to repair the damage Charlotte had caused by trusting Mr. Edgington. "I do not like it."

"I am sorry for that, but it does not change a thing. Mr. Card has gone to secure a special license. We will be married before the week is out, and we will all move to Crumbleigh."

Charlotte was poised to argue, but Maria looked at her earnestly. "You have taken care of me. Even before I moved here, I know you sent money to our parents. You introduced me to Westerham society. You took me to balls, hoping that I would have the love that you never had. Now I am benefiting from all the assistance you have given me. I will have a husband and a large house. It is my time to return all the favors you have given me in the past. Charlotte, let me take care of you."

"But the rumors…"

"I will not allow you to run away."

"I am not running away!" She was not running. Was she?

Maria's sardonic look momentarily cowed Charlotte.

"I know it will not be easy, but Mr. Card believes that your reputation will be restored in time, and I agree. People have short memories, and another person's scandal will make the town forget ours. Have not you told me as much in the past? And until then, Mr. Card's good name will carry us. You will see. We shall be happy and secure."

Maria paused and forced her sister to look into her eyes. The look Charlotte read there was sincere and almost pleading. "It is my turn to take care of you."

Her voice tapered off in a whisper, and Charlotte melted into her seat. She saw that Maria's mind was quite made up.

After Maria left the room, Charlotte indulged herself in an embarrassing display of emotion. Tears rolled unchecked down her cheeks, and her eyelids swelled under the strain of her sorrow.

As much as she hated to admit it, she had wanted to run away. Her situation practically demanded it. She had little money, and no one in Westerham would hire her. No one in Westerham would even hold two words' conversation with her! She simply had to leave.

Now Maria believed that her marriage would cure all the ills that had befallen them, but Charlotte knew it would not be so. It was true that society sometimes had a short memory, but Mr. Edgington still had her glove, and as long as it was in his possession, her reputation would always be in danger. Worse, once it became public knowledge that she had benefited from Lady Catherine's charity but was now shunned by her, she would be doubly shamed.

She began to consider tactics for talking her sister out of her impending marriage, but she discounted such persuasion almost immediately. Charlotte's interference would only serve to make matters worse. There was simply nothing to be done.

She would have a home, and for that she was thankful. She would have protection in Mr. Card and Maria. Mrs. Card, however, would heartily disapprove. She was known to have little compassion for people who have fallen prey to society's pressures or who have been accused of having done so.

Charlotte sighed, picked up her abused book, and placed it back in the trunk. In truth, she had little choice in the matter. Maria was an adult, and she had made her choice.

Maria would marry Mr. Card. It was as simple as that.

❧❧ ❧❧

Planning a wedding is never a simple affair. Planning a wedding in less than a week is utterly inadvisable. Charlotte and Maria had the advantage of already having prepared her clothing for her aborted wedding to Mr. Westfield. So new invitations had to be written and dispatched, and a messenger was sent post haste to Hertfordshire to inform Sir William and Lady Lucas of the date.

Thankfully, Mr. Card secured the license, the church, and the minister to perform the ceremony. Because the couple had not planned a wedding trip, etiquette dictated that Mrs. Card should hold a celebratory breakfast at her home, and Charlotte was certain that she went about her duties with as much joy as a cat in a tub of water.

The day of the wedding dawned bright and clear, but Charlotte still felt rather depressed, and when the Cards' servants arrived to transport their belongings to their new home, Charlotte felt even more disheartened.

She watched as two finely attired servants removed and placed her belongings—all contained in a surprisingly small number of trunks—on a wagon. When her personal possessions had been removed, they covered the furniture, which was to remain in the cottage, with dust cloths.

Charlotte was losing her home. She was losing her independence and would now be essentially in the care of her younger sister and her husband. Any pride that she might have harbored over her independent situation was now completely gone.

Maria entered the sitting room and found Charlotte perched on the edge of the cloth-covered settee.

"Are you well, Charlotte?"

"I am attempting to be well."

"The carriage will be here soon. What are you doing sitting in here?"

"I was simply saying goodbye to my dear old cottage."

"I know you will miss it, but Crumbleigh will soon become home. And it is ever so much bigger."

"Are you ready to be married?"

Maria gestured at her dress and said, "Yes, as long as you approve of my appearance."

Charlotte studied her for the first time since she entered the room. The dress they had chosen to serve as her wedding gown accentuated her slim form, and her hair curled elaborately around her face. She looked very beautiful indeed, and Charlotte told her as much.

Then, although she knew it was far too late to take corrective action, she made one last foray. "Maria, I am not trying to insult you. You are my sister, and I care a great deal about your happiness. Are you certain about this course of action?"

Rather than becoming angry, Maria softened. "I know you care about me, but you must stop worrying. I am at peace with my marriage, and so should you be."

Charlotte did not speak for long moments, considering. She would be no better than Mr. Westfield if she suggested that Maria abandon her betrothed on their wedding day. She must wed Mr. Card. "I shall be at peace. I shall."

"Good. Now, let us stop talking, for I hear Mr. Card's carriage approaching."

With that, Maria practically ran out of the room, leaving Charlotte alone again. She would have to get used to thinking of Crumbleigh as her home, but there had been something special about these stone walls. They had represented her safety and independence, and they had given her a life that she was sad to leave.

But leave she must.

Taking a deep breath, she followed Maria to the carriage and into her uncertain future.

৵৹৹ Twenty ৹৹৵

Maria and Mr. Card's wedding was a small, quiet assembly. The speed with which the wedding was organized prevented many people, including Maria and Charlotte's parents, from attending. Numerous members of the Card family were in attendance, however, as well as several of Maria's other friends. Mrs. Eff and Edward attended at Charlotte's insistence and sat unobtrusively behind the rest of the guests. Miss Farmington—the new Mrs. Westfield, actually—Mr. Westfield, and Mr. Basford, of course, had not been invited, and their absence was not mentioned, but it was felt by all. Only the first few rows of pews were occupied, but Maria and Mr. Card did not seem troubled that their wedding was not the society event of the season.

Charlotte sat in the front pew and watched as the couple exchanged their vows. Mr. Card cut a dashing figure in his dark morning coat, and Maria clutched a nosegay of flowers while light filtered through the church windows and turned her blond hair into spun gold. Charlotte was surprised to see tenderness in her sister's bright blue eyes. Perhaps it was true. Perhaps it was thankfulness. Or perhaps she would one day fall in love with Mr. Card. If that were the case, it would be good fortune indeed.

After the ceremony, the party was bound to return to the Card home for the wedding breakfast. On her way out of the church, Charlotte was arrested by Mrs. Eff.

"It was a lovely ceremony."

"Yes, Maria seemed happy, did she not? I do so want her to be happy."

"Of course you do, my dear," Mrs. Eff gave her hand a pat. "I do believe that she is very happy."

"She says that one day she will grow to love him, but will she?"

"One never knows about love."

"One never knows," Charlotte repeated.

They had reached the church door and were standing half in sun and half in the shade of the building. "I have news, and I thought it best you heard it from a friend." Here she paused and looked around. Finding no one within hearing distance, she continued, "I had it from a servant of Colonel Armitage that Mr. Westfield and Miss Farmington were already married when Mr. Basford discovered them. There was quite a stir, naturally, when he threw over your sister, but all is well now that Maria is married."

Charlotte nodded. This she had already known, thanks to Mr. Basford himself.

Mrs. Eff continued to speak. "They returned home briefly, but, they have left town again. Apparently, Mr. Basford has now arranged matters for them."

"I know of the occurrence at Gretna Green, but what other matters did Mr. Basford arrange?" Charlotte hoped she had kept her desperate curiosity from her voice.

"He booked them all passage to America, I understand."

"Oh? All of them?" He had said nothing about departing with the newlyweds.

"Yes, I believe so."

Mr. Basford was leaving. Although she had been quite certain that he was lost to her, it was a different matter entirely to have the truth so finally laid out. Mr. Basford was returning to Savannah. So far away. Across the ocean. And between them was only the lingering tension of the broken engagement between his nephew and her sister. She wished it were not so. She wished they could have parted in friendship. Or not have parted at all.

"I believe that neither Mr. Westfield nor the new Mrs. Westfield truly desired to undertake such a trip, but Mr. Basford insisted. And Colonel Armitage agreed, so it was settled."

"And have they set sail yet?" Charlotte's question was meant to be neutral, but she could hear the emotion in her voice. She concentrated on the scene before her. The carriages were filling and pulling away from the church one at a time. Dirt kicked up by the horses' hooves rose in the air, and Charlotte wondered vaguely if Maria was minding her dress in all that dust.

"I cannot say. But I do know that they are to visit Mr. Westfield's mother for quite some time before returning home to Westerham. If you ask me, we may not see them again. Savannah is said to be quite a beautiful place, and the trip, I understand, is rather a difficult one. Mrs. Westfield may not wish to undertake it again, despite the draw of family and country."

Only one carriage remained, waiting for Charlotte to embark. "I do wish them the best," she said, trying to feel as genuine as her tone of voice sounded.

Mrs. Eff gestured to Edward, who had been waiting in the vestibule. "We must be off, my dear. I do hope you enjoy the breakfast. I promised Edward a little something from the bakery."

Charlotte hardly heard her, but nodded just the same and watched them depart, walking together down the stone steps and rounding the corner of the church. Charlotte went to the waiting carriage, allowed herself to be handed in, and sat down as a wave of sorrow washed over her. It was odd how the prospect of losing something—or someone—could cause it to become so important to her.

❧❧ ❧❧

When Charlotte joined the wedding breakfast, the group, which had sounded animated when she was in the hall, seemed to become rather subdued, and she was quite conscious that it had mostly to do with her newfound reputation as a fallen woman. She attempted to remain on the fringes of the party, but Mr. Card and Maria continued to insist that she sit near them or converse with their group. It was rather kind of them to consider her feelings in that way, but it was also awkward and tiring.

Soon exhausted, Charlotte slipped away to a quiet part of the house. She opened the door to the library and peered inside. Vacant. Charlotte smiled. A few moments of peace at last. She chose a chair beside the window and did not even bother with the pretense of selecting a book. She knew she would not be able to concentrate on dramatic fiction, for her very life was a drama, and it was not fiction.

She was weary of being looked upon with suspicion. What must people say about her in the privacy of their drawing rooms? She longed for the presence of someone who looked upon her with kindness. Who did not contemplate her alleged lewd behavior with his peers. Who believed her when she said she was innocent. She longed for Mr. Basford.

Charlotte shifted in her chair and held back tears at the thought of him. This ought to be the happiest of occasions. Her sister had wed a kind gentleman who could support both her and Charlotte. She should not be contemplating a gentleman whom she was unlikely to lay eyes on again. They would never again share a chamber or sit together on a settee. But perhaps, late at night, she would see him often in her eye's mind. She would recall their conversations, their walk in the wood, and their dances. She would remember his dress, his scent. She would remember him.

She closed her eyes and indulged herself in her memories.

She had been alone in the library for quite a little while when the door opened and Mr. Card's mother invaded the room like a cold draft.

"Mrs. Card." Charlotte straightened on the upholstered chair. She felt like a child who had been caught in mischief. She did not know precisely what to say, so she blurted, "I am glad you are here. Will you sit with me? I wanted to thank you for allowing me to move into your home."

Mrs. Card puffed up her chest haughtily and did not take a seat. Her wiry gray hair moved stiffly as she shook her head, and her nose wrinkled. "I do not sit with women such as you."

Charlotte opened her mouth and then shut it. There nothing to be said.

Mrs. Card walked to a bookcase, and with her back to the room, she said, "Mrs. Collins, you know in the past I regarded you in high esteem."

Charlotte steeled herself. She had known that Mrs. Card would not be a bastion of support in her time of need, but she had hoped the lady would have been civil at the very least. "I appreciate that."

Mrs. Card turned, her skirts brushing the books on the bottom shelf, threatening to upend them. "But recent events have caused me to question my original estimation."

"I assure you those events have been grossly exaggerated."

Mrs. Card's chin rose slightly and her eyes narrowed. "As I understand it, Mrs. Collins, there is tangible proof."

It was useless to argue the merits of her case. Her character had already been decided. "It is not as it seems to be, Mrs. Card."

The older woman sighed. "I do want to believe you, but until further proof is laid at my door, I must protect myself and my family. I cautioned Jonas against this marriage, but he loves Maria. And Maria loves you. Therefore, you will live here."

"Again, I thank you."

Her eyes turned to flint. "Do not thank me. It is none of my doing, I assure you. Jonas had defended you quite convincingly, and I almost believe him. I just worry so about my son's reputation."

"I understand. Reputations are quite fragile things." Charlotte ought to know.

Mrs. Card sniffed, as though scenting the air for truth or the origin of an ill odor. "I find it best to retire to my house in London. I leave tomorrow."

She was leaving. It should have been a relief to have such a caustic presence out of her life, but grief rocked Charlotte. Not only had the slander caused her to lose her own home, but now it drove Mrs. Card out of hers.

She stood in protest. "Mrs. Card, I—"

"Do not speak. I am simply too old to bother with this type of nonsense." She sniffed again. Perhaps she had a cold. "Jonas reminds me that this is his and Maria's home now. She is the lady of the house. They must choose their houseguests themselves. It is no longer my place, no matter how heartily I disapprove."

The last words hung heavily in the air, and again Charlotte could think of no suitable reply.

Obviously expecting no response, Mrs. Card left the room, leaving Charlotte alone again. It seemed that being alone was to become her lot in life.

Charlotte's accommodations at Crumbleigh were more than adequate. Her cottage had boasted of a small bed chamber with moderately comfortable furnishings, but the Cards' home was luxury itself. Her bed was large and covered in soft, inviting linens, and she found that her clothing, which had been unpacked by the servants, did not even fill one of the wardrobes that decorated her bed chamber. Her toiletries had been arranged on her dressing table, but her books remained in their trunk. Charlotte decided to put them in the remaining wardrobe space, even though it was not the proper use for the furniture. She wanted to have them in her chamber, and moreover, she was glad to have a task to occupy her first morning there.

When at last she descended below stairs, she felt rather lost, disoriented in her new surroundings. A servant informed her that Maria and Mr. Card had not yet risen. Charlotte had expected as much, so she entered the breakfast room alone to find an elaborate buffet awaiting her. Perhaps living under the protection of her sister and her husband would not be so very dreadful, she thought as she filled her plate.

After finishing a large meal of sausages, eggs, and muffins and jam, Charlotte pushed away from the table and wondered what to do with herself. There was no menu to plan or shopping lists to make. She had no garden in which to toil, and she did not want to leave the property without wishing the newlyweds every happiness. Besides, she had no calls to pay.

So she decided to take a tour of the house. She had seen most of the public rooms in her visits in years past, but now that this was her home, she viewed things with new eyes.

Crumbleigh was certainly sumptuous, and the rooms were large and lushly furnished, but Charlotte was drawn to the smaller morning room. It was quite a bit larger than her sitting room in the cottage, but it had the same simple air about it that the other rooms home seemed to lack. The fabrics at the windows and on the furniture were light and cheerful, and the walls were a pleasing shade of pale yellow. A small fire in the hearth chased away the morning chill. She wondered who had chosen the décor, for Mrs.

Card certainly did not seem the type to choose such joyful accessories. Perhaps there was some goodness in her yet.

Charlotte remained in the morning room and settled herself at the escritoire, a much more elaborate version of the writing desk that had been in the cottage to write a letter to her parents and to her cousins the Emersons. She spent a great deal of time describing Maria's wedding and then found herself without much else to relate, so she closed the letters, sealed them with a wafer, and called a servant to see to their delivery.

Charlotte took several turns about the room and then selected a book of very poor poetry from a shelf and attempted to entertain herself with snide thoughts about the verse.

Maria and Mr. Card did not arrive downstairs until quite late that afternoon, and when they appeared, Charlotte found herself inordinately pleased to see them. She dropped the book, stood, and greeted them warmly.

The newlyweds sat together on the settee, and Charlotte found that she could not quite decipher Maria' mood. She wondered if her sister regretted her decision after only one night as a married woman. Mr. Card, however, was quite talkative, although Charlotte did not find the subject altogether pleasing. "I suppose you are aware by now that Mama left this morning for her house in town."

"Yes," Charlotte hung her head slightly. "I spoke with her yesterday at your wedding breakfast. I am afraid it is my fault that she has left her home."

"No indeed," Maria said. "She is just a closed-minded shrew who would not know the truth if it stepped on her foot!"

"Maria!"

Mr. Card arrested her with a quick hand gesture. "My wife," he blushed at the word and continued, "is quite correct, although I would not have used that precise wording. My mother has fallen victim to the unfortunate gossip that has been spread about you, but once we clear your good name, she will return home and all will be well."

"Mr. Card, you are very kind, but I do not believe there is anything to be done to rectify the situation." Charlotte glanced from Mr. Card to Maria. "I do appreciate your faith in me, but how can you possibly support me in the face of the evidence?"

"Time will make the truth evident."

Charlotte snorted.

"No, no. Listen to your new brother-in-law," he insisted. "If you will recall, Maria rejected my first proposal."

Maria's eyebrows knit together, but her voice was well-moderated when she said, "Oh, do not bring that up!"

"Patience, my dear." He turned back to Charlotte, his face set. "I have always loved Maria, and I knew that deep down, she loved me too. I just had to wait for the circumstances to make the truth evident to her. The same thing will happen to you."

Charlotte was not sure she believed him, but she smiled at his obvious fancy for Maria. If sister did not love him, at the very least, he loved her. And that was something. Perhaps that would be sufficient for a pleasant marriage. She said, "Until then, I intend to stay out of society."

"You will go mad in this house all the time, Charlotte."

"I knew you would prefer to stay out of society, which is precisely why I have taken it upon myself to make your time here more pleasurable."

"Oh, Mr. Card, what have you done?" Maria asked, concerned.

"I have made an addition to our staff. Mrs. Effingham and her son begin work in our household. Mrs. Eff will be your personal companion, Mrs. Collins. I think that you will soon be quite happy indeed."

Joy spread through Charlotte and she clasped her hands together. A smile stretched across her face. Maria appeared genuinely pleased for the first time that morning, and she spoke before Charlotte could muster a reply, "Oh, how thoughtful of you!"

"Mrs. Eff will work here?" Charlotte asked, testing the words and feeling the attendant pleasure they brought.

"Indeed she shall. I knew how attached you were to her, and I wanted to make you comfortable in your new home."

"I confess I am pleased indeed," Charlotte said, emotions rising in her throat. "You are very good to us, Mr. Card."

Hiring Mrs. Eff and Edward had been very kind of him. Not only would she have a companion, but she would have news—not gossip, news—from town and a little laughter.

Mr. Card rose and extending his hand to Maria. "Shall we take to stroll about the gardens? It appears to be a very fine day."

Maria seemed reluctant, but she took his hand and stood. "Yes, it is a very fine day."

Charlotte was quite sure Maria had not so much as glanced outside at the weather. Charlotte kept her place in the morning room and watched as they exited arm in arm.

She found that she was quite pleased at the turn of events. She had never expected Mr. Card to employ her former servants. And as uncomfortable as she was admitting that she required a champion, she was pleased to have Mr. Card to act on her behalf.

He had never struck her as the sort of man who would be a champion. Certainly, he had always been a very nice boy, but now he was acting as a proper man should. He was strong without being commanding, kind without being weak, and caring without being overly sensitive. Perhaps being married suited him, or perhaps finally being out of his mother's sphere of influence had allowed him to be the man he had always been prevented from being.

❧ Twenty-One ❧

Later that week, when the servant entered the morning room to announce the name of the caller who stood in the hallway, Charlotte could not have been more surprised, even if the butler had announced the name of the king himself. She jumped from the escritoire, where she had been composing a letter to Elizabeth, and tipped her chair backward. She caught the teetering piece of furniture just as the visitor entered the room.

The woman was plump and wore a dress of striped muslin, which defined the topography of her body, each bulging contour delineated in painful clarity. Her hair was done in tight ringlets that Charlotte knew had taken a maid ages to arrange.

But there was no bird in her coiffure at present.

Charlotte was shocked into immobility. She did not even think to curtsey. "Mrs. Holloway."

"Mrs. Collins."

The two women stared at each other. Tension radiated from Mrs. Holloway's face in tight lines that began at her mouth and stretched her puffy features until her eyes appeared thin and hard. Charlotte had the vague impression that Mrs. Holloway had arrived to demand a duel, and she sincerely hoped that Mr. Card kept no swords in the house.

"I had not expected.... Will you sit?" Charlotte gestured broadly at the room, and Mrs. Holloway chose a high-backed chair across from the escritoire. Charlotte continued to stand.

"I will come straight to the heart of the matter."

Charlotte nodded. Time seemed to slow, and she knew that something serious was amiss. She and Mrs. Holloway had never been companions. They had only one thing in common.

"This is about Edgington."

That was, unfortunately, the one thing.

Charlotte's fingers wrapped around the back of the desk chair that stood behind her. "Mr. Edgington?"

"Yes, Edgington." Charlotte began to fidget, and Mrs. Holloway stared at her again, undoubtedly noticing her discomfiture and lack of coherent response. "Are you daft?"

Why was Charlotte allowing herself to become so disconcerted? She had no reason to be intimidated by this woman. In fact, Mrs. Holloway may not be Mr. Edgington's lover, but an unwilling victim, blackmailed into an affair, just as he had attempted with Charlotte.

She felt her defenses fortify. "No, I am not daft." She turned the desk chair so that it faced her guest and sat down. "Tell me the purpose of this visit immediately."

"Edgington is mine."

Clearly, she was not an unwilling participant.

"I certainly have no connection to him."

"Do you not?" She produced something from her reticule. A piece of white fabric. She held it out and allowed it to unfold, the material sliding to dangle in midair. It took a moment for the object's identity to register in Charlotte's mind, but then she realized what it was. Her glove! "Does not this belong to you?"

"I...I..." Charlotte had never thought to see that glove again and certainly not in the hands of Mrs. Holloway. She inhaled deeply and tried to think clearly, but only questions came. Should she own it? What would that mean for her reputation? Was Mrs. Holloway also here to blackmail her?

"It has your initials embroidered here." She ran her fingers over the pale blue threads, much as Mr. Edgington had done the night he had stolen it from her.

If only Charlotte had not allowed Mary to stitch the cursed things! If only she had never accepted them from Mr. Edgington. Had never even met him.

"You may as well admit it, Mrs. Collins, for I have heard the gossip as well. You gave this to my Edgington as a token of your feelings for him."

Anger prompted Charlotte to stand. "I did no such thing. I have no feelings for him, except utter disdain."

Mrs. Holloway snorted like a nervous horse. "I also observed you with him at the theater in London." Charlotte stepped back. She had been observed with the man in London. Would her downfall never end?

"Do not appear so shocked. I concealed myself well. Even Edgington did not see me. Of course, I believed your meeting to be a product of chance, but then I saw the two of you dancing at the Armitage's ball. I knew then how you felt about him."

Charlotte remembered that dance, how he had leered. How she had blushed. "You misinterpreted."

"I think not, for in the coming weeks, I discovered this in his armoire, and I knew the rumors were true. You have been pursuing him!" She waved the glove at her. "He would have nothing to do with a woman like you. You are old and spindly. He prefers a woman with buxom qualities."

Charlotte gritted her teeth and strode across the room, rapidly closing the distance between them. When her skirts brushed those of Mrs. Holloway, she stopped and looked down at the surprised woman. Charlotte's eyes narrowed. So did Mrs. Holloway's. For a moment neither woman moved.

Charlotte leaned down and snatched the glove from Mrs. Holloway's hand. The fabric glided out of her chubby grasp with a soft whooshing sound. Without considering the consequences of her actions, she crossed the room and hurled it into the fireplace. She watched as it caught fire and listened to the crackle as it burned. Her anger smoldered.

When the glove had become nothing more than a charred mass, she turned back to Mrs. Holloway. She had not moved from her seat. Her back was rigid and her hands were balled in her lap. "I am pleased that you destroyed it," she said. "Now the evidence of your feelings for him is gone, and he will soon forget you."

Yes, the evidence was gone! He no longer had power over her. "I hope he never thinks on me again."

Mrs. Holloway looked at her for long moments, and then her face fell. When she spoke, her voice was softer, and she sounded like a young child. "I love him."

"Mrs. Holloway." Charlotte stumbled over the name. How could a married woman throw herself on the unmerciful Mr. Edgington? "I assure you that nothing is between your...companion...and me."

She nodded at the fireplace. "What about the glove?"

Charlotte hesitated. She did not want to give Mrs. Holloway power over her by telling her of the blackmail. She did not believe her to be an evil woman, but under Mr. Edgington's influence, how could she be certain? Still, she did not want her to believe it an amorous gift. Charlotte could only think to say, "It was nothing."

"You are not pursuing an affair with him?"

She could honestly answer in the negative. "I will have nothing to do with Mr. Edgington, I assure you."

Mrs. Holloway's face hardened again. The little girl voice was gone. "You may have gained his attentions in the past, but see that you do not come near Edgington again."

Charlotte looked at the ridiculous woman. Her leverage was gone, and still she spoke as though she had control of the situation. But the power now belonged to Charlotte. "See that you never mention that glove to a soul." Here Charlotte hesitated, considered, and then forged on. "For I will be forced to confirm the rumors that have been circulating about you, and I will name your accomplice. I will tell all that I know about your affair with Mr. Edgington. And I know a great deal more than you suppose."

Mrs. Holloway's eyes widened. In her anger, it was obvious she had forgotten her need to conceal the affair. Her mouth worked reflexively but only the following emerged: "I...I...."

"All of Westerham will know of your evenings spent with Mr. Edgington in London. About your forays to the theater." Mrs. Holloway's eyes widened to an alarming degree, but Charlotte pressed onward. "How do you suppose your husband will react when he discovers the truth?"

Charlotte could not fathom how Mr. Holloway might react. The sum of her knowledge of him was that his wife was unfaithful and that he had an uncommon love of porcine creatures. How was she to determine the mind of a gentleman of such tastes?

Again, the women stared at each other. One innocent, one sullied. The fire crackled in the background.

Mrs. Holloway stood. Her tense face cracked into a strained smile. "I believe we have come to an amicable agreement, Mrs. Collins, and I will trouble you no longer."

Charlotte wondered if this were some ruse, some trick to lull her into complacency. Would she now call for that duel?

But nothing untoward occurred. Both women curtseyed and bid each other good day. To any observer, the conclusion of their visit looked like any other benign call. Charlotte returned to her seat at the desk and watched as Mrs. Holloway's striped gown disappeared out the door.

Charlotte's bravado also disappeared.

What had just occurred?

She tried to think, but her mind seemed sluggish.

She had destroyed the glove. That, at the very least, was a benefit. However, she could not feel good about the methods she had used with Mrs. Holloway. Were they not the same methods Mr. Edgington had employed on her?

She sat many minutes, but soon she fancied that she could smell the charred glove amid the other fire scents. It choked her, and she took to her bed chamber where she remained until the next morning.

⚬⚬⚬

"Wake up!" a voice said all too cheerily. Charlotte heard a tray, presumably containing breakfast, deposited on the bedside table with a ceremonious thunk. She thought she could smell muffins, and she opened her eyes to confirm. Yes. Muffins.

She struggled to make her tired body sit upright and pulled the covers over her protectively. She reached for one and realized that the servant had not left.

"Mrs. Eff!" Charlotte jumped out of bed, the covers still tangled around her, and embraced her.

"Oh, go on with you now," Mrs. Eff protested. "It is not as if we have not seen each other in years."

Charlotte released her, ever so glad to have her there. "It seems like years to me. So much has occurred."

"Indeed it has. Look at you in your fine new home. And Miss Maria married. I suppose I should call her Mrs. Card now, should I not?"

"You may call her whatever you like, for I am just so pleased to see you. And how does Edward? Is he here as well?"

"He is working under the butler, a very kind man if my impression is correct. He will make a decent manservant out of my boy."

"Oh, I am so pleased, but I did not expect you so soon."

"Sometimes the unexpected can be good, and not evil."

"That has not been my experience."

Mrs. Eff observed her for some time. "Has something else occurred?"

Charlotte sat on the edge of the bed and revealed her encounter with Mrs. Holloway. "And I have descended to Mr. Edgington's level by extorting Mrs. Holloway."

Mrs. Eff had remained quiet during the recitation, her eyes serious. "I see no reason for you to experience such guilt."

"Do you not?" Hopelessness was in her voice.

"No, I do not, for you were innocent, but Mrs. Holloway is not. Moreover, she was threatening you. You had no choice but to act."

"There is always a choice."

"Oh, stop being so dramatic. Think of the good you have done. You have saved yourself. You destroyed the only tangible evidence Mr. Edgington possessed, and you have assured the secrecy of his consort. You are free."

Was she correct?

Was Charlotte free?

Mrs. Eff did not allow Charlotte the luxury of contemplation. She pulled her from her seated position on the bed. "Enough of this. Now, get up! It is time for you to get back out into the world."

Charlotte offered meek resistance while Mrs. Eff pushed her through her morning toilette and out the door, threatening to accompany her should she resist. So Charlotte did not resist. Mrs. Eff was unresistable.

The prospect of going to town had disconcerted Charlotte, but soon she became excited. Perhaps she had freed herself.

But as she walked through the shops, she was aware that people whispered about her. Of course, she should have foreseen that response. It was the treatment she had received since Mr. Edgington had slandered her. She should not be surprised, for it was the natural response of people who still believed her to be a fallen woman.

She was tempted to permit her spirits fall low again, but she had destroyed the glove! Mr. Edgington's power was effectually gone. She simply had to find a way to make her innocence known now that Mr. Edgington could no longer refute her.

Several hours had passed, and she was running out of shops to patronize and items to consider. She was beginning to lose hope of clearing her name. Not a soul had spoken to her, and she could not initiate the conversation herself, for that would only give the appearance of desperation.

Then, in the milliner's shop, she encountered old Mrs. Farmington. They quite literally bumped into each other while searching through a table of bonnets. She had not taken note of her, for older lady nearly blended in with the powdery white walls.

They each apologized, and when Mrs. Farmington was preparing to excuse herself, Charlotte stopped her, saying, "How have you been, Mrs. Farmington? And your family, are they all well?"

"Very well, thank you, Mrs. Collins. And you?" Her voice was dry and uncertain.

"Very well indeed." Charlotte steeled herself for a difficult conversation. "You have heard that my sister has married Mr. Card?"

"Indeed I have." Her words were awkward, hesitant, as if trying to determine the course of the conversation before it occurred. "May I wish them every happiness."

"And please convey our well wishes to your granddaughter and Mr. Westfield."

A flush spread across Mrs. Farmington's weathered, pale cheeks. Charlotte was pleased to see that embarrassment, for it meant that the older woman was not going to gloat over her granddaughter's capture of Mr. Westfield.

"The marriage did not occur the way we would have done it years ago. Children today, it seems, have a different way of viewing things." She turned her head to issue a brittle cough. "I am sorry for any pain it may have caused your sister, but I cannot help but be pleased by my granddaughter's fortuitous match. I only regret the manner in which it occurred."

"Pray, do not make yourself uneasy, Mrs. Farmington. The situation served a greater purpose. It taught Maria that she had always had a fondness for Mr. Card. Now, it seems that everyone is happy."

"I know my Constance experienced terrible pain over the affair." Mrs. Farmington winced at her own choice of words. "She had always valued your sister as a friend, and it was difficult for her to be in love with Miss Lucas's beau."

Charlotte fought the urge to roll her eyes. She doubted that Miss Farmington had experienced any such difficulty. "Maria harbors no ill feelings toward Mr. or Mrs. Westfield."

"That is very kind of her, for she is entitled to be quite angry, really."

"I can assure you that Maria is far from angry, and I know she would want to convey her best wishes to the Westfields."

Mrs. Farmington sighed in relief and the two women continued to carry on a very polite conversation until Mrs. Farmington finally said, "I am surprised to see you out and about, what with the things I have heard about you of late."

For once, Charlotte was pleased at Mrs. Farmington's bent for choosing inappropriate topics of conversation. She put down the bonnet she had been considering and gave Mrs. Farmington a steady look. This was her moment of vindication, and she would not spoil it. "None of those things are true, Mrs. Farmington. Why do you choose to accept his lies about my character?"

Her features seemed to harden slightly, and she huffed. "As much as I hate to say it, Mrs. Collins, I have heard there was proof."

"Have you seen this proof?" Charlotte knew that Lady Catherine had seen it, but had anyone else? Charlotte did not know if Mr. Edgington had simply hinted at the glove's existence or if he had displayed it for the townspeople to see. Had Mrs. Holloway shown anyone? Certainly not, for she had her own secrets to conceal.

"No, I have not."

"Has anyone of your acquaintance seen proof?"

Here Mrs. Farmington paused. Anxiety filled Charlotte. "No, I suppose not."

Charlotte sighed inwardly. No one ever would see that glove. She was safe.

Mrs. Farmington continued, "But it seems unlikely that Mr. Edgington would claim to have proof that he did not possess."

Charlotte was fortified by her newfound knowledge. "I am sorry to be harsh on any person, but Mr. Edgington is an unscrupulous individual and he meant to do far worse than merely damaging my reputation."

"So you claim that there is no proof?"

"Indeed, there is none. You may apply to Mr. Edgington himself, but I guarantee that he will not be able to supply it."

"Really?" Disbelief hunched in the creases of her skin.

"Truly. Ask him. Good manners prevent me from saying anything negative about that gentleman beyond the fact that he has done me a great disservice in this community. I will hide no longer. I am not guilty of that which he has accused me."

"You sound quite convincing." Mrs. Farmington eyed her. "I do so wish to believe you, if only because of your kind forgiveness of my dear Constance."

"You ought to believe me, for I speak only the truth, Mrs. Farmington. I do not deserve the censure of this town."

"Well, my dear, all I can say is that the truth will set you free. And I hope it does."

⚬◔ℓ ℓ◔⚬

As Charlotte had hoped, word of her encounter with old Mrs. Farmington spread quickly around Westerham. Although Charlotte had grown to despise gossip, she was thankful it moved so swiftly. According to Mrs. Eff, who had friends in many major households, it was generally agreed that Charlotte's insistence upon applying to

Mr. Edgington for proof had removed any need to do so. The fact that she was willing to offer such a course of action proved that no such evidence existed and that her poor reputation had been undeserved.

Soon, invitations, which had been scarcer than a daisy in December, began to arrive. Friends began to pay calls, and Charlotte cautiously began to enjoy Westerham society again.

However, the Charlotte who returned to society was ever so much more guarded. If being married to Mr. Collins had made her wary of her reputation in society, the situation with Mr. Edgington caused her to become extremely vigilant. Her reputation was all she had. She no longer had her independence or her cottage. She was very thankful for her small income and for her sister's generosity, and she would not dishonor Maria again by her actions in society.

While Maria and Mr. Card attended almost every event to which they were invited, Charlotte restricted herself to attending only small parties or gatherings held at Crumbleigh. She declined invitations to large assemblies and balls and was careful never to be alone with a gentleman even for the briefest of moments.

Maria had told her repeatedly that she was being ridiculous, but Charlotte would not budge, claiming that she preferred to remain in the morning room at Crumbleigh rather than risk humiliation again.

In truth, Charlotte found something lacking in the society to which she had returned. The parties were not as exciting, and the concept of a ball somehow lacked the intrigue that such an assembly had formerly possessed. The card parties were duller, and the dinners, while delicious, did not inspire her the way they once had. There was no sparkling conversation that sparkled enough or clever repartee witty enough to entertain her. She considered the reasons for this lack, but she was loath to admit the truth—that Mr. Basford was the missing element.

To her great frustration, over the intervening months, she found herself thinking of him more often than she wished. Sometimes he would slip into her thoughts as she sat reading letters in the morning room with her slippered feet tucked beneath her. He appeared in her mind when she was dressing herself for bed, which disconcerted her greatly. Why would he be so stuck in her mind? He was not a suitor; he was barely even to be considered a friend. It should not be such an ordeal to forget him.

She had practically succeeded in her quest to stop thinking of Mr. Basford, except for an occasional lapse—perhaps fifteen to twenty times per day—when the letter arrived from her cousin Mary Emerson in London and brought him back to the forefront of her mind.

She read the words quickly, eagerly consuming the news of her family and friends in town, but when she saw Mr. Basford's name appear in Mrs. Emerson's neat script, she read it very carefully. Twice.

> I have the most interesting news of Mr. Benjamin Basford. As you no doubt recall, I was acquainted with his sister before she moved to America. You may imagine my surprise even to hear his name mentioned in London, for I was quite sure you had told me that he returned to Savannah some months ago. However, I had the pleasure of meeting him at a dinner party given by mutual friends just last evening. After speaking at great length about his family in Savannah—all are doing well, by the way—I told him of my relationship with you, dear Charlotte.
>
> He inquired after you with more than a passing interest and was very desirous to know about your current situation. I related the happy news of your sister's marriage and explained that you are now living at the Cards' home. I had not expected the look of consternation that crossed his features. I confess I still do not comprehend the reason for it. Perhaps you will understand.
>
> Searching for a topic of conversation less disagreeable to him, I then told him that you believed him to be in America. He proceeded to give me the explanation for which you are undoubtedly waiting. He was, apparently, instrumental in securing passage for the new Mr.

and Mrs. Westfield, and he had originally intended to accompany them when they departed, believing, he said, that there was nothing left for him in England. However, he altered his plans at the last moment, electing instead to return to London where he has taken a small house. We had a pleasant conversation about the goings on in Westerham at the end of which he asked me if I thought he would be welcome to return despite his nephew's misconduct. I hope I did not answer incorrectly by telling him he would certainly be welcome. He seemed quite eager to be off, and I would not be surprised to hear that he beat this letter to you, my dear Charlotte.

For the remainder of the letter, Mary described renovations that she and Mr. Emerson had planned for their home, but after reading the news of Mr. Basford, Charlotte could not possibly concentrate on the merits of French interior design as opposed to the current rococo fashion.

Mr. Basford was to return.

He might be in Westerham already.

Charlotte untucked her legs and sat up straighter, looking around the morning room as though he might walk in at any moment. That was absurd, of course.

She reread the letter several more times, attempting in vain to interpret the precise meaning of Mr. Basford's conversation with her cousin. He had inquired after Charlotte "with more than a passing interest." What precisely did that signify? He could be concerned merely about her living situation, but her heart wondered. Could he possibly be concerned about her beyond the boundaries of casual acquaintance?

Charlotte had felt something more from him. He had been very attentive on their walk when they encountered each other near the cottage that day. They had danced together, and the experience was not unpleasant. They were, in truth, very pleasant dances indeed. Then, there was the time when they had been on the settee in her cottage and he had almost touched her hand.

She could not easily forget the sensation that shimmered through her body as she watched his hand draw closer. She had wanted to feel his fingers against hers. And she could distinctly remember the disappointment that cut into her when Maria had entered the room.

Certainly, Charlotte would never forget the way Mr. Basford had aided her that fateful evening at the ball when Mr. Edgington had begun his campaign against her. He had distracted her and fortified her. He had danced with her, and his every touch seemed to give her strength.

Although his attempt to marry his nephew to Maria was misguided, it was meant to protect her.

He had failed miserably, and Charlotte had been rightfully troubled, but with the benefit of a little perspective, she felt kinder toward him. A great deal kinder.

She only hoped that they would have an occasion to meet when he returned to Westerham. Despite the fact that she truly wanted to have the opportunity to speak with him, she would not break her rules. They would meet appropriately. They would be in a public place and among friends. She would ask his forgiveness for her earlier outbursts, and then they would continue as good friends.

She would not allow herself to hope for anything more.

Charlotte was an old widow, and Mr. Basford had displayed gentlemanly consideration of her. Perhaps he had felt kindly toward her, but it would be foolish to dare to hope.

However, Charlotte could not help herself.

And she called herself every kind of a fool.

⊗ Twenty-Two ⊗

"Pray, excuse me. Did you say something about Mr. Basford?" Charlotte asked. She was sitting at the breakfast table with her sister and Mr. Card and was enjoying some very fine sausages. She had been only partially listening to the couple's conversation, for their discussions could be quite tedious, when she thought she heard Mr. Basford's name mentioned.

"Indeed I did, Charlotte. Have you not been listening?" Maria scolded as she buttered a piece of toast.

"I do apologize. I cannot seem to keep my mind focused this morning." Or whenever the conversation centered on ribbons or methods for tying a stylish cravat.

Mr. Card put down his teacup and took up the conversation. "Maria and I saw Mr. Basford in Westerham yesterday when we stopped for lunch."

"We were quite surprised to see him," Maria interjected. "I thought he had escorted Mr. and Mrs. Westfield back to America. In fact, Colonel Armitage relayed that information to me personally. He was quite contrite over the whole debacle between Mr. Westfield and I, you see, and he wanted me to know that I would not have to come upon them unexpectedly in town and have to endure a difficult scene."

"It was a very kind sentiment, though I do not believe it was necessary," Mr. Card said.

"The colonel did not realize that nothing could possibly impede my happiness." Maria waved her butter knife in the air as though to emphasize her thoughts. "I am so content with my life that there is no room in my heart for sadness or awkwardness, even if I were to meet with Mr. and Mrs. Westfield every day of the week."

The couple smiled at each other, and Charlotte felt jealousy stir in her. Even if she was not in love, her sister seemed happy. Would Charlotte ever be so?

She steered the conversation back to Mr. Basford, asking if he seemed well.

"Indeed, he did," said Mr. Card.

"We spoke to him for a little while before our meal arrived," Maria explained. "He congratulated us on our marriage and was very kind indeed."

"Did he say how long he has been in town?" Charlotte kept her attention focused on her forked sausage.

"I believe he said he arrived last Monday and is staying again with his uncle," Mr. Card replied.

He had not called on Charlotte, and he had been in town since last Monday. More than a full week had passed. Perhaps he did not want to see her after all.

Charlotte tried not to allow herself to be disappointed.

"Mr. Card and I invited him to our dinner party on Saturday."

"And did he accept the invitation?"

"He seemed rather unsure, saying that Colonel Armitage had been keeping his schedule rather full of late and asked permission to check with him first. We assured him that he would be welcome, as would the colonel."

"I wonder what the colonel has him doing," Charlotte mused.

"Hunting, I expect. You know what a great hunter he is, and this cool weather often coaxes the deer from the woods."

"I do not see why he would choose to hunt all day and miss our party. It is possible, is it not, to attend both?" Maria whined.

"My dear, hunting is a taxing activity. Guns are much heavier than they appear. He may be quite exhausted after a day in the wilderness."

"Well, even if he may not attend the party, I invited him to call at our house any time that was convenient for him. I hold nothing against him."

Charlotte smiled at her sister's attitude toward her past circumstances, but the brightness of her smile could only be attributed to the news of Mr. Basford.

He had been invited to call.

Maria and Mr. Card continued their conversation, but Charlotte paid them little attention. Her anticipation rose even higher, causing her hands to shake slightly and her appetite to dissipate. She returned the fork and sausage to her plate and began to fidget with the napkin in her lap.

When would he come?

Would he come at all?

✦❧ ❧✦

By Thursday, several days later, Mr. Basford had still not paid a call at Mr. Card's home, and Charlotte fought her disappointment. She remained very distracted. With every knock at the door, she hoped it was Mr. Basford. Every footstep in the hallway toward the morning room was Mr. Basford's. Every voice sounded like his.

But still he did not come.

And Charlotte could not prevent herself from being disappointed. She could, however, prevent Mr. Card and Maria from seeing it, and she spent the majority of her time trying to distract herself with small jobs around the house with Mrs. Eff. That very afternoon she and Mrs. Eff were going to rearrange her wardrobe, putting away her summer dresses and taking her winter gowns and cloak out of storage. It was a rather dull task that she could have left to Mrs. Eff, but she needed to keep herself busy so Mr. Basford would not sneak into her thoughts.

Charlotte had just completed a rather fine afternoon repast with Maria and Mr. Card, but she barely tasted the sweet biscuits and Chinese tea and she hardly heard a word that was spoken.

"Charlotte?" she heard Maria say.

Guiltily, Charlotte met her eyes.

"Have you not heard a word we have said?"

"I do apologize. My mind has been at sixes and sevens today."

"That is not like you at all. Perhaps you are ill. Are you feeling quite well?"

Charlotte assured her that she was very well indeed, just distracted.

"Mr. Card and I are going for a walk after breakfast, would you like to join us since you are not ill?" She seemed to desire her company, probably to serve as a buffer from her husband.

"I think not. My mind is too preoccupied to allow me to be a proper companion. Besides Mrs. Eff and I have a project upstairs."

Maria rolled her pretty blue eyes. "Whatever you wish, but I do not see why you would turn down a walk on a lovely day for tedious indoor work."

"Do enjoy your walk. Do not worry about me. I am fine. Besides, tedium is sometimes good for the soul." Had not marriage to Mr. Collins been proof of that?

Soon, the couple departed, leaving Charlotte to her task with Mrs. Eff.

She climbed the stairs to her bedchamber, which was in a lovely part of the house that faced the front park. From her window, she had a delightful view of the small fishpond and the drive up to the house. The front lawn was elegantly manicured, and Charlotte not only enjoyed seeing it from the window, but she also enjoyed walking across the grass in the morning when it was still wet with dew.

Now it was later in the morning, and Charlotte stood in the window, waiting for Mrs. Eff to arrive and watching as sun descended through the trees that stood along the edge of the property. Their leaves had begun to change from lush green to radiant yellows, oranges, and reds.

Mrs. Eff had cracked the window slightly, allowing the cool autumn air to freshen the room. Although the air caused goose bumps to rise on her skin, she did not close the window.

Charlotte loved the fall—the scent of fallen leaves and the crisp feeling in the air.

Perhaps she should have gone on that walk with Maria and Mr. Card after all. Instead, she stood at the window and looked down the drive. She began to imagine. A single rider on a bay horse. Mr.

Basford's horse. He would come. He would be shabbily dressed, but his words would not be so shabby. He would propose and Charlotte would accept. They would be married and go together into the future. A secure and happy future.

Charlotte blinked away her thoughts. She focused her mind and gaze again on the driveway. There was no movement on the horizon, but as she looked out the window, she began to become conscious of movement in her soul.

She must see Mr. Basford. She must! And if he would not come to her, she would go to him.

She could put on her sturdy boots and walk to Colonel Armitage's house straightaway. It was not so long a distance, and it was a flat path. She would be home by supper, and no one need know the nature of her trip. Indeed, she would pay a traditional morning call. There was nothing untoward about that. And if she happened to meet with Mr. Basford and perhaps attempt to make her feelings known, then so be it.

No! What was she thinking. She must not do such a thing. Her recently tattered reputation was not fully mended. She must be careful.

Charlotte's hands gripped the windowsill.

Taking a deep breath, she turned and crossed the room to the wardrobe. Inside, she found the small wooden jewelry box where she had hidden the glove Mr. Basford had loaned her the night of Mr. Edgington's deceit. Underneath her accoutrements, she saw the fine fabric of his glove. She had not allowed herself to think of that glove since the day she had put it away. She had tried not to remember the kindness it represented, and she certainly did not touch its soft fabric as she was now.

She should destroy the glove. It should meet the same fate as the gloves given to her by Mr. Edgington. She glanced at the hearth, knowing what she ought to do. She would not be free of Mr. Basford until the glove, the only remnant of their friendship, was gone.

But she simply could not do it.

Running the tip of her index finger along the contours of the glove one last time, she closed the box. Mr. Basford was gone, but she was not ready to release him completely.

ఇత్ ఇత్

With each step of her boots, Charlotte vacillated between retreat and determination. Left boot, retreat. Right boot, determination. Left, right, left, right. Retreat, determination, retreat, determination. Her steps carried her onward, closer to Colonel Armitage's house.

She had planned to be careful, to be above reproach, and yet here she was, paying a call on a gentleman. What could she possibly be thinking?

She was not thinking. That fact was very plain. She was employing her heart, not her head, and she refused to allow herself to contemplate the wisdom of doing so. She simply continued walking.

In due course, she stood before the colonel's house. Of only moderate size, it seemed to tower above her now, looking ominous and foreboding. But Charlotte did not even consider the option of returning home. She had gone too far to allow her fears to dissuade her. Her heart was at stake.

Slowly, Charlotte walked up the front steps—left, right, left, right—and brushed the dust off her skirt. She checked her bonnet and tucked in stray wisps of hair. She was determined to look the best she could after such a long walk, even though she realized the low value Mr. Basford placed on fashion.

She raised her hand to knock, but stopped short, remembering to fetch her card from her reticule. Mrs. Charlotte Collins, it said in plain black script. So proper and detached. And she wondered if this prim Mrs. Charlotte Collins would recognize the slightly disheveled woman on Colonel Armitage's doorstep.

This time when she lifted her hand to the door knocker, metal struck metal, and the sharp sound seemed to echo around her. She heard the muffled footsteps of the butler approaching the door. It opened with a whoosh of air, and a large gentlemen greeted her. "Good morning, madam."

"Good morning," she handed him her card. "Is Mrs. Armitage at home?"

He took the card and glanced at her name before dropping it in the receiving bowl on the hall table, and Charlotte got the distinct impression that he did not believe the prim name on the card matched the woman standing before him. She brushed at her gown again.

"I am sorry, madam, but she is not at home this morning."

"Oh dear." What was she to do? She had depended upon Mrs. Armitage's being at home to receive callers this morning. Charlotte glanced behind the butler, hoping that Mr. Basford would appear as if by magic. But the hallway was empty.

Charlotte joined her hands in front of her gown and dropped her eyes. Was she to have gone all this way for naught? She could not allow that. She had already risked her reputation; why not see her task to completion? She raised her chin and found the butler still looking at her. "Is the family at home?"

"No, I am afraid they are all out this morning."

Out? Charlotte wanted to shout. All of them? The colonel? Mr. Basford? Everyone? How could they be out? She must see Mr. Basford. She simply must.

"Mr. Basford. Is he in?" Her words sounded tight.

"He too is out, madam." The butler was clearly losing patience. "No one is at home. They are all *out.*" The last word was annunciated as though Charlotte were an imbecile.

"Oh." Charlotte's mind raced. What should she do?

"My apologies," he said, slowly closing the door. "Good day."

The heavy oak door drew closer and closer to Charlotte's face, and she was frozen, wondering what course of action, if any, to take. If the door closed, she would have no choice but to return home a failure. Suddenly, one word escaped her tight lips: "Wait!"

Startled, the butler halted the door's progress and stared at her. Charlotte had startled herself and for a moment said nothing. What would she do? What could she do? She must say something. She could not stand here staring at the butler all day.

"May I be of service, madam?"

She gathered her courage. "Yes, you may. I would like to leave a note, if I might, for Mr. Basford. I require a quill, ink, and sheet of writing paper, if you please."

He did not appear pleased by her request, but he did not argue. "Yes madam." He opened the door fully. "If you will follow me."

The butler led her into the sitting room and to a small, well-appointed escritoire. She seated herself in the chair and immediately took up quill and paper. What would she say? She had never written a letter of this nature to a gentleman. The butler's voice broke into her thoughts. "I will return for the letter in a few moments."

Charlotte had already forgotten the butler and nodded in annoyance. She understood his message. She would not be left unattended long to write her inappropriate note. Her fingers tightened on the quill, and she began the letter:

Mr. Basford—

But the words would not come. She did not know how to convey all that was in her heart in a letter with a butler waiting to sweep her out of the house like yesterday's refuse. She huffed out a sigh. Perhaps this was a poorly conceived idea after all. She dropped the quill on the paper, causing ink to pool in the corner. She stared at the stain.

The paper was ruined. She was ruined. It was all ruined!

Charlotte grasped the paper in her hands and prepared to crumple it, but a dull sound entered her mind. The butler's heavy footsteps approached from a distance. She had no more time. He would escort her to the door and not readmit her. She could not allow herself to be indecisive.

Charlotte quickly replaced the paper on the desk and picked up the quill, and after dipping it in fresh ink, she began to scribble furiously. Her handwriting barely resembled that of a genteel lady. It looked more like an animal had danced across the page with muddy feet. But Charlotte paid no heed to her penmanship and wrote:

I had hoped to find you at home this morning, but since you are away, I must compose this note. I do so to hope to see you Saturday at the Cards' dinner party, for I greatly wish to speak with you.

The door opened and the butler appeared at her side. "Madam?"

"A moment, please," she begged, holding her left hand in stopping gesture.

Searching her mind frantically for a suitable closing, she could find none. The butler cleared his throat, and she glanced at his hard-eyed expression. She had no more time.

Before folding the paper in a hasty configuration and handing it to the butler for delivery, she wrote one word.

Charlotte.

✐ Twenty-Three ✐

Charlotte did not at first regret composing the letter to Mr. Basford. She imagined each day that he would arrive, unable to wait until the dinner party to see her. And each evening, when he did not arrive, the tiniest bit of regret crept in.

She had walked miles to pay a call on Mr. Basford. No gently reared woman would do such a thing. She had left a desperate note. No lady of sense would dare write to a gentleman, and certainly not out of desperation. And worse, she had signed her Christian name. Charlotte. No lady would do such a thing in a letter to a gentleman who was not her husband. And no gentleman would misunderstand the implication.

Perhaps Mr. Basford believed she still harbored resentment for his role in the incident between Maria and Mr. Westfield. But that could not be. Her letter was proof enough that she felt kindly toward him. Perhaps he was kindly rejecting her. A horrid thought.

By the day of Maria and Mr. Card's dinner party, Charlotte had neither seen nor heard from Mr. Basford or any of the Armitage family.

She did her best not to appear depressed when in company, but she felt her disappointment keenly. Her final hope was that Mr. Basford would appear at the party, but she knew the possibility was quite remote. He had told Mr. Card and Maria when they had issued the invitation that it was unlikely that he would be able to attend.

Still, on the evening of the party, each time the door opened to admit another guest to the sitting room where they had gathered to converse before dinner, Charlotte turned eagerly to discover who had entered. The appointed time to dine drew nearer and nearer, and still he did not come.

Charlotte talked with the guests, taking an eager interest in them. At least, she hoped she appeared interested. In truth, she had very little idea what had been said to her thus far that evening. She hardly knew to whom she talked. Perhaps she had spoken with the rector. She could not be certain.

Finally, dinner was announced, and Mr. Card escorted Charlotte into the dining room on one arm and his wife on the other. He mouthed the necessary compliments about his good fortune at having two beautiful women to escort, but Charlotte scarcely heard him. Mr. Basford had not come. Her mind cried out in sorrow, but she smiled to those around her.

The dinner consisted of numerous long courses, and each one was more highly lauded for its palatability than the last. Charlotte wished they had served only bread and cheese. It would have been faster.

She was seated next to Maria, who seemed very proud of her position opposite her husband at the head of the table. Speaking only when absolutely necessary, she listened as Maria and her guests talked and concentrated on attempting to push Mr. Basford's rejection from her mind.

The simple fact was that Charlotte would have to accept her life as it was. All in all, it certainly was not a bad life. She had financial security, a lovely shelter in the Cards' home, and the opportunity to buy a new gown now and then. She had a small circle of friends—most of whom were represented at the table—and she had Maria and Mr. Card, and she dearly loved them.

One day, she would be able to view Mr. Basford as a mere acquaintance. Until then, she would try not to think of him at all. Resolved, Charlotte turned her attention to the plates that appeared before her and ate without tasting a bite.

After dinner, the group returned to the sitting room to take tea and coffee and to engage in cards on the tables that Mr. Card and Maria had set up for the occasion.

Several guests left after the meal, citing the chilly night as the reason for their early departures, and the remaining guests chose to play at cards. Charlotte knew she would make a terrible participant in such an endeavor and took a seat on the bench near the fire. She purposefully kept her back to the door so she would not be tempted to look at every servant who entered the room in the vain, foolish hope that Mr. Basford had come.

Charlotte sat on the edge of a light blue brocade armless bench, which the servants had placed conveniently at the back of a settee to provide additional seating for the dinner party guests, with a book resting in her lap. The heavy oak door had been rather busy, admitting servants to clean up the tea things and to keep the fire stoked.

Charlotte had just congratulated herself for not turning around once to see who had come into the room when she felt someone sit on the settee behind her. She assumed that one of the card players from the table behind her had tired of the game and cried off to take a seat by the fire.

"Charlotte," a voice whispered.

Mr. Basford's voice. It washed over her like warm water.

Mr. Basford was on the settee behind her, with his back to her. He had come!

Suddenly weak, Charlotte's arm, which had been resting decorously on the book in her lap, fell limply at her side, her fingers brushing the brocade fabric on the edge of the bench. Her face reddened, and she glanced around, hoping no one had observed her discomfiture. Everyone was otherwise occupied with their games, and no one even seemed to notice that Mr. Basford had arrived.

"Ben." The whispered word fell from her lips unbidden. She had never used his given name before, and it felt brazen.

She could sense him at her back and smell his woodsy scent mixed with the odor of sun and horses, and she realized he must have come directly from a long ride. She wanted to turn and face him, but propriety prohibited her. Propriety and fear.

"I had to see you. In public, just as you wanted," Mr. Basford whispered.

They were silent a moment, voices murmured around them and the fire crackled softly beside them. His hand casually draped itself over the low arm of the settee, and his fingers brushed against Charlotte's. She jumped at his touch, and then a fire spread through her. His fingers sought hers, first tracing the backs of her knuckles, inviting her to open to him.

She lowered her head and glanced at the card players from beneath her lashes, but there was no one to witness their inappropriate behavior. Everyone was distracted by their games.

"Ben, this is…" she began as his fingers continued to brush hers. But she did not have the will to pull her hand away as she should.

"Inappropriate. I know."

His thumb now traced the contours at the base of Charlotte's hand, which had opened into a loose fist.

His voice was even quieter now, and she had to lean slightly back to hear him. "I am sorry for missing the meal. My uncle and I were at a hunting cabin. It was quite remote, and I did not return home and find your note until this evening."

Relief and understanding flowed over Charlotte. He had rushed to see her. Never had the scent of horses been so welcome.

"And about Miss Lucas and James. It was entirely my fault. I never should have interfered. But it was never about them."

Charlotte could not reply. Her voice would not function, apparently, when he touched her. She swallowed and attempted again to form reassuring words. But they would not come.

"For me, it was never about them." His voice was quiet but insistent.

"But…" she tapered off, trying to think of something practical to say. To explain that she had quite forgotten about Maria and Mr. Westfield and his role in the debacle. That she was not angry. That she had missed him.

"It was about you, Charlotte. I am in love with you." His voice paused, but his fingers continued to stroke the palm of her hand, encouraging her fingers to accept his. "You must believe me when I tell you that I cannot forget you."

"I have not forgotten either," Charlotte said, her voice barely a whisper. Then after a moment, she confessed, "I still have your glove."

She could feel the rasp of his fingertips across her soft palm.

"Marry me." His whisper was rough with restraint.

Charlotte could not speak words of either sense or nonsense at that very moment. Instead, she opened her hand and wove her fingers between his, shuddering slightly at the intimate contact. There they remained, holding hands with the fire as their only witness.

✦ Epilogue ✦

"I do not think that gentleman likes me one bit," Mr. Basford said as he joined his wife on the settee. He sat closer than propriety dictated, but Charlotte no longer cared. She only snuggled into his dark brown coat and inhaled deeply of his woodsy scent.

"Who? Mr. Darcy?"

"Of course. The Darcys are our only houseguests, aren't they? Mr. Darcy is the only male, I believe. Or is there something you wish to tell me? Have we other visitors hiding in one of the bed chambers?"

Charlotte ignored his jest and answered with as much seriousness as a woman in love can muster. "Mr. Darcy is a gentleman of contradiction. He believes in strict respectability and decorum, but Lizzie tells me he is a loving husband with a humor not visible to most acquaintances. And I know that he would go to the greatest lengths for her."

She smiled as she recalled Mr. Darcy's facial expression when, not more than a half hour ago, he had observed Mr. Basford's curious sitting habits. She giggled. "But I thought he would not be able to contain his disgust when you tilted back on the rear legs of that desk chair."

"I recall seeing that very same look cross your face when I first came to call."

Charlotte leaned back so she could look at him more fully. He had a handsome face, even when he chided her. She lifted her hand

and stroked his cheek. "I did not know you as well as I do now. You too are a gentleman of contradictions. You appear to be an uncouth lout, but in reality, your character has many things to recommend itself."

Mr. Basford took hold of Charlotte's hand and brought it to his lips. "And these recommendations are what convinced you to marry me?"

"Indeed. And the fact that I was desperately in love."

"Yes, it was all part of my plan." He grinned. "I gave you no option but to marry me."

Charlotte tucked her feet beneath her, snuggled close again, and thought back on their wedding, which had taken place on an autumn morning in Mr. Collins's former parish church. She found it appropriate that she would marry the man she truly loved in the church where Mr. Collins had delivered countless mind-numbing sermons.

The majority of the sanctuary had stood empty—much as it had for Mr. Collins's Sunday services—but Charlotte hardly noticed. She had begun to be influenced by Mr. Basford's beliefs regarding the need to gain society's good opinion, and although she had not yet done away with her concern completely, she certainly placed a great deal less emphasis on it. Her family and close friends had come to share in her happiness, but she was so besotted by him that she would have been almost as pleased to marry Mr. Basford with only a clergyman and a witness present.

As a wedding gift for his new bride, Mr. Basford had attempted to purchase Charlotte's treasured cottage, but he had met with the resistance of Lady Catherine, and even his charms— and a very large sum of money—could not persuade her to part with the property. Disappointed, he had confessed his attempt to Charlotte. She had been saddened at the news initially, but upon further consideration, she decided that Lady Catherine's unforgiving nature had resulted in a blessing, for the specter of her former patroness would no longer hover over her life.

Although Mr. Basford could afford to purchase a large country manor, the couple had decided to lease a moderately sized house in Westerham, which they christened Basford Cottage. Following the wedding, they took possession, electing to enjoy the peace of the house before departing on their voyage to the New World the following year.

Maria and Mr. Card were frequent visitors to Basford Cottage, and the two couples often went into society together. Mrs. Eff and Edward returned to positions in Charlotte's household. Mrs. Eff served as her lady's maid and confidante, and Edward became Mr. Basford's valet, which he declared to be the perfect position for the young man. Mr. Basford said, "The boy knows very little about fashion, and I find that essential in my valet. Another manservant might attempt to persuade me to adopt some *English attire...*" He spoke the last two words as though they were an epithet. "...and that is unacceptable."

And so their situation at Basford Cottage was ideal.

The Darcys had arrived several months after the wedding, and in the morning room of which Charlotte had become so fond, she and Elizabeth had been able to enjoy their friendship as they had in their youth.

Charlotte, suddenly serious, glanced at her husband. "I am glad Lizzie is here, even if you do cause Mr. Darcy discomfort."

"I believe our fishing excursions are helping him warm somewhat to my informality and casual bearing. Why just yesterday he loosened his cravat before making his first cast. Perhaps before he departs, he may tip his chair onto its back legs."

"I doubt that very much. But I am pleased that Lizzie sees that I have shed my preoccupations with money and propriety and followed my heart." Charlotte smiled. "Of course, she was equally delighted to discover that you could provide well for me, both in feeling and in the security with which every woman must concern herself."

Here Charlotte allowed Mr. Basford the liberty of a long and satisfying kiss. Or perhaps she was the one who had taken the liberty. Nevertheless, their lips met, and he hauled her across his lap, settling her so that more liberties could be taken.

At length, the kiss dwindled, but Charlotte remained draped across Mr. Basford's lap. She sighed into the lapels of his coat, for she knew that she would never have to fear for her security again. For the first time in her life, Charlotte truly believed that she had gained both happiness and security, which did not rest in a large income or in the good opinion of society, but in the relationships she had with her family and friends and in the love she shared with her husband.

✆ Author's Note ✆

I am most indebted to Jane Austen for her creation of the wonderful world and characters of *Pride and Prejudice*. I would also like to thank my family and friends, who ceaselessly supported my dreams. For their contributions to this book and to my life in general, I would like to express my deep gratitude to Bert Becton, Marilyn and Robert Whiteley, Octavia and Ed Becton, Laura Daley, Blaine Rankin, Brenda Godbee, Jill Huggins, and Beverle Graves Myers. Though any errors within this text belong solely to me, I will do my best to foist them upon someone else.

∽๑๏ About the Author ๑๏∽

Jennifer Becton works as a freelance editor and writer and is a lover of many genres of books, including historical novels, mysteries, and literary fiction. She lives near Charlotte, North Carolina, with her husband Bert and her cat Puttytat. She is also an avid equestrienne and owns a horse appropriately named Darcy.

Jennifer looks forward to hearing from her readers. Email her at jwb@jenniferbecton.com.

Check out Jennifer's website (http://www.jenniferbecton.com) and join her mailing list.

And don't forget to join Jennifer Becton's Facebook page (http://www.facebook.com/JenniferBectonWriter) and follow her on Twitter (http://twitter.com/JenniferBecton).

∽๑๏ ๑๏∽